A *LESS THAN ZERO* ROCKSTAR ROMANCE

FEARLESS

ENCORE

KAYLENE WINTER

A *LESS THAN ZERO* ROCKSTAR ROMANCE

FEARLESS

ENCORE

KAYLENE WINTER

Sensitivity Statement

READERS,

THE LESS THAN ZERO series dives into the highs and lows of rockstar life, inspired by the raw and real experiences of many in the music world. Across these stories, some characters face challenging themes, including abuse, sexual assault, mental health, fertility, and struggles with addiction. These topics are not universal to every character but are woven into the journeys of a few, which impact the entirety of the series.

At its heart, though, this series is about love—how it grows, heals, and transforms. Each couple's story ultimately leads to a well-deserved happily ever after, filled with passion, hope, and redemption. The band's journey supporting each other as "band brothers" also is a predominant theme throughout.

Please take a moment to reflect on your comfort with these themes before reading, and know that these stories are told with care and respect, sensitivity readers have vetted each one. Thank you for joining me on this emotional journey through love, life, and music.

With all my love,

Kaylene

Prologue - Present Day

LIFE IS FOR LIVING.

It's Da's favorite saying, so it is.

Life. Is. For. Living.

What the actual feck does that even mean?

I've been giving this too much thought, truth be told. In many ways, it feels like I've been barreling through my entire adult life. Ever since Da's accident when I was in high school. I can't even feckin' remember a time when I've not been in high gear.

Keeping the family business afloat when I was just seventeen. Sacrificing my own dreams to make certain my brothers made it through college. Finally being able to pursue my music career, only to be launched into the stratosphere of fame and fortune a couple of years later.

And, of course, then I met Ronni.

Ah, my Ronni. Fierce. Beautiful. Sweet. Strong. Independent.

And sweet baby Jaysus. Complicated. So feckin' complicated.

It's not a criticism. It's an observation. My woman never shies away from a challenge. Nothing stands in her way. She's fiercely protective of those she's loyal to. Willing to give two thousand percent. Which is feckin' admirable. It's just that...

Bollocks.

I'm tired. Tired of the hamster wheel. Tired of chasing some sort of elusive dream. Tired of always being on edge. Tired of drama with my band. Tired of being a rockstar. Mostly, I'm tired of being media fodder. It's too much.

I'm exhausted trying to protect my family.

So, so weary. All. The. Feckin'. Time.

So bleedin' spent.

So spent, I've wholly succumbed to my anger. My sorrow.

Ronni and I are through.

I crave a bit of normality. Some peace and quiet for feck's sake. I escaped. Fled the scene of the crime to hide out in my Irish sanctuary. Away from the chaos. Away from scandals. Away from everything—and everyone—I love.

Far, far away.

If I had my druthers, I'd stay here for the next year. Stare out at Belfast Lough. Wander the lush gardens my auntie, Saoirse, planted. Breathe in the violets and honeysuckle. Relish the silence.

Just be.

From the day and hour Ronni became my bride, all I've ever wanted was to be an excellent husband. A loving father. Play some music.

Simple. Nothing more. Nothing less.

Fat feckin' chance.

Not after the situation I find myself in. I'm a world-class eejit. I let my guard down. Thought everything was handled. Or, at least on the right track. Ronni and I had a plan in place. I felt comfortable for the first time in my life.

Safe, even.

For feck's sake, we deserved a break. Deserved to enjoy our lives together. Deserved to reap the rewards of demanding work and some heartbreak. I dove in headfirst.

It's all gone to shite. My entire identity is fucked. Everything I stand for—destroyed. In a blink of an eye, I'm suddenly persona non grata. If you were to believe the millions of articles on the subject, Connor McGloughlin is not a worthy human being. If you were to believe the social media trolls, I should off myself. Or, I should be offed.

Offing's a big feckin' theme when my name is mentioned these days, that's for feckin' sure.

I turn from the big picture window in my Belfast estate and head for the kitchen. Devour a bag of Spring Onion Tayto because there's no fresh food in the house. Put my dead phone on the charger. Slip out the back door and stride over the rugged stone pathway across the garden and up the stairs to the room above the garage that is still unfinished. The vast space is empty, save about thirty boxes that were delivered months ago.

Back when my life was on solid ground.

Back when my family was supposed to spend the summer here while Ronni worked on her movie.

I guess it's all relative. The past eighteen months haven't been easy. Not by a mile. Twin babies. Lawsuits. My band's implosion. Hell, I figured things were as low as they could go.

Oh, I had no idea.

None. Zip. Nada.

Methodically, I get to work. Rip open a box. Pull out the parts. Assemble. Consolidate the rubbage and repeat. The work is easy. My construction background comes in handy, thank Christ. I'm able to settle my mind for a bit with the meditative work. In fact, I'm so lost in my task, I don't hear someone come through the door.

"Connor." Her lyrical voice permeates the air.

I clutch the screwdriver for grim death, but don't turn around. My shoulders slump forward. My bearded chin hits my chest. Instantaneously, the permanent ginormous lump in my throat threatens to rupture.

"What is all this?" I hear her footsteps behind me as she navigates through the furniture I've put together.

I don't move. I say nothing. I don't look back at her. I can't. Not now. Maybe never.

The last time I saw her, Mae's face was contorted in agony and betrayal. I'll never forget her tortured screams for me to get out of the house. Not as long as I breathe.

So, no. I don't look because I'm a coward.

"Connor." Her voice is annoyed. Terse.

My neck prickles. My stomach roils. The crisps I ate earlier threaten to come back up. I curl my hand into a fist. Punch the floor. "What are you doin' here, Mae?"

The tat tat tat of her heels across the room toward me makes me tense up like a taut rope. Still, I keep my head bowed and my eyes riveted to the dusty hardwood floor. The tips of her black-leather, red-soled boots appear in my line of vision. My teeth clench. I squeeze my eyes tightly shut to block any visual of her.

I simply cannot face my wife. The mother of my kids.

Aye. I'm so feckin' low, I can't even look at her feckin' shoes.

Ronni's fingers thread through my curls. The tips of her fingers massage my head. Just the way I love. Little circular rubs. Light scrapes. I'm almost lulled into a sense of peacefulness. A sense that—maybe, just maybe—everything could return to normal. At least until she clutches my hair tight at the scalp and drags my noggin up, so I have no choice but to meet her gaze.

"Connor," Ronni growls through pursed lips. "You will look at me." Her startling green eyes narrow. Her milky skin is flushed with anger. She puffs away a lock of chestnut hair from her forehead with one forceful breath. "You owe me that much."

I hold her gaze for a second. I can't help but close my eyes again, even though I nod and whisper, "Aye."

Ronni unclenches her hands, snagging one of my curls in her wedding ring when she pulls away. The pain of a few hairs ripping out barely registers. How could it when my heart aches so bad?

I can tell by the clomping sound she's stormed across the room toward the windows facing our house. "Are you really going to just sulk there like a beaten dog, Connor?"

"I feel like a beaten dog," I mumble.

I hear her sigh heavily, then all goes eerily quiet. Unable to resist any longer, I open my eyes to find her where I expected. She's always a vision. The light streams through the big windows. Ronni's in perfect silhouette. One jean-clad hip is cocked though her head slumps forward. Her hands rest on the sill, but her stiff arms keep her upright. "Can you please pull yourself together? You don't have time for this woebegone bullshit," she snarls without turning around.

Rage spreads through my body like an Eastern Washington forest fire. After all I've put up with over the years, could she give me a feckin' break? Woebegone? Is she mad? It takes every ounce of willpower I have not to lose my shite.

Except, I do not raise my voice to my wife.

Ever.

"You know, every single thing about this is bullshit." Ronni turns toward me and waves her arms around the room. "Hiding out in Ireland isn't going to make this problem go away like magic. Trust me."

My problem, she means.

I hoist my six-foot-six frame up to standing and calmly cross the room to stand next to her. Fold my arms and stare out the window to hopefully hide how badly I'm shaking. I repeat my earlier question, "Why are you here, Mae?"

"Did you seriously think sending me a text telling me you'd give me a divorce was gonna fly with me? God, you LTZ guys and your stupid goddamn notes." Her voice catches, but she recovers in a flash. "Is that what you want? Be real with me. Please."

I keep my voice calm. Collected. I can't answer her directly, though. "It's for the best. For you. The boys."

"Wow. Okay." Ronni kicks the wall with the toe of her boot. I can't help but glance down at her to discover, despite her uncharacteristic display, she's wrapped her arms around herself protectively.

I'm such a feckin' arsehole. It kills me to lie to her. Divorce is the last thing in the world I want. Ronni's my everything. Life with her and our sons means...

"I'm not going to beg you. That's not who I am." Ronni's voice trembles. Pleads.

I'd never want her to lower herself that way. That she'd even consider it pierces my heart and makes me want to cocoon her in my arms. But, I can't do that.

I lost that right when I sent the text on my way to the airport.

So, I nod. Keep my face frozen and emotionless. Watch her storm across the room, kick the empty pile of boxes and slam the door behind her.

When she's gone, I break down. Wracking, silent sobs. I didn't expect her to follow me here, but the loss of her presence is beyond devastating. How will I survive a world where I can't breathe in her lemon-meringue-pie scent? Sip from her supple lips. Hold her tightly against my body after I've fucked her into oblivion. Cuddle with her and the boys and watch movies on a Sunday afternoon.

I won't. Survive, that is. Not intact. I'm already a shell of a man.

Who will I be when this is all over?

The better question is, will it even matter?

Chapter One

Fifteen Months Prior

THIS GARDEN IS MY absolute favorite place in the entire world. I'm lounging in the conservatory, a glass-and-stone structure with a 360-degree view of the grounds. Floor-to-ceiling panels unfold, so on a rare warm Irish day like today, I'm able to lounge on this incredibly plush sofa and work on rewrites of a screenplay I'm hoping to produce.

One day.

I've never lived in such a quiet, reflective location to just....be

Connor's estate is perfect. In the years since he bought this place, his aunt Saoirse has done wonders. She's renovated the entire mansion to be the perfect combination of modern amenities and traditional Irish cottage.

Her true contribution though, at least in my opinion, are these lush gardens. Her passion for horticulture and keen eye for detail have transformed acres of dense hazel and blackthorn greenery into magic. I'm surrounded by trees, woodland plants, ferns, shrubs, and flowers. Throughout the grounds are manicured lawns, stone planting areas and also whimsical flower beds that almost seem wild.

At this time of year, in the weeks before summer finally permeates the land, the fragrances are unreal. Gentle scents of honeysuckle, lilacs, hostas, daylilies, and crocosmia waft around me on the gentle breeze. Who needs candles when you have the real thing?

It's heaven on earth. Our very own Garden of Eden.

My oceanfront home in Malibu used to be my sanctuary. I'd sit outside for hours in one of my pods. Soaking up sun. Awash with the sound of the ocean, so incredibly meditative and soothing. Lately, it's not been as calming as it used to be.

Situated smack in the middle of a dozen celebrity homeowners, privacy didn't used to be an issue. Things began to change when a young TikTok influencer bought the house next door. The number of raging parties and photo shoots have made living there just about unbearable.

It doesn't help being besieged by a constant onslaught of paparazzi. Ever since word got out I was behind the demise of billionaire producer Don Kircher, it's been a shit show. I'd spent years cautiously covering my tracks. Careful to keep my identity secret, fearing it would ruin my career. I didn't want the credit. Or the notoriety. I just wanted him to pay for what he did to me and so many others.

It all changed when Connor slung me over his shoulder at that poker game in New York. Yeah, he saved my ass.

But, I was also exposed.

I'd let my guard down. A couple of months prior, we found out I was pregnant. I was desperate to speed up his downfall. Get on with my life with Connor. Unfortunately, a string of bad decisions and recklessness put me in real danger. Thank God for Kris Blakely, my best friend and producing partner. She and Connor stepped in to save me from myself. With their help, my plan came to fruition and Kircher was indicted for all his heinous sexual transgressions.

My role in his ruin went public and—to my surprise—I wasn't blacklisted. Quite the opposite. I've become a coveted triple threat: actor, writer, and producer.

When Kircher was arrested after the LA Times article, Connor and I happily stepped into the spotlight as husband and wife. My fans were not so happy. The past ten years of fake-dating mostly gay actors bit me in the ass in the court of public opinion. I wasn't quite cancelled—I'd exposed Kircher, after all. But boy oh boy were they pissed that I "dumped" Ty for Connor.

For a hot second, I was a bandwrecker. The whole reason LTZ went on hiatus.

Me, Connor, Ty, and Zoey did a series of interviews to counter the insanity. Ty's blissful reunion with Zoey, the woman he wrote all of LTZ's hits about, did the trick. Luckily, Less Than Zero's fans were ecstatic at their reunion so I was let off the hook. Soon, the world moved on to the next scandal.

With Kircher finally in our rear view mirror, Connor and I decided to spend LTZ's hiatus in Ireland so I could give birth in peace. Have some privacy. Allow space for our "scandalous" relationship to remain firmly as yesterday's news.

Holy moly, I'm so friggin' relieved the truth is out. Our truth. My impending motherhood, however, is not. As far as we're concerned, our babies are no one's business. Not yet. The way I see it, Connor and I have earned a few months of relative normality away from the public eye. As it turns out, Ireland is one of the safest—and most discreet—places to give birth to a celebrity baby.

Or two.

Connor has super sperm. He knocked me up with twins. We're blissfully hiding away from the entire world. Social media. Hollywood. The Billboard charts. Everything.

Until today, when our bubble will burst. Just a little.

"Ah, there you are, love." Connor tromps up the three steps to where I'm nesting. He's magnificent. All six foot six of him. His black shirt is tight, showing off his defined muscles. His long, curly, reddish-brown hair hangs loose. He sinks down next to me. Pulls me against his side. "Our guests have arrived." He nuzzles my ear.

My pussy clenches. He knows where every single erogenous zone is located on my body. Since I've been pregnant? Arousal times ten. Of course, I'm practical. I can't get it on with my husband when his bandmate and fiancée are waiting for us up at the house. I set my laptop next to me on the sofa. "I'm sorry I wasn't there to let them in. I lost track of time."

"No bother. They're both tired. They wanted to take a 'nap.'" Connor makes quotes with his fingers and waggles his eyebrows.

I can't help but laugh and shake my head. "I've never been around two people who are so, um...intensely physical. All. The. Time."

"Aye, I definitely got that vibe." Connor strokes my shoulder and leans down for a kiss. He sucks my top lip. Savors me before dragging his mouth down along my neck and laving my earlobe, sending electric zings straight to my pussy. "Gave me some ideas of my own."

Halfheartedly, I push back on his muscled chest. He holds me fast. "We can't get into this now, Ty and Zoey will wonder where we are," I protest.

"I beg to differ." Connor's fingers hook the hem of my skirt, drag it up my thighs and over my bump. He moves the crotch of my panties to the side and plunges two fingers inside me. His sneaky thumb flicks my clit.

It feels too delightful. I can't help but lean back to give him better access. I rest one leg on the back of the sofa. Orgasms at this stage of my pregnancy are next-level. I'm not turning one or two down by the sexiest beast on the planet. "Oh, jeez. Yes. Right there, ahhh."

"Ah, Mae. You are so feckin' wet." He works me to the brink and then abruptly pulls my underwear down and tosses it on the floor. Hovers his lips just above the surface of my inner thighs and my opening. His hot breath makes me squirm. He darts his tongue out for a lick here and there. Ramps up his intensity bit by bit. My hips cant and wriggle to make contact.

Connor cradles my bump gently to keep me in place. "Settle, Mae. You don't need to do a thing. Let me make you come, love."

God, I love when he takes charge.

"Aye," I lovingly say in an Irish accent as he places one of my legs over his shoulder. Leans down and suckles my labia with his pillowy lips. Swoops his tongue along my seam and along my folds. When my hips undulate against his mouth, he places his palm against my mound and presses to prevent me from moving. It's worth it when he traps my clit in between two long fingers. Laps it with long, languid strokes until he's essentially making out with my little nub. Licking. Swirling. Laving.

I'm panting now. Moaning. Squirming. Urging him on. He trails his fingers down my pussy and slips them back inside me. Rubs his rough pads against my little bundle of nerves with just the perfect amount of finesse. When he sucks my clit hard and keeps up the pressure, I can't help but cry out. I grab his head and hold him in place. He's relentless. I'm coming. And coming. Still coming. I fling my arm over my eyes. Unable to do anything but ride the orgasmic tsunami.

God, I love how he takes care of me.

"Beautiful." He smiles up at me, his lips and beard glistening with my release.

"Do you want to come on my belly?" I rub my exposed bump, which is covered with faint stretch marks. Twins are hell on a woman's figure, that's for sure.

Connor doesn't seem to care. He's too busy unbuckling his belt and shoving his black jeans down to answer me with anything but a grunt. Fisting his cock, he drags his crown through my pussy lips. I can't see him do it over my stomach, but oh how I feel it. The zings start flickering up and down my core again.

I draw my knees up and rest my feet on his chest. "Just dip your tip in a bit." I smile wickedly up at him. Knowing there's nothing left to his imagination at this angle.

"Holy shite, Mae." Connor's face is a grimace when he grasps my outer thighs to plunge in shallowly. My Irish honey looks utterly tortured. Well, he no doubt is tortured because, ordinarily, he loves to fuck me hard.

At nearly eight months pregnant, it's not possible for many reasons. At least in this position, I'm comfortable. We have just enough friction to push us both over the edge. It's the best we can do with my physical limitations..

But—holy moly—it's phenomenal.

My pussy clenches all around his crown. I'm on the brink of coming again. Connor pulls out and thrusts the underside of his cock against my pussy, careful not to enter me. Rocks his hips from side to side so his pubic bone grinds relentlessly against my sensitive little nub. I go over with a shudder. He follows, coating the underside of my ginormous belly with his release.

When our breathing returns to somewhat normal, Connor kisses my bump and cleans me off with the hem of his t-shirt. "Wee lads, I just can't help shagging your ma every day. I hope I'm not traumatizing you."

I run my fingers through his curls when he rests his bearded cheek on my stomach. He practically purrs when my nails gently scrape his scalp. "You're going to be the best papa." I gaze at the top of his head. "I'm so lucky you're the father of my kids."

Connor looks up with misty eyes. "Ah, you know how to gut me, Mae. This is all I've ever wanted in life."

"Me too, my love. But, as much as I'd love to spend the rest of the afternoon out here, I suppose we should be decent hosts?" I yawn and make no effort to move.

"Aye." He stands and buckles his pants then helps me put on my underwear. My belly lurches. We both watch in awe. Our sexy activities woke the babies, who are wriggling around like aliens under my skin.

"They're crazily active today." I place Connor's hand on my belly, mesmerized by how my bump moves and distorts as they shift position.

He caresses an elbow. Or maybe a knee. "Does it hurt?"

"Not exactly. It's the weirdest sensation. Uncomfortable. Sometimes they... Ugh—" A baby essentially stands on my bladder "He got me. I have to pee. Like now." I roll myself off the sofa and hustle to the bathroom to take care of business.

When I return, Connor holds his hand out. "Should we head up? I'm convinced they're done shagging the life out of each other by now."

"We gave them more than enough time." I can't help but smirk as we weave our way up the path to the house.

There's no sign of Ty and Zoey yet. We retreat to our room where Connor changes his sex-stained t-shirt. A bit of his spunk is visible on my skirt, so I change too. Opting for the comfort of an old, oversized LTZ sweatshirt and leggings.

Our guests are still "resting," so we decide to prep for dinner. Connor seasons steaks for the grill and wraps corn on the cob in aluminum foil with little pats of butter. I assemble a chopped salad. By the time we're done, the lead singer of LTZ and his fiancćc appear in the doorway looking, uh... fresh? Yes. They look fresh.

"Hey, Ronni." Ty, wearing his usual uniform of ripped jeans and a black Henley, embraces me from the side. He looks slightly terrified at the sight of my protruding belly.

Sporting black jeans and a light-gray sweater, Zoey almost shyly hangs back and studies us. I get it. She's still a tad uncomfortable around me. During our publicity-generated fauxmance, Ty and I were plastered everywhere as the world's "it" couple. Zoey had no way of knowing our romance was a ruse.

Connor hated everything about the stupid stunt. At least he knew it was fake. She didn't. Ty told Zoey the truth when they got back together. Let's just say she was not impressed and not afraid to say so. On the day we met, she harshly called me out. Which I respected.

"Zoey, take this." Connor hands her a can of Guinness. "Let me properly welcome you to Ireland."

Her smile is genuine when she throws her arms around my husband. She takes a swig of the stout and tries to hide her wince. "Thank you for inviting us. I'm so glad this worked out schedule-wise. Your house is stunning. This country is stunning, from what I've seen so far."

We spend a couple of hours eating, drinking, and catching up. When it starts getting late, the men leave Zoey and I in the living room while they clean up. "What's it like?" Zoey eyeballs my bump. "I mean, twins. Are you terrified?"

I realize I'm rubbing my stomach. It's become a habit. I love feeling my babies growing inside me. "I'm scared to death for all of it. I'm having a C-section, so at least I don't have to panic about pushing them out of me. Connor's aunt and mom will be here for a couple of months to help. After that? We'll figure out if we need to get a nanny. Or two."

"I can't wait to have kids, although, it's been wonderful having Ty to myself." Zoey relaxes back into the sofa.

"Well, you deserve some time together." I reach over and rub the top of her hand. "Ty seems the happiest I've ever seen him. The way he looks at you, Zoey? You're destined. It's so clear."

"I appreciate that, especially coming from you. I'll admit, it's still hard to believe I'm sitting here talking to you like this. You and I haven't had much alone time." Zoey's cheeks redden, but she manages to keep eye contact.

I'm self-aware enough to know Zoey's still a little weirded out about me. "Can I admit something to you? I always feel like an outsider because people are intimidated by this stupid fame thing. It was so fun to meet all of the LTZ ladies last year after hearing so much about you. I'm genuinely happy you and I are becoming friends. "

"Oh, thank God. Me too." Zoey visibly relaxes. She looks behind us toward the kitchen and whips back around. "Before they come back, could I ask you a question? You don't have to answer."

"Uh, sure." My hackles are up, just a little. The babies shift a bit and I have to readjust my position to get comfortable.

Zoey scrunches her nose, then surprises me. "Did Ty ever talk about his childhood with you?"

"No." I shrug. "Never."

"Ah, okay." She slumps.

I can't help but to be concerned about Ty. He's such a sensitive soul. "Is everything okay?"

"Oh, um. Yeah. I was just wondering. All that stuff with his mom and the press. He never wants to talk about it.

I don't want him to get hurt again." She waves her hand in the air to shoo herself. "I'm being overprotective."

She's clearly bothered, but I don't have anything to tell her. Plus, it's Ty's prerogative to talk to his fiancée. "Just ask him, Zoey. It's sweet that you want to take care of him. He hasn't had too many people in his life looking out for his best interests."

Luckily, I'm saved by the guys rejoining us. The four of us visit for a while, but soon I'm exhausted, and Connor and I say goodnight.

"Are you missing the band?" I murmur against Connor's chest as he strokes my hair in our big bed.

"Aye, a bit." Connor kisses the side of my head. "We'd been in each other's pockets for years. It's to be expected. Still, there's nowhere else I'd rather be than here with you."

"Promise?" Ty and Zoey's visit has punctured my bubble. Suddenly, the fact I'm giving birth soon feels too real. The nursery's done. Private birthing classes are over. We have every doohickey and gadget invented. Saoirse's planning on moving into the guest room. We're technically ready, but I realize I've been in denial.

Pregnancy's been like my greatest acting role. As much as I love and want my babies, have I just been going through the motions? I'm not prepared. Mentally, that is.

Holy hell. I'm having twins. In a less than a month. "Oh God, Connor. I can't do this…"

"You can. I'm ready, Mae. I can't wait for them to get here." Connor leans over and places a sweet kiss on my lips, soothing me. He strokes my brow with the tip of his finger, massaging my furrow away. "Stop worrying; they're going to be the best thing that ever happened to us. You're going to be great. I'll be by your side for all of it."

He never breaks eye contact with me. His radiant smile is infectious. He makes me start to believe in myself.

"Okay." I whoosh out a breath of air. "Okay."

He snuggles me close. Soon, I'm a bit calmer, but the boys kicking my ribs keep me awake for a long time after Connor's breathing evens out.

I know I need sleep. I should be stocking up considering once these two are born, I won't be getting much.

It's just impossible to ignore the prickling beginning at the base of my scalp.

Dreadful things happen whenever I feel this way.

Not this time.

Nothing bad is going to happen to my family.

Never again.

Chapter Two

Four Months Later

THE PAST FOUR MONTHS have whizzed by like a Formula One race car in Monte Carlo.

Twin babies have a way of speeding up time, so they do.

After Ty and Zoey left us to jet off to Italy, Ronni's specialist, Ronan O'Leary, advised us to push up our birth date. Her blood pressure was not in a range he was happy with. As he put it, "Ronni has done her job, it's time to get break these boys out of jail."

His failed attempt at humor aside, at thirty-seven weeks, the doctor determined it was safer for Ronni to give birth than to carry the babies longer. The next day, we were admitted into Ballybridge Private Hospital, an exclusive medical center near Belfast. We selected it because of its top-notch birthing facility. Pristine, modern, and impeccably designed. Ronni and I both swore we'd stayed in five-star hotels with fewer amenities.

As an added bonus, they built their reputation on privacy and extreme discretion. For us, this was not just important but necessary. The events of the past year required both of us to keep a low profile.

Look, I'm proud that Ronni brought down Kircher. I am. It's just that we lived through years of secrecy and lies. I shudder to think of what could have happened if I hadn't been in New York that night.

But, I was. I had my family to protect. And I think it's all been worth it.

Veronica Mae Miller is a heroine to everyone in Hollywood who's ever been exploited. Against the odds, she and I survived as a couple. We're finally public with our marriage.

It shouldn't matter that the blogs, fan clubs, and tabloids initially had such a visceral reaction, should it?

I get that Ronni's public fauxmance with Ty wasn't "faux" to our fans. Jaysus, though. It hurt my feelings. It feckin' killed me to endure the vile, horrific lies people told: I'm a woman-stealer. Ronni's a desperate, pathetic LTZ groupie who'd fucked the entire band and I'm the chump that got stuck with her. The worst? We feckin' cheated behind Ty's back.

I. Am. Not. A. Cheater.

A part of me is still infuriated our fans will never know Ronni and I have been faithful and committed for years.

Jaysus. Stop winding yourself up, McGloughlin. There's no point in reliving that shite.

Right. The bottom line is, there's no feckin' way I would allow her pregnancy—or any speculation about our babies' paternity—to add fuel to the fire. The second we found out we were having twins, I convinced Ronni moving to Ireland would be our best plan. Thank Christ she agreed. By the time we'd settled here at my estate, the media's focus had already shifted to Ty and Zoey's fairytale reunion and engagement. Ronni's fickle fans who hated us together now seem thrilled she's found true love with me.

I consider ourselves lucky the press hasn't found out about her pregnancy. Removing ourselves from the spotlight allows us to finally have some feckin' privacy. After decades in the public eye, Ronni's had the longest break since she was fired from Hawaiian High.

Impending motherhood forced her to prioritize her well-being. For once. I'm here to ensure she rests and takes care of her physical and mental health.

As far as our babies are concerned, Dr. O'Leary's team was second to none. Worth every single penny. Ronni's C-section went off without a hitch, and moments later our sons, Tristan and Torin, made their debut.

We're now parents to two perfect, squalling, wee lads.

Aye. Fatherhood. It's my favorite thing I've done, ever.

"Connor?" I hear Ronni's sleepy voice in the bedroom.

I pour some of the chicken soup I'm heating in a mug, place it on the tray with toasted brown bread and butter and bring it with me. The boys are still asleep. We have about twenty minutes before their ncxt feeding. "I brought you some dinner, my love."

Ronni stretches. Yawns. Blinks herself awake. I place the tray to her side. She wrinkles her nose. "I don't want the butter, babe. I have to lose this baby weight."

"Says who?" I boop her nose. "Not Dr. O'Leary. You are feeding two babies. You're supposed to take in additional calories to keep them healthy."

She swats me away. Picks up a piece of the bread and takes a bite. Chews. Swallows. Sticks her tongue out at me.

Torin stirs in his bassinette. I can't resist his little mewly noises. I bend to pick him up. Cradle him and watch in wonder when his tiny fingers grip my thumb.

"You're obsessed." Ronni's smile is cheeky. "He'll start crying if I don't put him on the boob. I better finish this while I have the chance."

She slurps down the soup and shoves the bread into her mouth while I continue to stare at my tiny son. Tristan cries out, kicking his wee feet frantically. I point to him. "There's no doubt Tristan was the kicker. He's destined to be the leader of the two."

"Mmm-hmmm." Ronni, who isn't paying attention to my predictions, sets the tray down and grabs the giant nursing pillow. She situates it to her liking. Unclasps her nursing bra. Motions for me to hand over the baby. "It's milk-cow time."

We have a system.

Feeding the twins at the same time is efficient. Gives her extra minutes to rest when sleep is an absolute luxury. Once Torin is latched, I pick up Tristan and hand him to her. She tucks him against her opposite side. Soon, both boys are happily suckling away.

"You're beautiful, Mae." I never get tired of the wonderous miracle of her feeding our babies. "You've taken to motherhood like a champ."

"Don't speak too soon. All I do is sleep, eat, pee, and feed these two. I literally have no energy to do anything else." She gently strokes the boys' heads as they nurse.

I cross the room to the changing table to get two nappies ready. "We've come a long way for two people who had no experience with real-life babies. Jaysus, when we brought them home, I was utterly terrified."

"I'm still terrified. And panicked. I've gotten used to being in our little Irish cocoon. I'm not quite ready to go back to LA." Ronni's voice has a bit of a tremor.

"Ah, Mae. Dr. O'Leary helped us vet an entire medical team. Kris is interviewing nannies, and you know she won't hire anyone who isn't legit." I sit on the edge of the bed and tweak her unvarnished toe. "We'll be grand. Better than grand."

Ronni is quiet. Contemplative. "Maybe you could postpone the band meeting. Or move it to LA. The guys will understand."

"I wish I could, but they're all in Seattle. I'm the lone wolf living in LA." I grip her ankle and squeeze. "Are you still worried about me being gone, love? I'm taking the jet; it'll be quick. Like I went out for coffee."

Her tear-rimmed crystal-green eyes tell me she's not happy about our separation. "I'm not confident I can balance everything without you. Even for a few hours. Kris is already setting up meetings to pitch the new show. We're supposed to start production on the movie. How did I ever think I could be a good mom and keep up the pace I was on? I can't even breast feed without you there."

"Should we hire additional staff?" I'm at a loss of how to reassure her.

Ronni's a strong, capable woman who simply doesn't know how to ask for help. Our relationship, for the most part, has been long-distance with spurts of me living with her in Malibu when the band had down-time. Neither of us ever consulted each other about our work schedules. We just did our thing and were together whenever possible.

Needless to say, my unilateral decision to attend my band meeting in Seattle did not go over well. It just never occurred to me there'd be a problem. I was wrong. Obviously, with infant twins, our lives are not our own anymore. I can't take back what I did, but I'll damn sure never prioritize anything but my family going forward.

Ronni doesn't answer. Instead, she unlatches Torin and hands him to me. She keeps Tristan but closes her nursing bra. We both sit them up in burp position. Rub their bellies. Pat their backs. A baby belch or two later, she finally replies. "I don't know, Connor. I think we'll just need to see. I hope you were serious about telling the guys we want more time. I know it's not entirely your decision, but I don't want you to miss your kids growing up."

"I don't either. I want all the time I can get with my wee lads." The thought makes me smile. "I'm happy to tell them I'm not able to start back up again for a while.

If it's a problem, they can let someone else take my place for a bit."

She visibly relaxes. "Thank you, my honey. I'm not asking you to quit, you know. I'd never do that."

"I know, Mae. I'm offering to take a step back temporarily." I kiss Torin's sweet head. "For the record, I'd never ask you to quit your career either."

The air around us feels ominous for a brief second before it dissipates.

"Feel like diaper duty while I shower? I smell like baby vomit and poo." Ronni thrusts Tristan in my direction, not giving me much of a choice, but breaking the tension.

"Gladly. Don't forget to use extra shower gel." I take my son and stick my tongue out at her.

While Ronni showers, I change the babies and place them in their bassinettes. Next, I strip the bed and put on clean sheets. By the time Ronni returns smelling like her normal lemony self, I'm leaning against the headboard with the boys nestled in the crooks of my arms. We're playing with their crinkle book. Torin loves staring at the black-and-white images. Tristan loves the squeaker.

She lays next to us and nuzzles Tristan's belly. "This is so nice," she mumbles. Her eyes close. Soon she's lightly dozing.

Torin starts to cry. Tristan joins him. I gather them close and head to the living room so Ronni doesn't wake up. I seem to have the magic touch. They always fall asleep when I rock them in a repetitive swooping motion. I return to our bedroom and place them in their cradles.

Cycle complete.

I look over at my beautiful wife. She's such a vision, so she is.

Her robe is untied. She's still naked underneath. I take a moment to simply admire her. My Mae's so self-conscious about her body these days, any nudity is a rare gift. Her breasts are luscious. Full. With big, rosy nipples from breast feeding. The scar from her C-section is hardly visible in her bikini line. Her obsession with fancy silicone treatments has worked a treat to heal it.

My dick hardens when she relaxes into deeper rest. Her knee is bent, allowing a wee glimpse of her pink pussy. I love that she hasn't shaved since giving birth. As sexy as it is when she's hairless, the wispy, reddish hairs framing her clit turn me on something fierce. What I'd give to lean over and breathe in her musk. Have a little taste.

Except, these babies are no joke. There's no way I'll disturb her rest.

Instead, I unbutton my jeans and shove my hand into my boxer briefs. Fist my cock. Squeeze the tip and stroke. Slow at first. Aye. Then, a bit faster.

Ayyyyyyye.

My right hand and my dick have become best friends these past months. My pace increases until I'm close. My hips buck. A zing takes root at the base of my spine when I hear my phone ringing in the kitchen. Ronni's eyes blink open and widen when she notices what I'm doing.

Caught.

"Are you going to answer that or finish?" She smirks. Skims her hand down her torso and rubs her clit with her finger.

Holy bleedin' hell. I'm too far gone to stop. "Ah, Mae. Oh, shite." I erupt in an arc that splatters her tits, chest, and chin.

Ronni laughs and wipes it off with the hem of her robe. "That was soooo hot."

"Let me make you come too, love." I reach for her.

"I'm okay. Not quite ready yet." She closes her robe and ties it. "You should really answer your phone. Someone's clearly trying to reach you."

I hadn't even noticed that my phone was ringing again. "Aye." I reluctantly trudge out to the kitchen and answer.

"Connor!" my ma cries into the phone. "Why aren't you answering your phone? Yer da's at the hospital. He's had a stroke. They're not positive he's going to make it. Seamus says you need to come straightaway, so you do."

Jaysus.

Ma is hysterical, but I manage to find out the basics. When we hang up, I initiate a group video chat with my brothers to fill in the gaps. It's not looking hopeful. Devastated, I return to the bedroom. Ronni's waiting. My strong, take-charge woman kicks into high gear when I let her know what's happening. Together, we hurriedly come up with our own game plan and set it into motion.

What a whirlwind mindfuck of a day.

I cuddle my wife close and shut my eyes. Ronni and I have been to both heaven and hell and back again.

Multiple times. My father's dire health condition is just another thing we'll navigate on our voyage.

Unfortunately, we have no choice but to abandon our blissful Irish hideaway sooner than we'd planned.

The thing is?

This is true life. Ronni's my feckin' soulmate. There's no one on this planet I'd rather have by my side.

The good. The bad. The known. The unknown. The triumph. The joy. The tragedy. The sorrow.

Together, we're stronger.

Now that we have our kids?

Our bond is unbreakable.

Chapter Three

A Couple of Weeks Later

CHAOS.

Utter. Total. Chaos.

I'm trying my best not to scream. Screaming would be stupid. Extraordinarily stupid now that the boys have settled down.

I've held down the fort on my own in LA for six full days. The longest motherfucking days of my entire life. The nanny Kris found quit on day two, despite my offer to double and then triple her pay. She met someone and is off to Europe, leaving me high and dry.

With me, myself and I to rely on, there's no choice but to take up swearing like a sailor. It's not on brand, I'm America's fucking sweetheart after all. I don't give two shits. Connor's in Seattle for at least another week to attend a band meeting after he's been there helping out after his father's stroke. I haven't had time to even think about posting an ad for a nanny.

Cussing's the one thing getting me through the day.

I flop down on my unmade bed. Close my eyes so I can't see my surroundings. The entire house is in shambles. I have food stuck in my hair. My breasts are leaking. I'm a flabby, out-of-shape blob. I'm starving, but too tired to eat. My gel manicure is peeling. To add insult to injury, my period came back today. The one-of-a-kind custom pearl-gray sofa I commissioned is ruined. I bled through onto it when I was napping with Torin splayed out across my chest.

The bubble has burst. This is not what I signed up for. My life, as I once knew it, is over.

God, what I'd give to turn back the clock.

Instantly, I feel sick I'd even have that thought. My babies are my world. I love them desperately. It's just—the day-to-day is so friggin' hard. It's all I can do not to sob.

My phone lights up. Connor. I accept the call, grab the baby monitor and crawl under the covers. The quicker the call, the faster I can grab a couple of hours sleep. "Hey."

"Are things any better? I haven't heard from you all day." Connor squinches his eyebrows together. He looks pale. Disheveled. Exhausted.

I shake my head. Bite my lip. He has enough on his plate without me adding to it. "No, I'm hoping Kris can let me borrow her admin for a day or two. At least set up some interviews."

"I wish you'd reconsider bringing everyone up here. At least we'd be together." Connor's amber eyes are sad. I know he's crushed at missing time with his sons.

I sigh. We've had this conversation a million times. My gut reaction is to refuse. My career has been on hold for too long. He's the one who unilaterally decided to go to Seattle before we had a plan. Or a nanny. Or help. "Babe, the problem is Kris has me in meetings for the next week. I'm lucky they're on Zoom, but the boys still need my boobs. The three of us are tied together for now. Once they're weaned, it will be easier if we need to be in different cities."

Connor looks away. Nods. "Aye. You're right. Uh...the thing is, Ty and Zoey are getting married. All of us are invited."

"When?" The thought of hauling the kids to a wedding is fucking daunting, but I'll need to be there. There's no question. It's too big of an occasion to miss.

He shakes his head and pinches the bridge of his nose. "Three weeks."

My mouth drops open.

"Hear me out, Mae." Connor doesn't give me a chance to respond. "Da's doing a bit better. The rehab facility is nice. Cillian's got Ma sorted out. We can both be back home in LA by December. You won't be working. We both know that Hollywood essentially shuts down for the holidays the Wednesday before Thanksgiving. There's no reason for us to be apart. Will you please come to Seattle? I miss you. I miss my boys."

Every part of my body melts into goo. The guilt at my earlier heinous thoughts goes through the roof, however- er. I'm a terrible person. A terrible mother. I've got to be better. I'm so lucky to have my little family. "Let me make some calls tomorrow. If I can, I will."

"Aye. Thank you, love." He takes a deep breath. Smiles at me. "What's in your hair?"

I roll my eyes. "Yogurt. Tristan thwacked it out of my hand when I attempted to eat something this afternoon."

"I'm sorry you're on your own, I'd do anything to be there. I love you so much." His smile is weak, but genuine.

"I love you too." I get out of bed when I hear joyful babbling on the baby monitor. I hold my index finger to my lip. "Shh, they're awake. I'm going to peek in."

Their nursery is in the room next door. My sons stare up at me wide-eyed from the crib they've shared since we moved back to LA. I flip the phone camera so Connor can see his sons. "Say hi to your papa, Tristan. Say hi to your papa, Torin."

"Well, hello, wee lads. Your papa misses you. Look at those smiles." I hear Connor through my phone. I let him coo at the twins until they start fussing.

I flip the phone back to my own face. "Duty calls, babe."

"Before you hang up, you forgot to ask me how the band meeting went." He grins at me. Even a glimpse of the babies gave Connor a pick-me-up from all of the drama with his family.

I can't help but slap a palm to my forehead. "Right! Well?"

"We're extending the break. No one is ready to immerse ourselves into LTZ. We also decided for any future tours, they'll be short enough so our families can come with us. We can even design our own custom tour bus." Connor scrubs his hands through his curls. "I'm so relieved."

As am I. "Well, that's great news."

"I know."

I gaze at his kind, amber eyes. God, I miss my husband. "I love you, Con. I hate to hang up, but I'm so tired. I'd like to get these guys back to bed so I can sleep."

"I know. I love you too." He puckers his lips and kisses me through the screen. "Think about coming up for a couple of weeks. It would be grand, so it would."

I nod. "Okay. It sounds wonderful. If I can swing it, I'll make it happen."

Thankfully, it doesn't take long to get the boys settled back down again. As for me, I'm wide awake. I didn't expect to change my mind about going to Seattle. Connor's been bugging me about it every night. Something shifted today, and suddenly I can think of nothing else. It's not even nine, so I call Kris.

She answers and waves at me through the screen. She's on the move, so I get a little seasick trying to watch her. "You must have ESP. Gulliver Rafferty's contract came in. They're putting the final budget together, but it looks like we'll be in Ireland in August through October. Postproduction here. Aiming for a holiday release to qualify for an Oscar."

"Wow. That's ambitious. I didn't think we had a shot in hell of getting the hottest Irish actor on the planet." I'm so giddy, it feels like a million sunbeams have entered my body. Funny the difference two hours can make in a girl's life.

Kris holds up a finger. "There's something else. I didn't want to say anything because you've obviously had your hands full." The screen pans to the floor and I hear a door shut. When her face reappears, I can see she's in her production office. "Okay, I wanted to tell you this behind closed doors. I had lunch with the Netflix execs today. We are a couple of days away from officially getting this series greenlighted. Apparently, there are minimal notes. As long as the contracts come through the way we negotiated, you and I have casting to do in December. We'll finish preproduction in the new year and film late winter-early spring.

I'm stunned silent. Hours ago, when I was losing my mind, I wanted to turn back the clock. Resuming my busy filming schedule seemed like a dream compared to changing diapers and feeling like a human feeding vessel. Faced with the reality, I'm so conflicted. I've worked my entire career for these types of opportunities.

Before I had sons. I don't want to miss a thing with them, despite my internal breakdown earlier. This schedule is insane. Even if I didn't have my babies to consider.

"Wow," is all I can muster.

Kris cocks her head. "I know you're a bit overwhelmed. Did you get my text? Allison will be at your disposal tomorrow; she'll have an excellent nanny hired within a day. She'll also arrange for you to have a full-time housekeeper."

"Thank you." I'm a bit choked up. Kris always looks out for me. I appreciate it. She sees me struggling. As supportive as she is being, she just doesn't get how hard it is. How tired I am all the time. How overwhelmed I feel just getting through the day.

How much I struggle keeping up with my side of our workload.

Or if I even want to keep up.

Kris smiles at me warmly. "Your dreams are coming true, Ronni."

I manage a big, fake smile.

"Oh." She holds up a finger. "I've hired a PR firm for our production company. They are adamant about turning the narrative around on the negative press you got about your relationship with Connor."

"What do you mean?" Most of the stuff with our relationship has long died down. My hackles are up. I've spent most of my acting career cultivating press. Knowing how and when to alert the paparazzi. Working my angles. Controlling the story. Hell, it's how I was able to build such an iron-clad case against Don Kircher—trading faux-relationships for press.

God, I don't want to put my real relationship in the spotlight. Not willingly.

Kris squeezes her eyes shut then lets out a breath. "You're going to hate this. They want to feature you, Connor and the boys…"

"No." I hold my hand up to the phone for emphasis.

"Hear me out. " Kris ignores me. "You aren't going to be holed up in your house forever. People are going to figure out you've had children with him. I think a holiday article—it doesn't have to be a cover or anything—with some well-wishes from Ty and Zoey would go a long way in quashing all of the negativity."

I palm my forehead. My breath feels erratic. I'm stressed. "I'll ask Connor. It will be up to him."

"It will legitimize your career shift." She regards me solemnly. In that moment, I know I have to do it. If I'm going to be taken seriously on the business side of things, having the public think I'm a band whore is not going to help.

God. It seems so superficial. No, it is superficial. My priorities are shifting. Of course I want to achieve success as a producer. But I want to prove to myself—and to

Connor—that I'm just as capable being a mom to these little guys.

Is exposing my little family to the press the right thing for us?

"What's up?" Kris taps her red-manicured nail against her lip. "I'm not getting the enthusiastic reaction I was expecting."

I prop up the phone against my pillow. "I am happy. It's amazing news about everything. I guess I'm just exhausted. I'm on the fence about the big press splash. I'd like those days to be behind me."

"Ronni. We're starting a production company." Kris is clearly surprised. Historically, I've been all about the press.

In the past.

Easily I make my decision. My family needs me, and I need them. "I'll let you know. For now, it's important the boys and I are with Connor. Ty and Zoey are getting married. The three of us are joining him in Seattle but we'll all be back in LA for the holidays."

"Well, that's fine. You can work remotely." She studies me. "Or are you trying to tell me something?"

"Honestly? I don't know. Let me talk to Connor. And Ty and Zoey. If they're all on board, an article should be fine as long as it's subtle. Did I mention the band met today and decided to extend their hiatus?" My eyes are growing heavy. Today's been a lot. "I want to do it all, Kris. I just need to work it all out. If I can take a raincheck on having Allison's help, maybe we all will come up with a plan to alleviate some of my domestic shit when I get back."

Kris's expression softens. She nods. "I'm sorry for pressuring you. I know things are different now."

"No, I'm sorry." My voice cracks.

"Don't be." She shakes her head. "Look, I've been after you for years to take time for yourself. I can't pretend to know what you're going through. The timing of all of this is what it is. It's got to work for both of us or not at all."

I put my hand over my heart. Kris has been my biggest advocate for most of my adult life. I don't know where I'd be without her. "I want to do everything, you know. We've worked so hard to get here. I just need to put the puzzle together."

"Just don't get knocked up again." She laughs.

God, she has a point. "I should've had the IUD put in when I gave birth. Connor talked me out of it. I blame the pregnancy hormones on a momentary lapse where I agreed to have a big, huge brood. I can't even imagine feeling that way now when I'm just hanging on with two."

We hang up. All I can think about is climbing under the covers and shutting my eyes. I consider showering to wash the yogurt out of my hair, but sleep wins.

Tomorrow, aside from taking care of my sons, my priority is chartering a flight to Seattle to reunite my family. I don't want to be without my husband. I don't want a life without my little babies, no matter how hard it is now. Because I'm lucky. I don't need to give up my career. Or even take my foot off the gas.

I'm not alone. Not anymore.

As long as we're together, Connor and I will be able to figure all of this out.

I've never been more certain.

Chapter Four

A Few Weeks Later

STANDING WITH JACE AND Zane in front of Ty & Zoey's grand fireplace opposite our women, we watch the happy couple recite their wedding vows. Well, some of us do. As for me?

I can't take my eyes off my wife.

She's a vision, so she is. Pale-pink, satiny dress. High heels with sparkly clasps. Chestnut hair partially held up by some sort of doohickey that allows little wisps of hair to frame her face. Her green eyes are rimmed with smudgy makeup. She licks her shiny, red lips.

So. Feckin'. Sexy.

As inappropriate as the timing is, my dick stirs then hardens to steel. Christ, I can't stop thinking about Mae's sassy, talented mouth. Jaysus. A couple of hours ago, when she and I were getting ready at my town house, she sank to her knees. Unzipped my slacks. Took out my neglected cock and sucked me off.

Staring down into her green eyes. Those pouty lips stretched around my shaft. Tits spilling out of her lacy push-up bra...

I came as fast as a teenager.

Hastily, I clasp my hands over my non-discreetly tented slacks. Jaysus, I cannot have a chubby. Not like this. There are children present. And my band. Their parents.

For feck's sake. I will myself to think of anything but the visual of my come dripping down Ronni's chin. Her pink tongue darting out to swipe up every drop.

Stop. It. Connor!

Wrinkly grannies. Wrinkly grannies. Wrinkly grannies. Cock. Still. Hard.

I shift my weight from foot to foot. Unable to stop sneaking glimpses of Ronni's abundant cleavage. Her dress is slightly snug around her breasts, which are still plump from nursing. I want to free those perfect tits and cup them in my palms. Roughly thumb her rosy nipples. Take her from behind and see them jiggle with every cant of my hips. Make her eyes roll back when I hit that place inside her that makes her let go fully. Feel her squeeze around me like a vacuum seal when she...

My cock lengthens and I can't help but stifle a groan. It's loud and inappropriate enough that Ronni glances up to catch me ogling her. Her gaze flicks up and down my body until she realizes my dilemma. Her eyes widen and dart back up to see me wince. The little minx winks. Licks those red lips. Scarcely suppresses a giggle.

The power this woman has over me. It's utterly devastating. Exhilarating.

All-encompassing.

Digging my nails into my palms, I try to get a grip on myself. Do everything in my bag of tricks to stop all thoughts of ramming my cock into my wife when I should be paying attention to these feckin' vows.

Wrinkly grannies. Wrinkly grannies. Wrinkly grannies.

Wrinkly grannies. Wrinkly grannies. Wrinkly grannies. Doesn't feckin' work.

The moment the ceremony is over, I hurry Ronni and the boys into a spare bedroom, claiming we need to feed them. Don't bother to worry if the others believe me or not, considering the boys are sound asleep. The second the door shuts behind us, I position their carriers to face the sliding glass door.

Beautiful view of the garden, I justify to myself.

It's best not to contaminate their little minds with what I'm about to do to their ma. As an afterthought, I tuck their stuffed twin elephants under the straps. If they wake up, their toys might buy us a couple minutes of fucking before they start wailing.

Satisfied that my fatherly duties are fulfilled for the moment, I turn around. Growl at the sight of Veronica Mae Miller watching me with an expression that's a mix of sex-kitten and doting mother. It's all I can do not to rip off my shirt. Instead, I unbutton it swiftly but carefully. Set it on an oversized gray suede chair in the corner of the room. Prowl toward her like a panther.

"Mae," I roar. Deep. Guttural. In a nanosecond, I free my aching cock and pump it root to tip as I move closer.

She backs up until her ass hits the bed. Looks around the room frantically. "Uh, Connor? Here?"

"Aye. Here. Now. Turn around and bend over. Lean on your elbows. Ass in the air."

Sweet Jaysus, she does it. Even spreads her long, luscious legs, clad in high-heeled pumps, wider. I fling her floaty dress over her ass. Shove the tiny scrap of underwear to the side. Pinch her swollen pussy lips to find her soaking wet. Fill her to the hilt with one thrust.

"Oh. My. God," Ronni whisper-yelps.

With no time for sweet nothings, I wrap my arms around her. Skim my hands down her arms and entwine her fingers with mine. I fold myself over her, blanketing her entire back. Still buried inside her, I whisper, "Is this okay, love?"

"Yessss," she hisses and wiggles her sweet ass against my balls. "Unbelievable. Thank God I put my IUD back in. I need this, baby. I missed this."

What? We didn't talk about her going back on birth control. If she's protected, it certainly explains her renewed interest in sex with me today. I'm still inside her, debating whether we should talk this out before we fuck. Except, wee Connor has a singular priority. There's no way he'll allow me slip out of her plump, pink pussy when she's squeezing my needy cock for dear life.

Not a feckin' chance.

Buried in her wet heat, I forget everything but how sensational it feels to be inside my wife. I cover her entire mound with one hand. Flatten the heel and press so her clit is stimulated against my dick as I fuck her from behind. She grinds against me. I rut into her. Fast. Furious.

I'm nearly out of control.

Ronni's mewling little moans grow louder. I cover her mouth with my free hand. Bury my face in her neck. Her pussy gushes around me when she goes over, unleashing a tremendous tickly, fluttery sensation up my shaft. One thrust and a jolt of electricity spreads throughout my lower stomach, intensifying into a blissful burst of joy through the tip of my cock.

I hold her tight against me as I overflow her with my come.

"Oh, shite, Mae. I've flooded you. Give me a second." I pull up my slacks, which were bunched around my ankles, and grab a handful of tissues from the en suite.

As I delicately wipe all traces of me from her pussy and thighs, Ronni laughs and shakes her head. "Did we just get it on in the middle of Ty's wedding? In Ty's house. All of them have to know what's going on in here."

"Aye, we did." I smooth her dress down her heart-shaped ass. "I don't give two shites. Truth be told, I blame the way your tits looked in that dress. I couldn't feckin' resist you."

She swats at me playfully. "Once a perv. Always a perv."

"Some of my favorite memories are of me fucking you proper before you'd head out with him to some feckin' red carpet BS." I weave my fingers with hers and bring her knuckles up to my lips. Kiss each one as I stare into her soul.

Ronni claps each side of my face. "I loved knowing I was full of you. Feeling you dripping down my thighs. Ooh. It's what kept me going."

I can't help but smile like the madman I am. Marking her as my woman is everything. Christ, she's my everything. She's mine and will be mine forever. Neither of us can wipe the happiness from our faces. Being apart during my da's health setback made us both realize just how much our priorities have changed. "You keep me going, Mae. We're not going to be separated again."

"Excellent." She presses her forehead to mine. "Family first."

Speaking of which, we both realize the boys are babbling away. Blissfully unaware of the shenanigans their parents have been up to. I help her get straightened out. Put my shirt back on. We grab bottles and settle on opposite sides in the overstuffed chairs. Feed. Burp. Nappy change. Done.

"We've got this parenting thing down," I say to Mae as we depart. I find Zane grinning at me in the hallway.

Feckin' hell.

"There you are. It's time for dinner." He glances at both of us, a knowing smirk spreads across his face.

Fee is behind him holding Mia's wee hand. "We didn't want to interrupt, but I'm glad you're finished feeding your babies. This one needs a potty break before we sit down to dinner."

"Oh, Mia. I'm sorry your cousins needed their dinner." Ronni strokes her dark curls and shoots Fee a knowing smirk. "It's too bad your mama didn't take you upstairs."

"It's okay, Auntie Mae. Daddy said we needed to check on you and Unka Connor to make sure you hadn't fallen asleep." Mia breaks free from Fiona, sashaying toward the bathroom without a backward glance. "Mama, don't follow me I'm going by myself."

Zane shakes his head at his adopted daughter's confident sass. "I can't get over how much she's just like you were at that age, Fee."

"God help us." Fee follows his gaze, clasps his hand and leans her head on his shoulder.

An hour later, we're all stuffed and happy. The toasts are complete. We're all enjoying hanging out together. With Torin tucked like a football in my arm, I sidle up to Jace, who's been quieter than normal tonight. "It's good they're getting their happily ever after, isn't it?"

"Yep," he drawls. I wait for him to elaborate, but that's all I'm getting from him.

Before our hiatus, Jace was fed up with Ty and Zoey's drama for a number of reasons. Considering Alex and Zoey are BFFs since birth, it's not like he's going to keep them apart. Or that he would even want to. "You're not still salty, are you?"

"Nah. I'm just over it. I love Ty. I love Zoey. I just want off the crazy train." I follow his gaze over to the area in front of the fireplace that's become an impromptu dance floor. Alex and Zoey are dancing with Lena and Mia. The rest of our crew are milling about in various conversation groups. "I really just want to focus on my own family."

Jace and I have a connection that transcends the band. It doesn't surprise me our feelings are consistent when it comes to our personal lives. What does surprise me is how little interaction we've had lately. It makes me a bit sad, so it does. "About that..." I fix him with one of my patented looks designed to elicit information.

"Life is good." The bollocks just shrugs like he has no bothers in the world.

"Feckin' hell." I can't help but roll my eyes all the way up to heaven. "Ronni's been with the girls at all of this prewedding shite. She said you got engaged. Were you thinking of telling me? When's the wedding? You're the last man standing."

His expression doesn't change. "We're married in spirit. Don't rush us. It will happen. We haven't set a date yet."

"What the hell does that even mean?" For feck's sake, how annoying can this man be? Then I realize. It's Alex. She's the one who is gun-shy, not Jace.

"Dunno. We'll figure it out." His tone confirms my thoughts.

Before I can reply, Ronni joins us with Tristan in her arms. She side-hugs Jace and wrinkles her nose. "Don't pressure him, babe. That's not cool."

"Thank you, Ronni." Jace glares at me. "You're the voice of reason."

Ah, hell. I decide to let it go. "Aye, that she is."

Except, most of the others overheard the conversation and have now joined us. To protect my band-brother, I divert the subject to hiring a new management company. The past couple of weeks of being together for Ty and Zoey's wedding hoopla make me yearn for LTZ to start things up again. Not how it used to be, though. We have to be smart. Our current representation still wants us to tour nonstop.

None of us want that anymore.

Unfortunately, Jace and Alex are still the hot topic. Zane and Fee grill Jace with similar intensity I employed earlier. I sort of tune out until I see Ronni touch Fee's arm. "She's dealing with some health stuff, Fee."

"Oh, God." Fiona's eyes widen with horror just as Alex walks up with Lena.

"What's going on?" She glances at Jace.

"I'm not sure." He sighs. They lock gazes, a look passes between them.

"Are you okay, honey?" Fiona tentatively touches Alex's shoulder.

Alex doesn't react to her touch, keeping her eyes fixed on Jace. "Um, yeah?"

"I think I said something I shouldn't have," Ronni pipes up next to me. Instinctively, I put my arm around her. "I didn't know you were keeping the situation private. I'm so sorry."

"What situation is that?" Jace grits out.

Alex sighs, the weight of the world on her shoulders, explains some sort of female reproduction issue the ladies all seem to know about. It makes me wonder if Fiona, Zoey, and Alex knew about Ronni's IUD before me.

I can see from Jace's annoyed expression, he's also not happy about personal business being discussed. "I didn't realize we were sharing yet, Poppy."

I'm about to say something to back him up, but Ronni beats me to it. "C'mon Jace. Lighten up. Female-related health issues have been a taboo subject for too long. It's important we share these experiences. Take it from me, keeping things like this secret is not okay. Did you know that the percentage of money spent on research into women's reproductive health is astonishingly low? You have a daughter. Think about it."

I look over at Zane. We're both so feckin' uncomfortable. Jace is pissed. Fee and Ronni stare us down defiantly. Willing us to contradict them.

Wisely, we stay silent.

Not Alex, though. She sees Jace's reaction and defends her man. "Jace isn't the bad guy here, Ronni. He's done more to help me than I've done to help myself. While I appreciate what you're saying, we'll make the best decision for ourselves. I'm happy to share what's going on, but our solution is not up for group discussion or debate."

Ronni's defiance crumples, but she nods. I know she was trying to have a "women-power" bonding moment with Alex, but she failed to recognize the hypocrisy in her statement. To me, her proclamation about transparency felt like a fresh stab wound. Does she not realize she kept her IUD implantation secret from me?

Now's not the time, though. November is a tough month for my wife. Wynn took his life all those years ago around this time, which has been the catalyst for her drive to seek revenge against Kircher and his cronies. Regardless of our own issues, I'll always give her grace when she speaks up for her friends, even if it comes across in a way she doesn't intend.

At some point, she and I will need to discuss birth control and our own family's reproductive health. No question. But it sure as feck won't be here. Or now.

"Maybe let's lighten the mood and play some music?" Zane asks hopefully.

I shift Torin to my other arm. Grab Ronni's hand and squeeze. Keeping my voice cheerful, I start toward the living room with my family in tow. "Aye. Let's."

She looks up at me, questioningly. I mouth, exaggeratedly, "Later."

While Ronni and I manage to enjoy the rest of Ty and Zoey's wedding day, I can't help but wonder about the state of my own marriage. In my heart of hearts, I thought we were past all of this. If she's still in the habit of keeping things from me, how does that bode for our future?

How do I trust her?

Without trust, what the feck kind of relationship do we have?

Chapter Five

One Month Later

How do all the women do it?

No, seriously.

I'm back to where I was before I joined Connor in Seattle. Only worse. Kris's assistant Allison can't find a qualified nanny—or even a PA— to save my life. I've interviewed young women, retired nurses, mannys, ex-teachers. It's been a disaster.

Out of thirty applications, three candidates made it through my interview process. Two have already been let go. Hopefully the third time's a charm.

Candidate one is a former preschool teacher. She looked great on paper and seemed to have an excellent connection with Torin and Tristan. By day two, I felt comfortable leaving her alone with them while I got caught up on my to-do list for the show. A couple of hours later, I decided to give them some cuddles. It was quiet, so I tiptoed down the hall and peered into the boys' nursery.

My heart nearly melted. She had them all dressed up in their little rocker outfits sitting on the zebra-upholstered bench. Then I took a closer look. Imagine my surprise when I realized she was wearing one of my LTZ T-shirts with her cut-off shorts. Oblivious to my presence, she knelt next to the twins, held her phone up, put her best duckface on and proceeded to take a selfie with my sons.

Hell to the no.

Let's just say I lost all semblance of decorum. Security was called. The photos were deleted. She received an incredibly stern legal letter reminding her of our iron-clad confidentiality and non-disparagement agreement. Good riddance to her. No way, no how will some LTZ fangirl bunny-boiler watch my babies.

The second candidate, a manny, seemed promising. His background was in nursing. He reminded me so much of some of my gay actor friends I used to beard for. I was excited. Visions of becoming BFFs, shopping trips, and fabulousness filled my mind. My dreams went up in smoke within hours, quite literally. I heard the boys wake up from their nap on my baby monitor. Then they started crying. And crying. Then wailing.

By the time I made it to the nursery, they were scream-ing, poopy messes.

As for my manny? He was sitting by the pool vaping, without a care in the world. Or a baby monitor. Security. NDA. See-ya.

The third candidate is supposed to start after the hol-idays. I'm not holding out much hope. It sucks being stressed about childcare in any city, but Hollywood has its own set of worries.

"Mae?" Connor calls from the living room.

"In here."

Seconds later, he joins me in my closet-slash-dressing room. I'm getting dressed for Christmas Eve at Ty &

Zoey's West Hollywood house. His giant frame always seems out of place next to my girly stuff. His smile is relaxed when he passes the racks of clothes and towers of shoes toward me. Which is a relief. He's been a little off since we got back from wedding festivities. We haven't had sex again. I've been scared to ask why.

I smooth my black sweater dress around my hips, which are still too full for my liking, and glance in the mirror. Swivel. No carbs for the indefinite future. It's fine. Nothing I can do about it today. "I'm ready."

He's behind me and wraps his arms around my middle. Rests his chin on my head. He's so much taller, I love how petite he makes me feel. "You look a vision, so you do." He catches my eyes in the mirror. That's when I realize I'm not imagining things, there's something sad behind his lashes.

"Are you okay? I know I've been busy on all these projects. Having you home to take care of the boys has been life changing for me." I fold my arms over his and tilt my head up so I can look at his real face, not the one through the glass. "And that's just one reason I love you."

He leans down to kiss me. "I love you too. I'd do anything for you, Mae."

I twist in his arms. Reach up and pull his head toward mine. Thread my fingers through his curls. "I'd do anything for you too, babe."

"Can I ask you a question? It's been bothering me since the wedding, but I have no idea how to talk to you about it." He strokes his palms along my sides. "I promise I won't be upset, but I just have to know."

I'm totally confounded. I squint at him. "Uh, you can talk to me about anything."

"I'm not positive about that, but I'll say it anyway. Why didja go back on birth control without talking to me?" He sighs like a weight's been lifted off his shoulders.

I guess it's been placed on mine.

I cast my eyes down to the floor. Shit. He's right. I did make the decision on my own. My body, my choice and all that. It never even occurred to me to talk to my husband. Gah. Back in Seattle, I'd called Alex to get the name of her doctor. Booked the appointment. When Connor was at Zane's practicing the wedding song they performed at the wedding, I asked his mom to watch the boys. Drove over. Had the device put in.

Didn't even mention it to him.

I glance back up. "I don't know how to answer that."

"Just tell me the truth."

"Okay. Well, the truth is, I don't know how to feel about this conversation. It's my body. I want to enjoy sex with my husband. I do not want to get pregnant any time soon. Maybe never again. Was I supposed to consult you? Get permission?" My voice is defiant. Defensive. Probably because I should be apologizing, not doubling down.

Tears well up against my will. "I was afraid you'd try to talk me out of it. No, I was afraid I'd let you."

His eyes cloud. "Oh-kay."

"Connor?" I move out of his embrace.

"What do you want me to say, love?" He sags into my makeup chair. "When I decided to extend my stay in Seattle for the band meeting, I felt bad for arranging it without discussing it with you. I should have done better. I'd already been away looking after Da. I left you in the lurch with the boys. Made a unilateral decision. But, I apologized. It was thoughtless but not deliberate. I need to know. Did you make this decision to get back at me? Bloody hell. An IUD Ronni?

Passive aggressive much?

I cross my arms. "Having twins has been a lot."

"Aye." He looks at me, waiting.

"I have so much on my plate. Responsibilities for my projects." I toe the floor with my boot.

"Aye." His expression remains unchanged.

"I don't want more kids." My voice gets caught on the word kids. Tears threaten to spill, but we're supposed to be at Ty and Zoey's house for Christmas Eve in an hour. I won't have time to do my makeup again. I choke them back.

He stands and envelops me in his arms. Cups my head and presses it against his chest. "Was it so hard to say that to me? Aside from the confidential Kircher shite you kept from me, I thought you always told me everything, Mae. We're supposed to be each other's safe places."

"I know," I mumble into his muscled pecs. "I'm sorry."

Ah, there it is.

He tilts my face up to his with his finger. "We're in our mid-thirties, love. If we aren't thinking of adding to the family now, then it's not likely going to happen. If you want my opinion? Our boys are enough. The four of us are a perfect family. You are my honey. You will always be my honey."

"You're not mad?" I throw my arms around him. Squeeze.

"Aye. I was. Still am a little." He kisses my head. "Not because you went on birth control. Not because you're done having babies. Not because I don't love you. I'm upset you wouldn't talk to me. I'm upset you didn't think I'd have your back no matter what. It feels a little like déjà vu. I most definitely don't want to go back to secrets. Secrets are shite."

I disentangle myself from him. "I don't either. I was wrong to do it without discussing it with you. I knew I was being inappropriate. I just couldn't seem to stop myself."

"Okay. Thank you for saying that." He watches as I freshen myself up.

"I really do love you, babe." I sling my purse over my shoulder. "There's not much else to say."

He follows me from our bedroom to the nursery. "I really do love you, Mae. I know you're stressed about not having a nanny. Put that worry away. I don't have much going on for a bit. I love taking care of our sons."

My God, this man reads my mind. I've got to remind myself when I'm wound up that I can trust him. I. Can. Trust. Him. He loves taking care of me. Would it kill me to let him do it every now and then?

Now that the weight of keeping the IUD secret is, at least, over, I'm ready for our sex life to get back to normal.

———

As usual, traffic sucks. It takes an hour to get from Malibu to Ty and Zoey's house. Her parents, Mike and Olivia, greet us at the door and lead us into the living room.

"They're getting so big!" Olivia makes googly faces at the boys, who stare up at her. "It's only been a month since the wedding, and I swear they're twice the size."

Zoey joins us, kneeling next to her mom. "May I?" She waggles her fingers at Tristan. Then at Torin. "You always dress them in the cutest matching clothes. I never asked how you tell them apart."

"It's easy now." I unbuckle the boys, who wear matching ugly Christmas sweaters, and hand Torin to Zoey. "Torin has a little freckle on his temple." I touch the tiny spot.

Zoey snuggles Torin to her bosom, clearly at ease holding a baby. Some women are born to be mothers, and my bet's on Zoey. It wouldn't surprise me if she and Ty start popping them out, one per year. Ty watches her intently as she strokes Torin's head. My little guy grips her red-tipped finger. She wiggles it. Kisses his rosy cheeks about a hundred times. "I need one of these, Ty." Zoey beams when she catches Ty gaping.

"You're more than welcome to take one of these lads off our hands for the night." Connor slaps Ty on the back. "They seem calm and sweet now but get 'em both going and holy bejeezus."

I lift Tristan out of his carrier and snuggle him to me. Stick my tongue out at my husband. "You aren't giving my babies away. No matter how hard you try, Connor."

"Damn." Conner swoops over and plucks our son from my arms and hands him to a dumbfounded Ty. "Here, Ty, don't listen to her. He's yours."

I dash the two steps to where Ty's holding Tristan like a sack of potatoes. "Just support Tristan's neck and place him against your chest."

As awkward AF as Ty is, Zoey's smile lights up the room when she sees her husband with the baby. "You're doing great, babe."

"Um, I gotta check on dinner." Ty's veins bulge in his neck.

I take my son back. "You did great. You'll be a great dad, Ty."

A look of bewilderment washes over his face before Ty turns on his famous rockstar charm and hurries back the kitchen. "I'd stay, but it's time to baste the turkey."

Connor catches my eye. Raises an eyebrow at Ty's inadvertent sexual innuendo. I stifle a giggle.

Not long after, we sit down to eat. Ty's and his mother-in-law Olivia's dinner is fantastic, as always. Connor and I feed the boys and put them down, refraining from shagging this time. Olivia and Mike head to their room, leaving the four of us to visit. Ty and Zoey both sip cups of tea. Connor and I each finish a glass of red wine left over from dinner.

"What are the others up to for the holidays?" Connor sits opposite from me on the couch, my feet are tucked under me. "I haven't talked to them in a couple of weeks."

Zoey, who is snuggled in Ty's lap, lifts her phone to show us a darling picture. "Alex and Fee did a holiday photo shoot with Lena, Mia, and the horses. They want all of us to do it next year as a new LTZ tradition."

"I loved spending Christmas in Seattle. It was nice to be around family." I unfurl my legs and nudge Connor's thigh with my toe. "I think Seattle should be our tradition."

"Oh, really?" Connor caresses my foot and kneads my arches with his strong bass-player thumbs.

Zoey leans her head on Ty's shoulder. "I'd love that, Ronni. Next year, the boys will be running all over the place. Maybe we'll have a little one to include in the horse picture."

"If we don't, it won't be for lack of trying." Ty waggles his eyebrows, his eyes locked with Zoey's.

Connor shoots me a look that says, "A schmooopier couple there never has been."

"Isn't it cool how far the four of us have come?" I lean back into the sofa. "By the way, thank you for the 'we're so freakin' happy for Ronni and Connor' quote for the Variety article. Kris thought we'd need it to put this stupidness to rest once and for all."

Ty's expression clouds and then, in an instant, he pastes on his "I'm the lead singer of LTZ" smile. "No problem, Ronni. You helped me out when Zoey and I went public. We were happy to do it for you two."

"Yes, we were." Zoey's brilliant smile convinces me. "It's time for all of us to live in truth. You guys are parents now. We can't wait to have our own baby. We're the couple who's known each other the longest yet we're playing catch up to the rest of you."

"It scares me a little..." Ty glances around uneasily.

I can't help but laugh at my not-so-distant memories. "The first few months are tough, but once you get the hang of it..."

Connor sighs contentedly and finishes my sentence. "...it's the best job you'll ever have."

We stay late talking and visiting. By the end of the night, Connor's convinced Ty to help him produce Fireball, his twin brothers' band. Zoey's offered to help watch the kids for a couple of weeks if we can't find a nanny by then.

Apparently, the glowy, golden light of the gorgeous Christmas tree creates a magical energy in this room. Enhanced by the candles flickering all around us. I come to a realization. For the first time since my mom passed away, I feel secure. Like I'm truly part of a big family.

Connor's folks and siblings, of course. But, also the band, their spouses, and our children.

They know the real me. I belong here.

Out from under the lonely cloak of being famous. Finally.

I've built my life and career in LA. Never considered living anywhere else. But why? This town is superficial. Cold. Calculated. Transactional. Fake. Everyone's values are all screwed up. Mine were too.

Plus, it's downright exhausting. Everyone wants something. I can't even find anyone trustworthy to help me with my kids.

Come to think of it, I really don't like it here. It doesn't feel like home anymore.

God. My babies. I don't want to raise Torin and Tristan in this privileged, entitled environment.

Being with Connor changed me. Living with Connor in Ireland showed me what and who we could be. Who we are. I've just been too overwhelmed as a new mother to stop and absorb it all. I slipped back into old patterns out of sheer exhaustion. I don't want to keep anything from Connor ever again.

Maybe it's time for us to think about moving. Permanently. I could do most of my work from anywhere in the world. The movie's filming in Ireland. The series will shoot in Vancouver B.C., which is only a three hour drive from Seattle.

Yeah. That's the solution. I feel it in my bones. I glance over at my gorgeous husband, who's listening intently to a story Ty's telling about one of his foundation kids.

He's my dream come true. I can't wait for us to figure out our next steps.

Together.

Chapter Six

A Few Weeks Later

I'M FINDING MY TRUE creative groove.

I feckin' love it.

Until now, I'd never been a huge fan of the studio. So much sitting around doing nothing. I never took the time to understand the craft. It's not to say I wasn't intrigued. It's kind of like...hmm. Intimidation, maybe?

It probably dates back to the beginning of LTZ. Zane's dad, Carter, legendary guitarist from Limelight, took us under his wing. We practiced at his mansion on Lake

Washington. He pushed us to get into the studio. Produced our EP. Hooked us up with his management company. Was at every single show we played when he, himself, wasn't on the road.

For feck's sake, the man was so intense about steering the band in the direction of success. Gave us lots of unsolicited advice. Incessant talk about condoms. Warnings about groupies and drugs. At the time, my own da was a raging alcoholic who stole money from the family business, leaving me to pick up the pieces. It was hard to wrap my head around a guy like Carter who was just so...involved.

With all the pressure I was under at the time it was always touch and go whether I'd have to quit LTZ. Which would have gutted me. At twenty-five, I'd already given up playing in a band with my wee twin brothers, Padraig and Liam, to support my family. I had the weight of the world on my shoulders.

A burned-out rockstar doling out advice to me, of all feckin' people, was incredibly annoying.

Now that I'm a dad, I have perspective. Carter lost years with Zane due to his own severe addictions. Zane's best friend, Ty didn't have a father figure in his life. In retrospect, Carter was making up for lost time. Doing penance, I guess.

He took complete charge in the studio to record an EP of four songs Ty and Zane wrote. I don't think the three of them ever took a break. Well, aside from Ty shoving his tongue down Zoey's throat every chance he got. Jace and I often felt like hired-gun musicians. I'm confident it wasn't deliberate. We were the newer guys in the band. Outside of recording our parts, we offered no input, nor were we asked for it.

In the years since, we've become collaborative as songwriters. Hours on the bus gives the four of us lots of opportunities to help shape LTZ's music. Zane, our musical savant, can pick up and play any instrument. Jace's steady rhythm gives the band a backbone we can all count on. I'm exceptional at pinpointing a harmonic pulse that ties each song together.

But Ty? Holy shite. He's a feckin' master in the studio. Focus. Attention to detail. Mindfulness. A stickler for creating the appropriate vibe. He knows what to add and when something's missing. A drawn-out base note here. A drum fill there. A sprinkling of violin. A dose of cowbell (I couldn't feckin' resist).

Case in point? Our second album, Z, blew us into the stratosphere. LTZ won Grammys and countless awards and accolades. Despite Carter's credit as head producer, word spread swiftly throughout the industry that Ty was not only the greatest vocal talent of our generation, but the actual production genius behind the LTZ sound.

In the years since, Ty's worked behind the scenes on dozens of hit songs for many artists. Across genres. If I were a betting man, and I am, I'd wager his personal income is easily double or triple the rest of us. He's stealth though. And humble. He never talks about his experiences with any of us. We hear about it when the tracks he worked on hit the Billboard charts. Or win awards.

Which is why I asked Ty if he'd help me produce my brothers' band, Fireball.

Liam and Padraig started the group in college with a fellow student, Felicity Clark. She left the band when my brothers wanted to move in a different creative direction. It took them years to recover. After stints with four or five singers, they found their permanent band member, Avonna Parilla.

The trio's been grinding and grinding for years on the underground circuit. They're unconventional, but excellent. Strong Celtic influence. Avonna weaves a bit of her Spanish heritage into the mix. Their harmonies are haunting. Fireball is special. A huge cult following, but they haven't perfected a radio-friendly sound as of yet.

Recently, one of their tracks became the theme song for a popular streaming series. With a little taste of success and royalties coming in, my brothers asked if I would help produce Fireball's latest album. Initially, I said no. I'd hate to screw things up when all of their hard work was paying off.

At Christmas, I tried to get Ty to take my place. His condition for working on their album is if I'd coproduce with him. Obviously, I couldn't say no. Ty's golden touch could propel my brothers' band to the next level. Plus, I figured I'd learn something.

The timing worked out, too. Ronni and I hired a full-time nanny. Yolanda came highly recommended by one of Ronni's colleagues. She's young, energetic, and great with the babies. My wife's been buried in prepro-duction on both her projects. The Netflix series and the

Finnegan O'Rourke film. With the kids in capable hands, I have flexibility to work with my brothers.

"I think Liam's a little pitchy." Ty chews on the cap end of his black sharpie. He holds up a finger to my wee brother, who's waiting for direction in the vocal booth. "Let me play it back again so you can listen."

He rewinds and presses the button so all we hear is the isolated track of Liam's vocal. Undoubtedly, something's off.

"It's his enunciation. If he drew out each word at the end of the chorus, he could ease into the note. It would give the song some edge, and I think it'd be grand." I find myself tracing some imaginary notes in the air with my index finger as I explain my solution to Ty.

"Let's try it." Ty presses the mic button to communicate to my brother. "Liam, if you can hold out the word 'lost' at the end of the chorus. Play around with it. We can do as many takes as you want. Go raw."

Padraig joins us, slumping in an oversized chair behind where we're sitting at the console, his long legs crossed in front of him. "He never has the confidence to just let the fuck go."

"He's in a safe place here, so he is." I crane my neck around. "We'll get him there."

Liam adjusts his headphones. Shakes out his hands. I know my brother. He's nervous for some reason. He makes the adjustment and the next take is better, but it's still off. We try a dozen or so takes, each a little better but not quite there.

"What did you think?" Ty nudges me with his elbow.

I glance at Padraig. He just shrugs. "He's tense. He knows our entire future is riding on this album."

Ty winces, then calmly pulls his hair back and knots it at the base of his neck. He glances over at me and says quietly so Padraig can't hear, "Do you remember how it was for me the first time we went into the studio?"

"Uh, no," I admit.

"I was scared out of my fucking mind. Carter didn't mean to, but he made it seem like the band's future was in my hands." Ty leans forward in his chair. "Liam, come out here for a bit. Let's give you a break."

We watch him take off the headphones and toss them down in frustration. He leans against the doorway adjacent to where we're all sitting. "I'm fucking this all up. I know it. I can't get it right."

"Where's Avonna?" Ty taps the Sharpie on his hand. "You're together, the three of you?"

"No, they fucking aren't." Padraig stands and glowers at Liam. "Are you?"

Liam sits on the edge of the sofa. "No." He hunches over. Chews on his thumbnail.

Linus O'Donnell, Fireball's manager, slips into the room from the hallway. "Hey. How's it going?"

"Could be better." Liam gazes up at him for a beat longer than I'd expect before looking back at the ground.

"Do you know where Avonna is, Linus?" I gesture to my Apple Watch. "We need to shift the dynamic a bit, and she's late."

Linus' face reddens. He looks at Padraig, then at Liam. "Um. I thought she was here."

"Let's take an hour." Ty stands. Stretches. "Get your house in order, my dudes. Remember, this is supposed to be fun. There's no pressure. Nothing's riding on any of this shit. We're having a kick-ass time making music. Connor, you hungry?"

We leave them downstairs and head up to the kitchen. Ty pulls out some ground beef, onions, tomatoes, and buns. He seasons the meat and mixes in chopped onions. "Burgers on the grill?"

"Sure, I'll check in with Mae while you cook," I say to his back as he walks out the sliding door.

When Ronni doesn't answer, I wonder if I should call Yolanda. Decide against it and grab my sunglasses and join him on the patio. Zoey is lounging in the pool in a tiny black bikini. Ty's busy cooking so I take off my shoes and sit on the edge, dangling my feet in the water.

She paddles her swan floatie over to me. "How's it going?"

"Ty's a genius, you know." I avert my eyes from her body and focus on the clear, blue water. Just because she's nearly naked doesn't give me the right to look at my band brother's wife. I've already seen her tits twice, though, through no fault of my own. Years ago, I walked in on them going at it in the practice room at Carter's house. Last year, Ty had her pressed against the window in their bedroom, not realizing Zane and I were down here at the pool with a bird's-eye view.

Perhaps sensing my discomfort, she rolls off the floatie into the water so her body's submerged. She hangs on the side of the pool and rests her cheek on her arms.

"Oh, I know. He's spending all his time down there. I don't see him much during the day. Sometimes he's down there all night, too."

"Aye. Sorry about that, Z. We'd hoped to make better progress but there's something going on with my brothers. It's affecting this recording session. I know how badly they want to make a hit record. It's frustrating, so it is." I swish my feet in the cool water.

Ty startles me when he comes up behind me holding out a giant beach towel for Zoey. "Liam, Linus, and Avonna are together. That's what's going on. It's pissing Padraig off because he feels like the odd man out."

"What the feck?" I pull my feet from the water and stand. "Liam denied it. And Linus? My brother's never been into men as far as I know. Why do you say that?"

He wraps Zoey in the towel when she climbs up the pool ladder and says carefully, "I saw them together."

"He did, Connor. Yesterday, after you left. Padraig did too. He wasn't happy." Zoey shakes out her hair. "I'll leave you two to discuss. I have a couple of calls to make anyway."

"Wait, babe." Ty dashes to the grill and assembles the burgers. Brings one to me and hands the second to Zoey. "You need to eat."

She gives him a quick kiss and heads inside, leaving the two of us to dissect the situation.

I scratch my head. "So, they're in a thruple?"

"I guess. I think that's what the kids call it today." Ty takes a bite of his burger.

"What do I do?" I'm completely out of my depth. And shocked if I'm being honest.

Ty studies me for a second as he finishes chewing. "Nothing to do. It's not your call to make. As far as recording goes. Talk to Padraig. Reassure Liam it's okay to love who he loves. He has such great potential as a vocalist, but he's closed off. Maybe he's afraid of being accepted for who he is."

"Are you still seeing that therapist? She's rubbed off on you, so she has." I nudge him with my shoulder.

The look on his face is unreadable. I notice he doesn't answer me.

"I was asking for Liam."

He nods. "Lisa Kinkaid. I'll text you her number."

"Thanks." I pick up my own burger. "For the record, I don't care who my brothers love. As long as they're happy. Who am I to judge?"

"I'm glad you feel that way. Maybe go play big brother?" He starts toward the door. "I'm going to finish my lunch with Z."

I can't help but roll my eyes. Everyone knows what that means by now.

Truth be told, I'm grateful for some time alone. Grateful my own life is drama-free. I'm not much older than my twin brothers, they can figure their own shite out without my interference. Or opinions. I'll be here to support them, of course.

As for now? I'm going to soak up the sun. Eat my burger.

And enjoy a little peace and quiet.

I've earned it.

Chapter Seven

A Few Weeks Later

SUN STREAMS THROUGH THE filmy blinds when I wake up.

My mouth is incredibly dry. I reach for my bottle of pineapple Hint water on the nightstand. Drink what's left and set the empty down. A couple of yawns later, I pat the bed next to me.

Empty.

It's a devastating pattern. Missing time with my husband. My family. Then again, my work schedule is mostly to blame. The past couple of weeks, I've crawled into bed hours after Connor and he's up long before me to take care of the boys.

I pad across the plush carpet to the bathroom. Pee. Pull on joggers and my favorite old LTZ sweatshirt and head down the hallway. I hear little giggles and Connor's deep voice coming from the nursery. I lean against the doorway and watch for a minute. My husband is beaming at Torin and Tristan, who are standing on their own. Assisted by the denim sofa they both cling to in order to keep themselves upright.

"Wow, they're both standing." I cross the room to sit next to Connor, who's freshly showered and dressed in jeans and a t-shirt. My boys squeal when they see me and fling themselves into my arms. I smother them with snuggles and kisses.

He pulls me and the boys to him. "Morning, love. I let you sleep in; it seemed like you needed it."

Tristan plops himself in my lap. Mama's boy through and through. I smooth his reddish-brown wisps around his ears. "They're at such a critical age. I feel like I miss something every day."

"It's temporary. I'm happy to step up," he reassures me. I know he's trying to be supportive, but it doesn't make me feel any better.

Connor plucks Torin up and sets him next to his brother. Then stands and strides to the door. "Why don't you spend some quality time with them this morning? I'll go check to see if Yolanda has their breakfast ready."

"Stay." It comes out shriller than I'd intended.

He stops and turns. "Okay." He closes the door behind him, pads back over and crouches so he's at my level. "What's up?"

"Nothing. I just miss my family. And my life's about to get busier." I kiss the tops of my boys' heads.

Connor drops to the ground opposite me and encloses us all with his long legs. "You've worked ridiculously hard to get here. Once you see these projects through, they'll be plenty of time to reassess. All of this was in motion before you got pregnant."

"Yeah, I know. I appreciate you being so supportive, babe." I attempt to keep the boys in my lap, but they don't ever sit still for long, so I let them squirm away. We watch as they crawl like little bandits toward the pile of stuffed toys in the corner.

Connor cups my face and draws it toward his. Kisses my lips softly. Slips me a little tongue. Scoots closer. He grabs my ass and pulls me flush against him. Dips down for another kiss when the door flies open.

"Oh, jeez. Crap. I'm sorry." Yolanda's big, brown eyes gape at us in horror. "You're...uh. Um. I'll come back."

I lean back on my palms. Connor crosses his arms over his knees. We weren't doing anything but kissing, so her reaction is a little dramatic, but I certainly don't want her to feel uncomfortable. "Yolanda, wait. I'll help you feed them breakfast."

"Oh, okay." She peers warily into the room. Her long, black hair is in a braid that reaches her butt. She wears cut-offs and a black t-shirt. Nothing revealing, but she's most definitely a pretty girl.

Connor stands and pulls me to my feet. He shoos our nanny away with a smile. "You're grand, love. We'll grab the boys and see you in the dining room."

She blushes at the endearment and skedaddles.

My face is red for a distinctive reason, but I don't say a word. Not yet.

Minutes later, side by side, Connor and I feed the twins mashed eggs, sweet potato, and applesauce. I decide to leave Yolanda with the task of cleaning them up and changing their diapers. It's nice to participate in my family's morning routine. The ritual makes me feel somewhat normal.

"Yolanda seems to be working out." I give Connor a side look to check his reaction. "I mean, she's great with the babies."

"She's fine, but she's not you." Connor slings his arm around my shoulder. Kisses the side of my head.

"You called her 'love.'" I pull back and stick my tongue out at him.

My phone starts buzzing on the counter before he can answer. I dash over and see it's Kris. I hold the phone up to show Connor, who nods and tosses his head toward the patio and mouths, "Go." Outside on the patio, I nestle into a lounger pod overlooking the ocean and take the call.

"Is there any way you can swing by my office so we can review the audition tapes for the Sam role? Martin dropping out puts us in a bind. We need someone well-known for that cameo. I'm drowning, babe. I know you have stuff going on at home, but our backs are against the wall." It's just past eight in the morning and Kris sounds like she's about ready to lose her mind.

I've given her ten hours each day. Mostly working from home. She's not overtly said anything, but Kris is becoming impatient. I don't blame my partner; our current situation is not how we envisioned working on these projects. Back before I got married. Then pregnant.

I look out at the ocean. Waves crest and crash along the shoreline. This used to be where I'd find peace. Now, it's just a reminder that I'm in over my head. "Kris, did you know the boys are standing now? I missed it. I hate disappointing you, but I can't do much more. How can I let the nanny be there for all their firsts and not me?"

"Look, babe. I know you're juggling a lot. We need to have a serious discussion about what's next for us. We've made commitments. People have invested money into us. I'm not trying to put pressure on you, but we slid everything for a year so you could give birth. The year's up. I know the timing is brutal, but we won't get this chance again." Kris is stern, but not mad. I totally get it. Both of our reputations are on the line. "And if you could ask Connor about LTZ's schedule, that would be great.

If we need to factor it in, it's best to know as soon as possible."

"Okay. I'll be there around noon." I say nothing else before I hang up. I know I'm not pulling my weight. The transition from actress to producer is a big one. Even with the positive press we got with the article about the birth of the twins, there's still so much publicity about Kircher's demise. There are definitely plenty of men in this town who'd love for me to fail spectacularly.

I close my eyes and breathe in the salty sea air. With a heavy sigh, I know it's time to get the day going. I turn to find Connor standing in my line of vision. He sits down and takes my hand. "Want to tell me what's going on?"

"Something's got to give. I don't see how it's possible for me to continue doing both the series and the movie." I pull him into the pod and curl around him. "I thought having Yolanda here would help me, but I don't—"

"Want her to have all the boys' firsts. I overheard you say that to Kris." He wraps his arms around me. "For the record, I call all the guys' wives 'love' too. It's a fairly common term of endearment in Ireland. I didn't realize I said it to Yolanda, our employee. It's inappropriate. I won't do it again."

"Thank you. It might be common, but I didn't like you speaking an endearment to Yolanda. I still get tingly when you say it to me. I don't want her to get the wrong idea. Let's not go down the stereotypical path of the nanny falling in love with Daddy because the wife is always at work." I squeeze him tightly to me. I love smelling his fresh, linenly, manly smell.

Mine.

"Ah, Mae. You're the one I want to tingle. There's zero chance I'm ever going to cheat on you, let alone with our feckin' nanny." He kisses my head. "Now tell me what's going on. You don't need to bear the weight of the world on your shoulders. Let's figure this out."

"Well, as you know, we've spent the past couple of months in preproduction in the hope that the series would be greenlighted. Most of the scripts are done, except some polishing. Locations are scouted. Production team is mostly hired. When we got the word a couple of weeks ago, we mostly just needed to finalize the paperwork. Kris took care of most of that stuff." I stroke his hard abs up and down. "It's my creative baby, though. My idea. It's not a chore. I want to be involved in everything. Did I tell you Netflix wants us to film it in Vancouver?

Our plan is to shoot it like a feature-length movie and edit it later to save actual filming time, but it will require careful planning."

Connor shifts so he's facing me. "Veronica Mae Miller, you can do this. You should do this. If we all need to go to Vancouver, we can bring Yolanda or we can find local help. Maybe even both. Now that Fireball's album is done, when you're holed up in the office, my excitement is limited to taking the boys to the park."

"With Yolanda." I pout.

He rolls his eyes. "You are the one who hired her. And no. I usually take Barry."

"Well, at least I know you have security with you and the boys. That makes me feel better." I flatten my palms against his chest and stroke his pecs.

"Isn't a tighter shooting schedule better? You'll be done sooner?" Connor brushes the hair out of my eyes. "Is the movie still on track later this summer?"

"So far." I sigh; the idea of doing the movie seems better than doing the movie at this point.

"Well, I'm looking forward to spending time with the boys in Belfast, so I am. Saoirse is over the moon to help out when we're there." He nuzzles my neck.

I grip the sides of his face. "Except, what the hell is going on with LTZ? You've said nothing."

He presses his forehead to mine and then flops over on his back, pulling me into his side. "We're going to chat about it soon. I'll go down to Seattle for a meeting when it's scheduled. I know we need to fire our management company, but I'm not in any hurry. Although, when we're in Vancouver, my plan is to work on the types of customizations for our bus. I'm thinking big playroom. Giant bed to fuck you on..."

"Are you serious?" I sit up and smack his bicep.

He smiles up at me. "Aye. I told the guys that I can't commit to any schedule until you've finalized your schedule. There's no way I can be in the studio or on the road when you're so busy. Besides, Fiona's opening her restaurant next summer. Alex and Jace are, well, Alex and Jace. Who knows what's going on with Ty & Zoey now that they're married, but if I'm a betting man—and you know that I am—she'll be knocked up soon if she's not already. I have one commitment: rehearsing for a live show we're playing at The Mission for Gus's opening night. That's a ways away."

"Ohmygod. Connor. I've been this woebegone drag for weeks. I had no idea you were sacrificing your own career to let me further mine." I straddle him. Lean down. Kiss him.

"Ah, my love. There's no sacrifice. We're truly blessed. We have all the money we could ever spend. I have the most beautiful, talented, badass wife to ever walk the planet. My sons are the finest specimens ever born. Why would I want to leave my family? If we ever go out on the road again, you're all coming with me or I'm not going." He grips my hips and moves me back and forth on his hardening cock.

I splay my hands under his shirt. Lean over. "You are a silver-tongued devil. Speaking of coming, I want you inside me. Now."

"We can make that happen." He unzips his jeans while I strip off my joggers.

When I'm pantless, I resume position and sink down on top of him. Ride him. Roll my hips. He grips my ass and moves me faster, watching where we're joined. God, the way he looks at me. The way he treats me. I'm the luckiest woman in the entire universe. He's always one step ahead of me. Anticipating what I need. Looking out for my best interest. My family's best interest.

"I love you, Connor. I still feel like I won the lottery when you chose me." I pant, leaning over him. Bracing myself on the pod to gain purchase as he drives up into me.

He sneaks his thumb to my clit and taps then circles it. "I want to watch you come, Mae. I've got you. Let it go."

The electric current starts deep within my core and permeates my entire being. I squeeze his cock as hard as I can manage when I get there. I want to bring him over the edge with me. It works. He groans and fills me with hot warmth. He and I have made love on these pods too many times to count.

It never, ever gets old.

A loud bullhorn startles us both. Jesus. It's just past nine a.m. The influencer house next door begins its daily assault on our little oasis. House music thumps to life. Loud, raucous voices can be heard just below us on the beach. Connor lifts me off him and wordlessly hands me my joggers. He tucks himself into his jeans.

"Little feckin' bastards," he mutters when he holds out his hand. I take it and we head up to the house. Yolanda is waiting with the boys dressed for the park. She reaches for her sweater, but Connor holds up his hand. "Maybe you can box up some of the clothes they've outgrown for the donation bin? Barry and I will take the boys this morning."

She gives him a puzzled look but heads to the nursery.

"Thank you," I say when she's out of earshot, feeling a bit ashamed that I had an iota of weirdness.

He doesn't make me feel foolish. Instead, he leans down and kisses me. "You go kick ass, my love. Your tribe of men will be here when you get back."

Our talk and sexcapade gives me a boost. Now I'm ready to take on the world. I've always been ambitious. My ambition has led to great success.

But having the love of a man like Connor behind me?

I truly feel like I can do anything.

Chapter Eight

A Few Weeks Later

SUPPORTING RONNI'S CAREER AND putting mine on the back burner is not too shabby. A man could get used to it, so he could. At least I could. Spending all day with my wee lads is more fun than I ever thought it could be.

For the past several weeks, we've been living in Vancouver BC in a two-bedroom suite at the Sutton La Grande Residence. Our little entourage takes up an entire floor. Yolanda has her own one-bedroom. Ronni's personal assistant, Paxton, has another. Our security boyo, Barry, has the fourth. Yolanda and Paxton are now BFFs. Between the two of them, they've been phenomenal in helping us manage Ronni's brutal filming and production schedule.

I'm hopeful my pep talked helped. Although she always seems stressed, she's juggling both the series and preproduction for the movie like the champ she is.

As for me? It's not bad living in the middle of a big city. LTZ stopped here on tour, but I've not spent much time in Vancouver here even though it's so close to Seattle. Now that my schedule is so flexible, immersing myself in such a thriving, cosmopolitan location is an exciting experience.

With Barry in tow, Tristan, Torin, and I spend clear days taking a dander around Stanley Park, eating lunch on Granville Island, or strolling along the pathway by Coal Harbor. When it's pissing down, we duck into the aquarium or Science World. Sometimes we stay in our hotel suite in loungewear all day.

At night, once the boys are asleep and Yolanda's on nanny duty, I sometimes nip out to the pub for a Guinness. Visit with some of my fellow musician friends who live here. Just last night I hung out with Brody Mason, who manages both Dirty and the Players, bands we've played with on and off throughout the years. We mostly caught up, but I walked away with excellent perspective on how to vet new management for LTZ.

Even with a little business thrown in, all in all Vancouver's been like a vacation. A vacation with a feckin' amazing opportunity to immerse myself into my boys' lives each day.

It's the one thing I stressed about when Ronni got pregnant. LTZ spends months on end on the road, and I refuse to miss my kids growing up. I've never felt love like I do for my wee lads. Fatherhood is a tremendous thing.

Tristan is slightly bigger than Torin. He's run the show from the day and hour he came out of Ronni's womb. Now that they're getting older and interactive, he's the boss. Just as I predicted. Tristan decides what games they'll play. He picks the books. He was always the first to nurse, and now he's the first to eat. Torin is laid back. He watches his brother and follows suit.

The one thing I'm a bit glum about is Ronni's missing so many things in their little lives. She's already gutted about it. I try not to go on and on about each new milestone. It's not like she has a choice, there's no reason for me to make her feel worse than she already does.

Tonight, she's off early. Which, for her, means eight p.m. I've ordered dinner from the hotel restaurant. The doorman is keeping an eye out for her and will signal the kitchen to deliver it once she's home. The boys have been bathed and are now down for the night. I've got roses set up on the dining room table. Candles lit. A little rosé on ice.

I might not be the most romantic bloke around, but there's something to be said for taking extraordinary care of your woman when she's worked hard all day.

Shortly after eight thirty, I'm in the bathroom running her a bubble bath when I hear the key card. "Connor? What's all this? Where are you?"

"I'm in here." I swish my hand in the water to test the temperature. The lemony-lavender bubbles fill the air with a fresh, soothing scent. Ronni appears in the doorway, looking like the day's flattened her. "Come take a bath, my love. I'll wash your back." I hold my hand out.

"It smells amazing." Like a mermaid to water, she moves toward the oversized tub. I swoop her into my arms and rain soft kisses along her cheeks. Taste her lips. I deepen our kiss until she literally melts into me.

She's already shoeless, so I set her down and peel her tight, black jeans down her legs, taking her tiny black thong along for the ride. Unclasp her black bra. Slide my palms up her waist and tug her black t-shirt over her head. When she's fully undressed, I pick her back up and place her into the bubbles. Take off my own t-shirt and sit on the tile ledge beside her.

"Connor, this is heaven. Pure heaven. I was about to tell you I had work to do tonight, but no. Just no. I need this." She sinks lower so just her eyes and forehead are visible.

I grab a little pink puff and squeeze some lemon-vanilla body gel on it. Dunk it in the water and begin to wash her. Ronni's eyes remain closed as I cleanse her inch by glorious inch. When I'm done, I wonder if she's asleep, so I whisper, "Mae, are you hungry?"

"Famished. Utterly and totally famished. I could eat an entire pizza myself. That's how hungry I am." She doesn't bother opening her eyes.

"Up, you." I kiss her forehead. "Let me dry you off."

I help her step up and out from the water. Her rosy-pink nipples pucker when the cool air hits them. As I towel her off, it takes every ounce of willpower I have not to bend down and taste them, but this isn't about my desires tonight. This is about taking care of my woman, who's clearly been zapped of all energy. I wind her hair up in a towel. Help her slip into the oversized, cozy bathrobe.

By the time we're done, Barry let the hotel staff in, and dinner is set up on the dining table. "Connor, are you serious?" Ronni's eyes are wide when I lead her out to the living room.

"Salmon in butter sauce. Wild rice. Assorted veggies. Healthy. Delicious. Nurturing," I rattle off things I heard described on a cooking show I watched earlier today when the boys were napping.

She sits at the table and devours her meal. "Ohmygod. This is the best thing I've ever eaten." She smiles up at me with her mouth full.

"Our meals at Matsuhisa were equally as delectable if not better." I laugh, thinking of our favorite sushi restaurant in LA.

She points her fork at me. "Yeah, maybe technically. But this is something you thought about and made happen. The experience is what makes this the best meal I've ever had."

All I can do is grin like an eejit.

"Soooo... Have a question to ask you." Ronni slides her dinner plate away and scoops up a spoonful of lemon chiffon mousse.

I lean back in my chair. "The answer is 'aye.' I'm happy to go down on you for thirty solid minutes."

"Oh, I'm taking you up on that." She dips her spoon into the dessert and leaves it there. Runs her magenta-tipped nail along the rim of the glass. "I think I'll save this. I'd like to lick it off your cock while you're licking me."

Instant. Feckin'. Boner.

"Well, that's settled, I accept your fine offer." I move to stand.

She holds her hand up. "Wait, I did have an actual question for you. I know you're going to say no, but before you do, I've just gotta say I think it would be amazing and you'd be perfect..."

"Ronni. Just ask me. I want to move on to the licking." My voice is low. Commanding.

She sighs. "Will you play the hot construction guy neighbor? There's not too many lines. His role is to kind of shock the FMC out of a bad marriage. There's no nudity or love scenes. Just a couple of scenes of him building something without a shirt that she fantasizes about."

Well, that's not what I expected.

"Hold on a second. Are you seriously saying you want me to be man-candy in your series?" I cross my arms over my chest. "What's an FMC?"

She claps her hand over her mouth. "Sorry, didn't mean to acronym you with set lingo. It means 'female main character.'"

"I don't act, Mae. Surely there's someone better qualified than me." I shake my head, baffled beyond belief.

"No. We've struck out completely." She pouts. "We've auditioned dozens of dudes. None of them look like they've spent a day outside, let alone can convincingly hold a hammer. I mentioned it to Kris today that we needed a Connor—jokingly—and a lightbulb magically appeared above her head. She demanded that I ask you tonight. Please. We can bring the boys to the set. I'll have a room set up with their toys and everything. I might even get to kiss them goodnight before they go to high school."

I'm still gobsmacked. "I have no idea what to say."

"Say yes. It's three episodes. That's it. Easy." Ronni leaps from the table and straddles me on the chair. "Your character was written as a transition role. His attention sets her free to start to a journey of self-discovery."

"When?" I grip her hips. Grind her bare pussy against my cock, which is aching to be free of my jeans. Lean down and suckle her earlobe.

"Ohhhh." She throws her arms around my neck. Leans into my nibbles. Squeezes her thighs around mine. "Next—Uhhhhh. Ohhhhh—Week."

I untie her robe, freeing her fantastic tits. Lean down and take a nipple in my mouth. Lave it. Ronni winds her arms around my head, caressing me. Watching me suckle her. Still bucking her hips against the bulge in my jeans. Her little mewls and breathless pants tell me she's already close.

Releasing her nipple from my lips, I look down and see her pussy's soaked the front of my pants. With a growl, I roughly move her back and forth against me, so her clit gets friction from the denim. She squeezes my head between her arms, so my cheek is mashed against her tits. "Come, Mae. Fucking come all over me," I growl.

She buries her face into my neck and keens and shudders through her release. We stay like that for a spell. Breathing heavy. My hands stroking up and down her back. Soothing her. Preparing her. I'm not nearly done, though.

When she manages to lift her head, I'm ready. Our mouths mash together. It's not pretty. It's passion re-captured. I grip her ass and stand. She winds her legs around my waist as I carry her back to our bedroom and kick the door shut.

I toss her on the bed. "Mae, change of plans. I've got to taste you, but I want to be inside you when I come."

"God, Connor. You're making me even wetter." She opens her knees and I dive in. Licking. Suckling. Lapping up her sweetness. I spread her lips with my thumbs and flick my tongue against her still-throbbing clit. I'm rewarded by her sexy moans. She digs her heels into the mattress and thrusts up against me. Wild. Writhing. Chanting, "Oh. Oh. Oh." When I slip a finger inside her, she explodes.

According to my internal calculations, I'm just shy of thirty minutes of the promised licking, but I can wait no longer. While she rides out her orgasm, I tear off my jeans. My cock is literally weeping, it wants inside her so badly. Using my palms to press her thighs apart, her puffy, soaked pussy beckons. I nudge her opening then watch myself disappear inside my woman. Inch by glorious inch. Methodically, I glide in and out of her. Admiring how wet she's making my dick. Relishing the squelching sounds of our merging. Inhaling the intoxicating smell of our passion.

"God, you're such a sex god." Ronni's up on her elbows watching us together, too. "I wish you could live inside me. You unlocked something in me all those years ago, Connor. You're my key. My only key,"

"Ah, Mae." I collapse on top of her. Showering her with kisses. "That's because we're meant to be together, my love."

We roll our hips in unison. Lazily, now. In this moment, I savor feeling her tight, wet heat around me. I don't want this to end anytime soon. My arms wind around her so there's no air between our bodies. Like we've been absorbed into one being. We move together for what seems like hours until my cock can't take it anymore. I roll us to our sides. Keeping her hip hitched up on mine so I don't slip out.

My release floods her. Exhausted, Ronni falls asleep straightaway, tucked against me as I still pulse inside her

I love her. It's simple, but true.

I already knew I'd traverse oceans for her.

I guess pretending I'm an actor will be slightly less difficult.

Maybe I'll give it a go.

Chapter Nine

A Few Days Later

I CANNOT BELIEVE I talked him into it.

I also can't believe how impressive he is.

Years of acting lessons. Decades of being on set. Blocking. Rehearsing. Table reads. It's like breathing to me now, but it took so long.

My husband? An absolute natural. Positively riveting on screen. The camera adores him. The way he effortlessly delivers lines with just precise timing has everyone on set swooning.

I'm swooning.

He is, after all, a world-famous rockstar. A great performer. Not as showy as Ty or Zane, but he holds his own. He belts out the backing vocals. Engages the crowd. All while maintaining the pulse of the band. Zane relies on Connor to keep him grounded. Jace and Connor have been a rhythm section for so long, they're essentially telepathic. As for Ty? Connor gives him stability.

Who knew these skills would translate so well. He's a natural actor. That's the truth of it.

The premise of our dramedy is simple: a woman is in a loveless marriage with a doctor who expects her to be a perfect wife and mother. She embodies the role for years but finds out he's leaving her for one of his residents at the hospital. On the day her divorce is finalized, her best friend challenges her to date diverse types of men before getting serious again. They call the challenge, The Essential Hunk List, which is also the name of the show.'

It's been grueling, even now that I have Paxton helping me. Most days, I feel like I'm an imposter. Sometimes, I'm so over my head there are no words to describe it.

What's surprising, though, is being behind the camera is more appealing than being in front of it. As a performer, especially as a woman, there's so much pressure to look a certain way. Be a certain weight. Stay young.

Still, this entire experience has me conflicted. Is missing time with my family worth any of it?

I'm so ready to be done. It's excruciating feeling like a third wheel in my own family. Connor and Yolanda are, essentially, parenting my kids. They feed them. Read to them. Clean up after them. Do the laundry. She keeps "forgetting" to include me in texts about the boys. When I have rare free time to spend with my sons, she leaves me lists telling me what their schedule is and how to do this and that with my own sons.

God, it pisses me off.

I can't risk losing her at this time, so I say nothing. She's fantastic with the kids. Connor likes her. He needs help and I'm not available. It took so long to find a quality nanny like Yolanda, I won't let my own insecurities mess up the status quo.

It's not forever. I can suck it up. Ignore she's demonstrably friendly with Connor and chilly with me. Disregard my feelings of unworthiness as a mother. Pay no attention to the times when the boys reach for Yolanda and not me. Push down my feelings of jealousy at the amount of time she spends with my kids. My husband.

Connor's not a cheater, thank God. Still...

Crap. I'm making things up in my head. It's guilt. The bottom line is—I'm just not there for my family and Yolanda is. I'm gone for twelve to sixteen hours a day. I've made this choice and it's eating me alive.

Conversely, Connor is his amazing, supportive self. Assuring me this is all just temporary. Complimenting me on my ability to multitask. Convincing me he's grateful to have bonding time with his sons. Confirming he's taken over all decisions about Tristan and Torin so I can focus on work.

His words, not mine.

To think my plan was to star in the series as well as produce it. Fate had different plans. The reason I'm not on camera is because the Netflix executives told Kris—given the expedited schedule we're on—I didn't have time to get my body into the shape they expected. It hurt to hear. It always does. Things don't change, though. This industry is brutal on a woman's self-esteem.

How could I argue, though? The reality is my body hasn't fully bounced back yet.

How could it?

At the end of the day, I'm choosing to look at it as a blessing in disguise. If I had to memorize lines and act, well—there's just no way. I'm not even hanging on as it is.

I recast the part with a long-time friend of mine, Clover Callahan, whom I met on the set of Hawaiian High. In the years since, she's had a couple of pop hits. Been through a horrific divorce, complete with cheating scandal. Though she hasn't acted in over a decade, Clover is fantastic. Regardless of how the show is received, I think she'll have many compelling opportunities after this.

Connor agreeing to play the first "hunk" means we'll stay on schedule. His role as a tall, muscular construction guy suits him to a "T." Ironically, he's the last of the hunks to film this season. We're at the end of the shoot. Once Connor's scenes are filmed, we'll wrap.

So far, Connor's work has consisted of slow, panned shots of him wearing nothing but jeans and a tool belt as Clover and her BFF ogle him from her porch. The

"hunk" catches her staring and delivers a self-depreci-
ating remark, for comedic value. He's nailed each one
and even came up with an ad-lib of his own, which
we're using: "Holy bejeezus, have you seen where I
left my shirt?"

Today is Connor's final day on set. The only kissing
scene and it's with my friend Clover. He claims he
isn't nervous. Even if that's true, I'm nervous enough
for the both of us. Quite honestly, I'm not looking
forward to it at all. Even though I'm a professional actor and have kissed—oh, hundreds of actors over the
years—including years when I've been in a committed
relationship with Connor—I can admit I'm irrationally
jealous.

There, I've said it. I don't like the idea of my husband kissing another woman. Even if it's pretend. How
he put up with it, I do not know. The man has the
self-confidence of...well, a saint?

I guess I'm not a saint.

Like most sets these days, we have an intimacy coordinator. Her job is to set boundaries so actors are
comfortable filming love scenes. In the consultation,
Connor was adamant that he wouldn't go further than

touching lips with Clover. She agreed. They both want to be respectful of me, which I appreciate.

My production challenge is the scene is written as a passionate, breaking-out-of-her-shell moment for Clover's character. A midlife sexual awakening with the hot construction guy. It's got to be believable. We're using camera angles and blocking to make it seem realistic, but I'm anxious all the same.

To soothe my nerves a bit, I'm up early with the twins. They're so cuddly in the morning. If I have time, I love to sit on the couch and read to them before I head off to set. I treasure every second.

"Mae, you're up unusually early." Connor joins us on the couch, his hair as wild as a lion's mane in a wind tunnel. "I missed my morning cuddles."

I shift so the three of us are ensconced under his arm. "I couldn't sleep. The boys were up babbling in their secret language, so I thought I'd get a little extra time in today."

"Cool. You stay here. I'll go make us something to eat." He kisses my head and crosses the room to our tiny kitchen. We keep just enough groceries on hand for morning breakfast. Eggs. Bacon. Cereal. Milk. Oatmeal and Cream of Wheat. It's a rare treat to be home to sit with my family. Mostly, I run out the door with a tub of yogurt and some fruit.

Now that they know their papa's awake, Tristan and Torin are a bit squiggly and fussy. Our quiet time is over, so I set them in the playpen with their favorite toys. It's hard to believe how much I hated the idea of playpens until I had twin toddlers. We never leave them in there long, but when I have to pee or make a meal, or go kiss my husband, it's a life saver.

I stroll up behind Connor and wrap my arms around him, resting my cheek in the middle of his back. "Are you ready for your big kissing scene today?"

"Can't feckin' wait." His voice is animated, but he doesn't stray from his current task of cracking eggs into a bowl.

I pull away and spank his ass. "Can't wait?"

He turns and rests his big palms on both my shoulders. Catches my gaze. "Mae. I was joking. Remember, you're the one who got me into this. I've already set my boundaries with that intimacy woman. My lips will barely touch Clover's. Truthfully? I want to get it over with. I'm ready to go back to being just a bass player in a rock band."

"Me too. I'm kinda sorta regretting casting you a little bit. I don't want to see..."

"Seriously." Connor's annoyed now. "I do not want to kiss another woman for pretend or otherwise. You're a professional actress, surely you realize this isn't going to change how much I love you. How much I'd rather be kissing you. My plan is to nail it in one take and be done."

My head thunks against his chest. "I'm being so stupid. I know it. How did you put up with me kissing those men all those years?"

"I'm a feckin' saint, so I am," he mutters and kisses the top of my head before turning back to the counter. "Go shower or something. I'm already nervous enough."

While Connor finishes breakfast, I do shower. By the time I return dressed and made up, Yolanda's sitting next to Connor and the boys at the dining room table. Leaving me with the seat at the end. I take a spoonful of yogurt and watch her cut bits of sausage and feed bites to my sons. The gesture, even though it's her job, causes a pang deep inside me.

I'm missing out on being their mother.

Connor's ease with this particular domestic scene is infuriating. He's not doing anything deliberate. It's his—their—normal daily routine. He looks to Yolanda, not me, to feed our sons. To wipe their mouths. To get their juice. Glumly, I stir my yogurt.

I'm the fifth wheel here, not our nanny.

The second we wrap, I'm doing something about this.

On the way to the set, I'm quiet. Connor and I clutch hands in the back seat of the car. He fidgets, which is unlike him. I feel bad that I said anything. Rather than being a professional, I put all my insecurities on him when I should have just done my job. I was supposed to make him feel comfortable. At ease.

"I want to apologize for my behavior this morning, babe. I didn't mean to stress you out. I trust you. I trust Clover." I thread his fingers with mine and squeeze. "You know your lines. You've brushed your teeth. It's going to be a piece of cake."

He brings our clasped hands to his thigh. Kisses the side of my head. "Aye. It'll be fine. While I've enjoyed our time in Vancouver for a while, I'm ready to get back to normal."

"What's normal?" I keep my voice light and teasing, but inside my heart is pounding.

He leans back against the soft, black leather of the car. "Dunno. I'd like for us to figure out what our normal is. Together."

I rest my cheek against his shoulder. I know how he feels.

For all the mental buildup, the scene goes off without a hitch. If anything, Connor blows everyone away. When I look through the camera at the playback, my producer mind can't help but think what an incredible star he could be on screen. The fact he has no interest in it whatsoever most likely gives him the electric vibe we're capturing.

Because he could really give two Fs.

"Thanks for letting me borrow your man, Ronni. If you don't need me this afternoon, I'm gonna jet." Clover sneaks up behind me and throws her arm around my waist. "Wouldn't it be great if they cast him opposite my character next year?"

I purse my lips playfully. "Oh, I'm not sure he'd be down."

"Well, if you want to know the gossip, everyone's convinced you picked the best rockstar in LTZ," she teases.

I shoo her away. "I don't care about gossip. Everyone knows Ty and I were just a publicity relationship. Connor's my man."

"A fine man he is. And funny. You did amazing, my friend." Clover pulls me into a hug. "See you on Monday."

"Thank you." I wave as she leaves.

I stroll around the set as the crew gets the afternoon shot set up, looking for Connor. I don't get far. Kris stops me to get feedback on PR and marketing materials. Before I know it, an hour's gone by. I have no idea where Connor is. As it stands, I have just enough time to grab a piece of fruit before it's time to shoot the next scenes.

My phone buzzes. It's a voicemail from Connor.

"I'm in a car on the way home, I didn't want to interrupt your meeting with Kris. Yolanda called, Tristan fell. He has a little gash on his forehead. Apparently, it's not serious but I wanted to get him to the emergency room right away."

Instant. Total. Panic.

I dial my husband. He answers on the first ring. I don't give him a chance to even say hello. My fury level is on eleven. "I'm on my way. In the future, if one of my sons is hurt or sick, that is more important than anything I'm doing at the minute. It's not cool to leave a message telling me you're taking my baby to the ER, and you didn't want to interrupt me. That will never. Ever. Ever. Be. Okay."

"Look Mae, I'm home already let me..." Connor sounds a bit panicked.

"Find what's going on and text me where to meet you." I'm nearly out of breath as I run to the production office to grab my purse. "We are going to have a serious talk about Yolanda's judgement."

"Okay, sure...I'm at the door now. I'll call you..." He yells for Yolanda and the phone goes silent.

He hung up.

If furious described me before, multiply that times one thousand. I'm irate. Fuming. Incensed.

Scared.

That prickly thing along my spine that always tells me when something's off is engaged in a big way. In my rush to get to the car that's waiting for me, I don't notice the slight, waif of a woman who grabs my sleeve as pass her.

"Veronica Miller?" she says loudly, causing a couple of the crew to look up.

"Yes. Look, I have an emergency, I'm in a hurry..."

She shoves an envelope into my hand. "You've been served."

Chapter Ten

A Few Weeks Later

IT'S STRANGE TO THINK we won't live here for much longer.

Today is unusually windy. I don't mind, I've always loved the smell of the ocean out here on the deck. Not that I have time to enjoy it much. Too much to do. Too many decisions to make. Another deep breath and I walk up to the house where movers are packing up our—Ronni's—furniture under Paxton's direction. His final task as her PA. So I overheard. Apparently, he's taking a job with a PR firm.

I set the baby monitor down on the kitchen counter. The boys are still sound asleep so I make myself an espresso before the kitchen gets packed up. Sit at the counter and watch a guy wind cellophane around the living room furniture. Reflect on what an insane turn of events the past two weeks have been.

Don't get me wrong, as happy as I am we're temporarily moving into the Seattle townhouse—we'll get to celebrate the twins' first birthday with my family—Ronni's swift, unilateral decision has my brain feckin' whirling.

She's been mental since the day Tristan bumped his head in Vancouver. I'm still working through what brought us to this point.

Never, in a billion years, did I think I'd enjoy the acting gig. But I did. It was fun. I got into it. When Ronni told me I'd be shirtless? I was surprised, but I work hard to stay fit. I'm not ashamed of my body, so it didn't matter a whit to me.

Of course, it took me by surprise when Ronni got weird about my kissing scene with her friend Clover. It wasn't even remotely feckin' real. My wife's the one who taught me about love scenes years ago when she was still on her sitcom, She's All That. For this show, we rehearsed with the on-set intimacy coordinator. Everything was set. I was nervous. I'm not an actor, after all, but I felt okay. I was willing go outside my comfort zone for Ronni.

Only for Ronni.

So, I can't lie, her uncertainty about the kissing scene left me feeling a little annoyed.

I've never, in the entirety of our relationship, given her any feckin' reason to worry about me being unfaithful. From the day and hour I met her, I've never had eyes for anyone but her. Even when I was forced to stay behind the proverbial curtain during her dreadful faux relationships with various actors.

She was the one in the public eye holding another man's hand. Smiling at him. All the while I was kept hidden.

Her reasons were altruistic, sure. But, oh how I hated it. Excruciating.

What really sucked? Her fauxmance with my own feckin' bandmate, Ty. What started out as a lark to clean up Ty's image turned into insanity. The world went bananas for them as a couple. It killed me every time someone mentioned he, and not me was her soulmate.

I wanted to shout from the rooftops, "I'm her soulmate. Me."

It was a feckin' mess.

I'm sitting in my dressing room feeling abandoned. I just don't get it. My scenes were spot on. The crew all congratulated me when I was done. Not Ronni, though. I haven't seen hide nor hair of her. I figured she'd keep things professional on set, then meet me here. I'd give her a real kiss. Maybe even fuck the absolute bejeezus out of her.

Show her she's the only woman my cock gets hard for..

Instead, she was so immersed in a conversation with Kris, she didn't even see me walk past. It's confusing. Disappointing. As the minutes ticked by while I waited for her to join me, my mind started whirling. Is she mad? Did I fuck things up?

Anyway, my thoughts were elsewhere when I took Yolanda's call on autopilot. The girl seemed frantic. Distraught. Which made me panic. I gave no thought to my actions. I knew I needed to get to my son. On my way out, Ronni was still deep in conversation with Kris. She didn't even notice me walk by. I figured whatever they were talking about must be important. I didn't want to disrupt her work when I wasn't positive what was going on.

In retrospect, she's my wife. Tristan's and Torin's mother. I should have interrupted, no question. Luckily it was only a wee nick, Tristan didn't even need stitches.

I've been in the doghouse ever since.

I've never known Ronni to act this way. Ever. She's been distant. Short. Erratic. Angry. Eerily quiet.

What's worse, her unilateral decision-making is back in full force. Like arranging for a private jet to bring us back to LA a couple days early. Like firing Yolanda when we were all packed up and ready to catch the plane. She handed her a thousand dollars in cash with a first-class ticket back to LA. Like the day after we settled back in here, telling me she'd hired realtors to sell this house.

I've tried to keep my mouth shut. I know she's processing some heavy shite. It's not every day the man who horribly abused you and so many others sues you for defamation and demands a hundred million dollars. Her name has been in the headlines for weeks. She's hired an expensive team of some of the highest-powered attorneys in the country who are defending her. It's scary stuff.

Not to mention our security is at risk. We have paparazzi camped out at our front door 24/7. Barry's handling my detail, but we hired five rotating security guards to patrol the property and another to be with Mae at all times. Doesn't matter, with the telephoto lens technology that exists, there are shots of her and us every single day on the blogs and tabloids with scathing and salacious headlines.

All of this has taken a toll. No doubt.

Today? The movers showing up without me being informed has me raging.

I hear the front door click open. Ronni walks in dressed like the powerhouse badass she is. White pantsuit. Sky-high white pumps. White purse with a gold band. Her chestnut hair is tied back into a low bun. Oversized sunglasses swallow her face.

"Hey. I met with the lawyers." She sets her purse down and surveys the room where dozens of men are working. "Wow, they're fast."

"Were you thinking of telling me they were coming today? Did that thought cross your mind?" I say through gritted teeth.

She cocks her head. "Of course I told you. We're leaving in a few days. They're just packing everything except our bedroom and the boys' nursery so they can stage it while we still live here. It goes on the market the day we fly up to Seattle."

"Ronni." I pinch the bridge of my nose. Take a breath. "When did you say we were leaving?"

"In three days, to be exact. I'm scheduled to meet with the lawyers again tomorrow then I'm free for a bit." She takes her sunglasses off. Kicks off her shoes.

My palm slaps the granite on the counter. She gives me a puzzled look.

"It's time for a serious conversation. We obviously can't do that here with the movers around. Should we take the boys on a drive?" I keep my voice calm in an attempt to be reasonable. Mindful that there are ears everywhere, including Paxton's.

I'm boiling mad.

Ronni picks up her shoes and walks back toward the bedroom, motioning me to follow. Her voice is cool, decisive. "We can talk back here, I'm not leaving people in our house unattended."

I follow her back to the bedroom, fuming. She disappears into her huge closet and comes out wearing leggings and a tee. I stand there gaping at her like an eejit as she takes off her earrings and places them in her jewelry safe. Wanders into the bathroom and washes her face.

Like she doesn't have a feckin' care in the world.

When she returns to the bedroom she sits on the chaise and curls her feet under her. Points at me. "Okay. I'm ready. Let's talk. What's going on?"

"I could ask the same feckin' thing." I remain standing but move toward her. "I've said nothing for the past couple weeks, but I can be silent no longer. You're taking complete charge of our lives as though I have no goddamn say in it. What the actual fuck, Mae."

"Oh, now you're angry." She looks down at her perfect manicure and back up at me. Her expression steely.

"I don't think angry begins to cover it. We're supposed to be married. I'm telling you, I'm not going down this road with you again. The secrets. The unilateral decisions. I thought we resolved this when you went back on birth control without telling me. Not to mention all the feckin' years you were..."

She holds up her hand to silence me. "I had to take some control back in my life, Connor. Can't you understand that?"

"I could if it was just your life. But it's our lives. Mine. Yours. Tristan's. Torin's. This is not the feckin' Ronni Miller tells everyone how it's gonna be show. If you want it to be that way, then why the hell do you need me? For my dick?" I pound my fist into my hand. I may not raise my voice to my wife, but I'm so frustrated.

"I'll ignore that last comment because we're moving to Seattle for you." She looks at me incredulously. "You're the one with all the band stuff coming up. We've been focused on my career for months and now it's your turn."

God damn it. "Gee, thanks for deciding that for us, Mae." My voice couldn't be filled with more sarcasm if I tried.

"What do you want from me?" I see her bottom lip tremble. In the present moment, I'm not moved.

Still, I'm a gentleman. I kneel at her feet and take her hands in mine. "I want what we agreed to. For us to talk about things. Make decisions together as a couple for our family."

"Like you did up in Vancouver when you just took over the boys schedule? Spent all your time with Yolanda?" She rips her hands from mine as she spits out our former nanny's name.

Like a knife in my gut, that comment is. "That's unfair. We agreed that I'd step up for the boys while you were working, Mae. To give you the time to fulfill your commitments. Now, if you have something on your mind about my faithfulness, you best tell me outright." I'm incensed.

"Oh, I don't believe you'd be unfaithful to me. You're just clueless. That girl was up to something, mark my words. She undermined me at every turn. Took over my role as though my children were hers. Called you and not me when things were happening with my babies." Ronni jabs her finger at me.

I seriously have no idea what she's going on about. As I saw it, the nanny was being a feckin' nanny. Things have been building in her mind and no matter how pissed I am at what's happening now, I will never undermine my wife in her role as our boys' mother. "I'm sorry you felt that way. Why didn't you say anything?"

"Why? You wouldn't have listened to me." She buries her face in her hands. "And then Tristan got hurt. I got sued..."

Tears do me in every time, I can't help but soften. "Mae, Tristan was fine. Nothing was happening with Yolanda, I promise. I think you're under too much pressure. Pushing me away isn't cool. Neither is taking away my say in our lives. If you're angry with me, tell me. So I can fix it. Don't let it build up like this. The deep freeze has been excruciating."

Suddenly, Ronni's wracked with sobs. Like a dam has burst. "What am I gonna do, Connor? I'm trying to keep all the balls in the air and I'm not handling myself well. I don't want to disappoint you. Or the boys. Or Kris. And now this lawsuit's going to cost me everything if it goes to trial. I'm 50K into it already."

"Come here, babe." I enfold her in my arms. My sweet girl. Still suffering alone. "I'm wondering—and please don't take this the wrong way—if maybe you and I should call that counselor that Ty and Jace used. She's here in LA. She specializes in trauma."

Ronni looks up at me, her startling-green eyes spilling with tears. "No, I don't need a shrink. I just need to get out of Los Angeles. Can we focus on that please? I want to be the one supporting your career for a bit. My movie work is manageable remotely for a couple months."

"Is that for the best? Can you fill me in about the lawsuit? You haven't spoken to me about it. Please, babe. I want to be here for you." I smooth her hair down.

She sniffs. "My legal team is amazing. They're convinced Kircher is grasping at legal straws, but because of how I went about gathering information for the documentary, things are complicated. Staying behind the scenes hurt me as much as it helped the others. Or something. Anyway, they're working all the angles. Trying to get it dismissed. It's just so disturbing to think he's using the press to turn this around on me."

"It's been a lot. For both of us. I'm in this relationship too." I squeeze her back into my embrace.

Ronni wrenches herself free. "Yeah, well, you're not the one on the front lines."

Ouch.

"Look, there will always be times when we inadvertently hurt each other, but deliberate hurting is a hard feckin' no for me. I didn't realize you felt the way you did in Vancouver. You never said anything. Instead, you reacted. Now you're lashing out. As though I'm supposed to read your mind." I scrub my fingers along my beard. "I'm no psychologist, Mae, but these patterns need to be broken. I get you're going through something hard. I get that you weren't happy with me about how Tristan's injury went down. What I don't understand is why you're deliberately treating me like dog shite. I don't deserve it. I, uh... I'll just say it. I don't know how many more of these incidents I have in me."

"Is that supposed to be a threat?" She steps back. "You left me once before."

I cock my head, frustrated. "Yeah. I did. It was a long, long time ago. For the identical reason. Don't you see? When you keep things from me on purpose it's destructive. When you deny my ability to participate in my own life? No. Just no. I'm a grown feckin' man, Mae. You're not the boss. Neither am I. We're supposed to be doing this together."

"I keep pushing you away. To the point where you want to leave." Tears pool in her eyes again.

"You're infuriating, woman. No. You tell me what I'm doing. It drives me mad." I boop her nose to try to diffuse the tension. I speak softly, "Aren't we in the same boat? Don't we have a couple of passengers now?"

Ronni groans. "God, I'm awful."

"Mostly, you're wonderful. The kindest and gentlest woman in the world. I'm begging you to work on this issue." I pull her up from her seat and hug her tightly.

"I was so mad, Connor. I felt like my kids were bonding with someone else. I couldn't stand it." She melts into me. "I do stand behind my gut feeling about her, though."

I speak quietly into her hair, "Next time, try 'Connor, I'd like to talk to you about serious concerns I have about our nanny.' Or 'Connor, I'd like to sell the house, I need a change, what do you think?' Or 'Connor, wouldn't it be great to spend an extended amount of time in Seattle while your band is trying to come out of hiatus?'"

"What if I told you I knew what I was doing and did it anyway?" She pulls back to look at me, wincing.

I shrug. "You think I don't know that? That's why we're having this little chat."

She slaps the palm of her hand to her forehead. "It's official, I am awful."

I nod solemnly. "Okay. Fine. Yes, I agree. You are awful. And I forgive you." My ears perk up because I faintly hear the boys fussing from afar. I realize I left the baby monitor out in the kitchen. "Shite. I wonder how long they've been up."

"Connor. Would you come with me to check on our sons?" Ronni stands and holds out her hand.

I can't help but smile and clasp it in mine. "Aye. That's more like it."

She grips my hand very tightly. I feel slightly better, but my ego is still bruised. She and I don't fight often but it always comes down to this consistent issue. I'm not going to drop the subject of counseling with Ronni. I'll even go with her. I think there're many things she thought she dealt with but hasn't.

Same goes for me, honestly.

I'm not willing to sacrifice our relationship to past demons. I truly don't think she is either.

Am I ready to face my demons? Hers?

Aye.

Family is everything.

And I'll do anything for minc.

Chapter Eleven

The Next Day

MY INSIDES FEEL LIKE wriggling worms on a fishing hook. Not that I've ever gone fishing. I haven't. But I've seen A River Runs Through It about a million times. I can visualize a wiggly worm, and that's how...

Jesus. Or Jaysus, to quote Connor.

I'm losing my mind. I shouldn't be worried, Kris is my best friend. My closest confidante. My older sister. She's my only family.

She's not going to hurt me.

Oh, Kris will give it to me straight. But, she's not going to hurt me.

I think.

I've been doing my best to ignore the defamation lawsuit Don Kircher filed against me. My lawyers assure me he doesn't legally have a valid case against me, but he's well-funded and angry. He's also protecting a slew of wealthy, famous people who participated in his debauchery for the past couple of decades.

So, I'm under no false pretense this is going away anytime soon. Or that I'll emerge unscathed. My commitment to secrecy all those years was for a reason. I might have been altruistic in my pursuit of justice, but I was selfish too.

My story wasn't meant to be part of the narrative. The only two living people in this world who know what happened to me are Kris and Connor. Well, and Kircher, of course.

I didn't want my name associated with his takedown, so I was blindsided when the LA Times christened me the second coming to the #metoo movement—a title I didn't covet. I certainly didn't want. Or need. All I wanted was for Kircher to get his comeuppance.

I thought I'd succeeded fairly unscathed.

One saving grace is the documentary I made has never been released to the public. It was part of the evidence the authorities used against Kircher. Nearly everyone I filmed has agreed to testify against him, so they don't need to rely upon the film itself. When Kircher is convicted, it will be based on eye-witness testimony.

If his case goes to trial.

I push through the glass door to my office building. Wave to the security team and get into the elevator. The production offices I share with Kris are on the twenty-third floor overlooking Wilshire Boulevard. We're located in a Hollywood power tower, as they like to say.

Kris is waiting in our modest lobby, wearing a fitted, black dress. "You look gorgeous." She surveys my pale-pink suit that I've paired with a black, sleeveless blouse and rose-gold jewelry.

"You are my inspiration." I hug her tightly. Kris' sense of style has always been impeccable. It's taken me years to operate in a similar realm as her.

"Your office or mine?" Kris stops in the hallway in between our two doors.

I walk into my office and motion her to follow. "Let me multitask. I haven't gone through my mail in weeks."

We sit across from each other. The mood is tense, which I knew would be the case. I know today's going to be heavy, no matter what.

"Tell me where everything is at with this lawsuit." Kris leans back in her chair. "I've read the complaint and the answer you filed but give me your take on it."

I sigh. "He's claiming defamation, emotional distress, and 'impersonation over the internet,' for the interviews I conducted. His defense is predictable: when I was on Hawaiian High, I came on to him and he rejected me. When he fired me, I held a grudge and enticed the so-called victims to come forward by paying them with my dating services. There's a bunch of additional stuff that's related, but essentially, he's innocent and I framed him using illegal tactics."

"What about the documentary? Isn't that what he says defames him?" Kris steeples her fingers and cants her head.

I nod. "Yeah. But I never planned on releasing it. My intention was to obtain proof for law enforcement. My defense against his legal threats is through Anti-SLAPP laws."

She stares at me blankly.

"Basically, an Anti-Slapp law prevents people like Kircher from intimidating people like me to speak out. If I prevail, he'll have to pay my attorneys' fees and I'll be dismissed from the lawsuit."

"God, considering how much time and effort you put into this. Was it worth it?" Kris squints. "I mean, considering?"

"If the victims' stories help prevent disgusting predators like him? Unquestionably."

Kris fidgets in her seat. "He's denying all allegations. Claiming what he's being accused of is a distortion of reality. That his relationships were consensual. Blah. Blah. Blah."

"Oh, I know. He's cancelled. No more projects. Dropped by his agent. Criminal and civil lawsuits. Other people have come forward with horrible stories." I shrug. "I guess this will play itself out, I just hope I'm out sooner rather than later."

"There's been blowback." She leans forward, placing her beautifully manicured hands on the edge of the desk.

Absentmindedly, I shuffle through my stack of mail as we chat, but her comment catches me off-guard. "The shitty press I'm getting is essentially either calling me a liar, slut-shaming me, or cancelling me for gender misappropriation because I pretended to date gay men."

"Don't be flippant, Ronni. You're not just some actress anymore. Do you know how fucking hard it is to be taken seriously? Do you understand what I've needed to do to get to where I am without sucking a lot of dicks?" Kris furrows her brow, clearly displeased with me.

"What are you saying?" I'm shocked senseless. Kris has never spoken to me this way. Ever.

"I'm saying I've given you this opportunity and you're treating it carelessly. What is your plan?" Kris, perhaps realizing that she lost some of her decorum, calms herself. "I don't want you to lose your career over this asshole."

I sit in uncomfortably silence. I guess ignoring the situation and hoping the lawyers could handle it isn't enough. I try to gather my thoughts, but I decide honesty is what is most important. "I know I've let you down, Kris. The transition from actress to businesswoman hasn't been intuitive for me. At heart, I'm a creative."

Her expression softens considerably. "Yeah. I know, babe. You're a new wife. New mother. It's been a transitional couple of years."

"I'm not doing well at any of it." I can't help but slump forward.

She stands and walks around to my side of the desk. Sits on the edge. "There's no easy way to say this. Until things calm down or smooth over, the financiers want you to step down from the movie, Ronni."

My head snaps up. "Wait. What? Can they do that?"

"Yes. They can. Unless you can get this sorted in the next couple of weeks. My advice is to do what you can to contain the narrative..." She peers down at me. Concerned, not angry now.

My jaw sets. I ball my hands into fists. "Fuck them. I'll fight this. I worked hard to get this movie..."

"Ronni. Please. Think before acting. You could bring me down too." She closes her eyes, takes a breath, and recaptures my gaze. "I want to help you navigate this, but..."

"You want to break up our partnership?" All the wind leaves my body.

"No. I don't want that." She gasps. "Of course, I don't want that. But you've essentially been M.I.A., Ronni. Now this. You have great lawyers. I believe you'll overcome this bullshit. I'm asking you to take a minute to consider the long game. Our business. Me."

Call me bewildered. Tongue-tied. "I. Uh…"

"Case in point. Were you going to tell me you're selling the Malibu house? I mean, where are you and Connor moving to?" Kris regards me with annoyed curiosity.

Leave it to Ronni Miller, burning bridges left and right.

"I was going to tell you today. The stupid TikTokers next door have made life unbearable. I thought we'd just go stay at Connor's in Seattle until you and I go to Ireland." I cross my arms over my chest. "Besides, I thought the rule of thumb is to ignore—the press will move on to someone else."

Kris stands again and paces. "No, Ronni. Not in this case. You need to hire crisis PR. Immediately. They'll work with your attorneys to hopefully get this put behind you. Come up with some sort of strategy to get Kircher off your ass. God, I'm sorry I didn't prepare you better. I hate what's happening, but the truth is you can't stay on the film in any official capacity until you get this figured out."

"Don't talk to me like I'm a child." I'm the one who's furious now. I can see my career slipping through my fingers and I'm wondering what the hell I can do to stop it.

Kris clasps her hands to the side of her head. "I'm sorry, there's no way for this conversation to be pleasant. I guess I might as well get all the news out there. The Netflix execs called this morning. They're on my ass too. I can't say this more plainly— you have a tiny window to fix this. I have a list of crisis PR firms you should talk to. I'll be right back." She whisks off to her office, presumably.

With a moment to catch my breath, I stand and look down at the hustle and bustle of Wilshire. I'm trying to remember why I wanted to produce so badly. Why I've essentially stopped acting. Why bringing down Kircher was so important to me.

Why? Why? Why?

Through the window, I can see a group of men on the sidewalk laughing and talking. Heading into Spago across the street. It's where every Hollywood exec lunches when they want to be seen.

The fact is, I've done nothing wrong. Yet, I'm getting ostracized. My career's being threatened all because I had the audacity to shine a spotlight on abhorrent behavior that needed to end. It's not fair. Then again, life's never been fair for a female executive in the entertainment industry.

I'm royally pissed off. I realize it's not at Kris.

The game is fucking rigged.

Kris returns and hands me a printout. "You and Connor should vet these together, babe."

"Thank you. I'm sorry for getting heated. I understand why you need to do this. Distance yourself." I flick my eyes up to hers and hold her gaze. "I need a week or two. There's a couple of legal process things that are going on with Kircher that may or may not impact all of this. I'm so, so sorry I brought this down on us. I really am. I'm also pissed. We should not have to pay the price for that man's misdeeds."

Her eyes mist a bit. "You're absolutely right. I never thought it would go this way."

"But, this is where we are." I pull her to me. We cling to each other for a long while. "We're heading back up to Seattle. I'm happy to do whatever you need me to do. Behind the scenes. Incognito."

"I'll let you know. No matter what, we'll get through this." Kris grips my shoulders. "For the record, I think Netflix is just bluffing. They love you. They love the show."

"I know," I lie, but it's what she needs to hear.

On my way back home, it occurs to me everything in this town is such a fucking illusion. When I think of my gorgeous giant of a husband, my two adorable babies and the family we have up in Seattle?

That's what's real.

I'll go through all the motions. Hire a stupid PR firm. Defend myself in this dumb lawsuit. Hell, maybe I'll do some private sessions with Lisa Kinkaid, if that will help me retrain my brain a bit.

What I won't do?

Compromise the people I love.

Never. Ever. Again.

Chapter Twelve

The Same Day

RONNI AND I ARE gradually getting our groove back.

Both of us carry a wee bit of hurt. Big misunderstandings have a way of doing that in a relationship. The boys' first birthday party was a success. We're not far off our second wedding anniversary, and I'm beginning to get the picture of what marriage is. An ebb and flow of tides, which carry unique obstacles for us to navigate. Some are like a playful splash. Others are like riptides, dragging us out to sea.

My wife and I are learning how to work together to steer the ship when things get a little choppy.

For two stubborn souls like us, our biggest relationship blunders don't seem all that insurmountable. We need to learn how to make decisions together. About everything. Where we live. How we want to raise Torin and Tristan. Our careers.

Careers. Jaysus.

It's genuinely like we're trying to merge two distinct cruise ships. Each of us have people depending on us. Responsibilities. Schedules. Demands. Now that LTZ is back in the mix, things are getting complicated. If I know one thing, it's this: I will not be separated from my family.

One saving grace is Ronni agreed to couple's counseling with Lisa Kinkaid. While I'd not ordinarily be all that sussed on talking to a shrink, this particular woman helped my bandmates. She specializes in celebrity shite, so she seemed like a decent choice. We'll work with her remotely when we get settled in Seattle.

I pile my clothes into the giant portable wardrobe and cross the hall to the boys' room. Ronni's meeting with a crisis PR team. The backlash from the defamation lawsuit has put my wife in the crosshairs of the court of public opinion. Currently, it's fifty-fifty for and against her, which doesn't bode well. Whatever happens, me, Torin, and Tristan will be behind her.

"Wee Tristan, where do you think you're going?" I scoop up my wayward son, who's halfway over the wall of his crib. He wails in protest. "Torin, you need to talk some sense into this one."

I change Tristan's diaper and set him on the ground, making sure the bedroom door is closed. Next, I get to work on Torin. "Jaysus, son. What have we been feeding you?" I dispose of the stinky mess in the Diaper Genie and clean him up and set him next to his brother.

The boys are walking on their own a bit now. They look like lurching zombies at the moment, but it won't be long before we're going to need some sort of device to keep track of them. Both are obsessed with building blocks, so I dump out a huge container onto the floor and the three of us get busy.

I can't help but check my phone every so often. I'd hate to miss a call from Mae.

We're deep in play mode when Barry knocks on the door. "I hate to bother you, but your nanny is at the front door. She's asking to speak with you."

"Yolanda?" I'm confused. It's been nearly a month since Ronni fired her. I thought our housekeeper had boxed up her stuff, but I guess it's possible she left something here.

"Double Ts, you'll have to entertain yourself for a bit." I hoist my tall frame up from the floor. "Dude, can you watch them for a sec? This shouldn't be long."

Barry squints at me. "Uh, I'm your security, you have an unauthorized visitor..."

"Ah, you're grand." I wave him off. "I'll just be a minute."

"Fine. She's on the front porch. Shout if you need me." Barry sits on the floor with the kids. He's like an uncle to them at this point.

I jog to the door. Through the sidelight I see our former nanny sitting on the bench. Deciding it's best not to let her in the house without talking to Ronni, I step outside. "Hello, Yolanda. What brings you by?"

"Connor, I came here to talk to you about something personal. It's important." She clutches her blue cardigan with both hands. Looks up at me with teary brown eyes.

Now, I'll admit, even though this woman worked for us for months, I never took the time to get to know her much. As far as I was concerned, she had one job and that was to help with our kids. Of course I engaged in conversational pleasantries here and there. Mostly in Vancouver when Ronni was away so much. But nothing deep. Nothing personal. So, I'm feeling trepidatious.

"Okay. Ronni's not here now..." I try to deflect because I'm so uncomfortable. I choose to step back and lean against a stone pillar a couple feet away from her.

She bites her lower lip. "I'm getting approached by powerful people who want me to sell my story. I've talked to a lawyer and he feels like the non-disclosure agreement is void. It violates my first amendment right of speech."

"Okay." I set my jaw. So, this is a shakedown. I know how to deal with this shite. "This conversation is over. Have your lawyer contact ours. We'll go from there."

"I don't think you want what I have to say to go public." Her eyes lock with mine. She tilts her head slightly.

Poor little lamb. She has no idea that Ronni and I have been dealing with this shite for a decade. "As I said..."

"No, I'm talking." She holds her hands up. "Your wife is a terrible mother. We both know that. You and I were a great team taking care of your sons and that's why I was fired. She was jealous. Of my relationship with your kids. And with you."

Whoa. I want to set her straight, but I have to be careful. "Yolanda. You're way off base. We needed your help because Ronni was working. Then we didn't."

In a flash, she stands and moves toward me. "Don't fight it, Connor," she says before she grips my shirt and kisses me on the mouth.

"Jaysus." I push her off me and step back. "Not on your life, woman. You need to leave. Right feckin' now." I point to the walkway.

"Don't send me away. I'm in love with you." She lurches toward me again, wrapping her arms around me like she's clinging for grim death. She drops to her knees and reaches for my belt. "Let me suck your cock. No one will ever have to know..."

I struggle to get her off me. Cursing myself for falling into this stupid feckin' trap. Cursing myself for being outside where Barry can't hear me. When I manage to break free, I dart toward the door and turn the handle, backing in while keeping my eye on her. "Yolanda, I don't want you. I never wanted you. I love my wife. Stay away from us. I'm alerting security. Don't you dare ever come back here. If you try anything, and I mean anything, it will not be pretty. I mean it."

When the door shuts behind me, I lock it. Check all the outer doors on this level. Frantic, I run back to where Barry is to find him rolling around on the ground with the boys.

He looks up. "All good?"

I'm not sure what prevents me from saying anything. Maybe it's the absolute shock of it all. "Aye. She's gone."

"Great. Mind if I grab something to eat?" He gets up from the floor a hell of a lot smoother than I did.

"No, go for it," I say as he walks past me. "Hey, Barry. Wait. Before you do, can you make sure the doors and windows to the outside are locked?"

"No problem." He salutes me and takes off down the hall.

"Oh, and when you're done, get me a backup of the video from the front door. Just in case," I call after him, pinching my nose with my fingers.

"Connor, you'd tell me if there were something to be alarmed about?" He turns and cocks his head. Studies me.

I shake my head. "I don't think so, but Ronni will ask when I tell her about this. I want to follow our protocol."

He nods deliberately. Then turns and walks away.

"Pa Pa." Tristan lurches toward me and I sweep him up into my arms. Lean over and pluck Torin up as well.

The two boys tug at my beard when I bring them into the kitchen and set them in their highchairs. I doubt I'll ever get used to the hairs of my chin being yanked out by the wee fists of my babies. Today, I ignore the jolts because I'm trying to make sense of what just happened. "Should we get some lunch before your ma gets back, my boys?"

Ronni's obsessed with feeding them all organic homemade baby food. She tried to make it herself for a while, but now we have a service. I take out their favorites, yogurt, chopped fruit, and chicken and place the food in their dishes. Grab their tiny spoons and sit in the stool facing them. A dangerous location, I'm bound to get pelted with some of their lunch.

It's hard to get worked up over a bit of food on my shirt when I'm worried about how to tell Ronni about this shite with Yolanda. Don't get me wrong, after our previous missteps, I'm telling her. I just can't bear to add additional heartache to her plate.

Bollocks.

I guess when the winds are gale force, we must power through. Once we're in Seattle, I have a feeling things will be a little easier. Having our friends and family around us will soften these blows.

I just hope my warnings to that cunt of a nanny are heeded.

No one messes with my family.

I won't stand for it.

Chapter Thirteen

A Few Weeks Later

I CAN'T HELP BUT stare in fascination at Fiona as she bustles around the kitchen.

I thought my kitchen in the Malibu house was impressive. The kitchen at Ty and Zoey's is spectacular too. It made me realize what #kitchengoals should be.

But this? It's the size of a small cafeteria. Modern but rustic if I had to describe it.

The cabinets are a warm, golden color with black handles. Each wall is set up like a cooking station. On the far side, two eight-burner stoves are separated by a butcher block counter that's easily four feet long. A hood that spans the entire wall. The back wall is taken up by a floor-to-ceiling wine refrigerator, the actual refrigerator—which must be custom, because I've never seen anything like it in my life—and a freezer.

Next to the freezer is an oversized door, which opens to the pantry behind it. Lined with floor-to-ceiling shelving, it's the size of a coffee shop. If that wasn't overkill, four wall ovens are installed next to cabinets that are filled with every size and type of plate, dish, and serving vessel you could dream up.

Twin waterfall islands run down the middle, connecting the kitchen together. One island is covered in marble. The other is covered in stainless steel with plush mid-height barstools surrounding it. Bi-fold glass doors open to a conservatory-type room with a dining room table and glass doors out to a patio, which overlooks Seattle.

"My God, Fee." I can't stop gawking at the amount of food that lines the islands. "I've never seen anything like this, and I've been to some swanky parties in my day."

Fee's at the oven pulling out trays and trays of tartlets. "I do most of my recipe testing here so I can be home with Mia. My sous chef, Justice, is here so much Zane jokes that he lives here."

"Can I help? I can't promise anything, my kitchen skills are nonexistent," I offer, but hope like hell she doesn't take me up on it.

Fee gestures to a pile of dishes, glassware, silverware, and napkins. "Are you any good at table design? Maybe set the table for ten?"

"You got it." I get to work on placing everything just so. Fee also has a cabinet full of candles, glass beads, flowers, and essentially anything you'd need to make a table look like it belonged in a Martha Stewart magazine. I choose subtle pieces and sprinkle little packets of blue glitter for some sparkle.

Fee joins me at the dining table and hands me a glass of white wine. "Well, there's a talent I think you've got down pat. Alex just texted, she's on the ferry. We have about an hour or so before they arrive."

"I'm so in awe of you, Fee." I raise my glass to her. We clink them together. "You're so incredibly talented."

"Smoke and mirrors. I feel like I'm always on the brink of disaster." She sinks into a plush dining room chair.

"It's tough balancing motherhood, marriage, and career. Connor and I are trying to figure it all out. I'm having a hard time giving up control," I can't help but blurt out. Fiona's a great listener and I don't have anyone else to talk to about this stuff from a woman's perspective. With my production company going through a rough patch and the scandals looming over my head, I just don't feel comfortable bringing Kris into my personal life.

Best to let her have plausible deniability. For now.

"Zane wants a baby so bad. I do too. It's just...I put my life on hold when I gave birth to Mia. I wouldn't change anything because she's my world, but once Gus is up and running..." She looks out the window, a flicker of sadness tinges her expression.

"I had my IUD implanted without telling Connor. He knows now, but he was not happy." My hand flies up to my mouth at my revelation. A few sips of wine and, apparently, I have loose lips.

Fiona's head snaps back in my direction. "Ronni Miller. Taking control over your own body. Was he pissed?"

I nod. "Very. Not because I did it. Because I didn't tell him."

"If I can give you some advice you're not asking for, the two of you are adorable together. I've known Connor a long time and he's never loved someone like he loves you. Don't make the mistake I made with Zane. We lost too much time because of my inability—or fear—to simply talk to him." Fiona grips my hand, which is wrapped around the base of my wine glass.

I shake my head. "We're in counseling. I've been taking care of myself for so long. For most of our relationship, Connor's been away with the band. It's been an adjustment over the past couple of years since the wedding. Now the kids."

"True. You guys have had a lot going on. Speaking of which, are you okay?" She releases my hand and drains the rest of her wine.

I suck in a breath. "I'm scared. The powers that be are threatening to remove me from the movie to avoid negative publicity. Kircher is bound and determined to take me down with him. I'm trying to get a handle on the narrative to let me keep my job, but he has trolls and bots everywhere. It's like whack-a-mole." I decide to keep the bullshit with Yolanda to myself. Man was I pissed when Connor told me what happened. So far, nothing's come of it. Why tempt fate by saying it out loud?

"Even if that happens, weather the storm. You have a decent, respectable man. Beautiful boys." She leans over and hugs me. I'm so moved, I can't help but hug her back tightly. "Do you mind if I go change real quick before I finish the food?"

"Of course not. I want to check on our husbands. Who knows what the hell trouble they'll get into." I finish my wine, follow her back into the kitchen and pluck an olive off a charcuterie board that looks like flowers and vines. "Things have been quiet on the kid-front too, it always worries me a little."

Fiona shrugs. "If I know Mia, she's pretending like the twins are her dolls. Olga's there too so everything's probably fine. I'll pop in to check, though."

I wander out the front door under a blue-and-white balloon arch. Connor and Zane are diligently tying blue balloons of every shade to the lights along the walkway. "Looks great. I'm positive no one will need to ask twice what's happening here."

"Look, I've never been to a baby shower before. I'm doing the best I can." Zane grins cheekily. "Plus, there can never be too many balloons."

"Shouldn't you guys get outta here soon?" I check my phone for the time.

Connor comes up behind me and wraps his arms around my waist. "You wanna get rid of me, my love?"

I swat him. As if.

Zane checks his phone. "My mom's gonna be here in a second. I want to see her before we take off. Zoey and Alex's moms should be here soon too."

The three of us go back inside. Connor and I check on the kids, who are all napping. Fiona and Zane's middle-aged nanny, Olga is also napping. I close the door behind me and turn around into a wall of my studly husband. He grips my face in his hands, leans down and kisses me passionately.

"You look delicious enough to eat, so you do." He nibbles on my neck.

I hook my thumbs in his beltloops and cup his tight butt. "Ah, I think that's you. Residual from when all the girls on set called you eight-pack behind your back."

He blushes. "I'm so glad that's over."

"You know I've got to tell everyone, right? If they find out just by watching it, you're gonna catch so much flack." I squeeze his buns for emphasis.

He rolls his eyes. "If you do, I'll have to tell the guys. They'll never, ever let me live this down."

"Let you live what down?" Zane suddenly appears in the hallway.

Connor palms his forehead. "Ah, bollocks."

"If I tell you something, do you promise not to tell Ty and Jace?" I release my grip on Connor's ass. "It's a big secret."

"Don't you dare tell Zane then. He can't keep anything to himself." Fee appears, looking beautiful in her party attire, pink hair flowing around her shoulders.

Zane clutches his chest. "Why do you wound me so?"

The doorbell rings to save us. Lianne Rocks, Zane's mom, has arrived. Zane grabs an armful of baby gifts and hauls them to the living room. I can admit, I'm fascinated by Lianne. She's ethereally beautiful, like a strawberry-blonde fairy. She glides in and immediately asks about Mia. I can't help but study her. My mind's always thinking about casting these days.

Then I remember. I'm persona non grata.

Seconds later, Zoey's mom, Olivia arrives with Alex's mom, Andrea. Piles of packages. A couple of pies. We're all here but Alex and Zoey. We assemble in the kitchen and ooh and ahh over the feast Fiona's prepared while we wait for them to get here.

Fee motions for Zane to come over. "You and Connor should get moving. Alex should be over at Ty and Zoey's by now, and all of you guys are supposed to be in Poulsbo, not in West Seattle."

"You're right. Connor? Let's blow this popsicle stand," Zane hollers. Connor manages to sneak in a goodbye kiss and they're off.

"Okay, now that it's just us ladies." Fiona brings five champagne flutes to the island we're standing around. "Sparkling rosé anyone? Miraval? A little nod to Brad Pitt. He may be old, but he makes a fine wine."

We all clink glasses. I look around at the women, and even though I still feel a little out of place, my comfort level rises every time we all get together. I'm grateful no one else but Fee has even mentioned the lawsuit. It's bad enough that the monster who abused so many of us on set is suing me for defamation. It would be worse if I had to talk about it with my girlfriends.

"Ronni. Tell me the truth. How tough is it having twins?" Fee nibbles on a piece of cheese. "Zane is so jealous, he can't stand it. I'm stressing about having one baby, but two would put me over the edge."

"You know, the first couple of months were great. We were in Ireland in our little cocoon. Connor's auntie was our personal lifesaver. When we moved back to LA, it felt like a nightmare. Connor was up here for two entire weeks when his dad moved into the rehab facility. I was in LA with no husband, no nanny, two hungry boys and a work deadline." I shudder for dramatic effect.

"It's not easy being on your own with a baby." Lianne nods. "Carter was so involved when Zaney was an infant. By the time Zane turned two, Limelight was on the road leaving me to fend for the both of us. I was just lucky Fiona's mom, Faye, helped out so I could still dance. Otherwise, my career would have been shot."

Fee grabs another square of cheese. Her eyes glaze over a bit. "Yeah. I couldn't have made it through Mia's first years without my mom."

"Wait, is Faye your mom, Fiona?" Andrea asks innocently.

"Sometimes." Fiona raises a brow. "Depends on the day. Ooh. Saved by the buzz." She holds up her phone to show us Alex and Zoey are coming up the driveway.

Zoey's clearly blown away by the fact we're all here to celebrate her and Ty's baby. I'm a little envious when the group feasts on the platters of food Fee prepared. I'm still trying to take off four pounds of baby weight. If I have any hope to play a character in the movie I'm directing, I have to take it off. Today, I'll have to choose judiciously. Spiced lamb and chutney. Roasted eggplant and feta. It's delicious, of course.

The group of us sit at the modern dining room table and eat and drink for a couple of hours. I'm feeling a bit lubricated when I stand and tap my champagne flute. "Zoey, on behalf of all of us here, we welcome you to the mother club. It's an experience like no other."

"Absolutely. And to your third trimester. Heartburn, constipation, giant tits, and the inability to ever get comfortable," Fiona joins me.

Everyone else stands up and toasts a clearly uncomfortable Zoey. She sits down suddenly, almost out of breath. It's time to lay off the libations and get to the gifts.

"Let's get you into the living room. Once that belly pops, the discomfort starts. Get used to it." Olivia takes her daughter's arm and helps her to a cushy couch.

"I'm getting so fat." Zoey wrinkles her nose. "Ty doesn't seem to mind, though."

Zoey's belly isn't huge by any stretch of the imagination, but she definitely looks pregnant. "You should have seen my belly when I hit five months. I never thought I'd look like myself again. Well, I don't, but man, I was twice your size. The twins, God love them, have fucked-up my body big time." I squish my middle a little to show her.

Alex sits next to me and scoffs, "You're gorgeous, Ronni. But, to your point, I can't say I'm envious. I didn't have to go through any of that shit and I have a beautiful daughter."

Well, then.

Fee follows us in with a tray of faux-mosas, her concoction of orange and passion fruit juice with seltzer. "With those stupid migraines, I'm so glad you're taking such good care of yourself, Zoey. When I was pregnant with Mia, I developed preeclampsia. I don't want that for you. Not with all of the complications that go with it. It fucking sucks."

While Zoey unwraps gifts, me, Fee, Lianne, Andrea, and Olivia share pregnancy woes. By the end of it all, we're all laughing. Alex has a strange smile on her face, almost like she's zoned out but doesn't want to interrupt. Zoey's clearly horrified but too polite to tell us to stop the share-a-thon.

"Ah, Z. You won't remember any of it other than fondly the minute you hold your baby." Olivia notices her daughter's reaction and hugs her.

God, I miss my mom so much.

Then, I look around at all the women, who have become trusted friends. I think of my sons and how much they'll miss if they don't grow up with their band cousins. A while ago, before the series was shot, I'd considered talking to Connor about moving here permanently.

Given all that's happened, we're essentially hiding out in Connor's town house. Seattle's beginning to look like our best option for our family's home base.

We'd be away from Hollywood and the paparazzi. Connor and I could focus on being parents away from the spotlight. We could work on our relationship. He'd be closer to his family. His dad. Most of all, we wouldn't risk the boys growing up to be spoiled Hollywood brats.

They'd have real friends. Real family.

I'd have this amazing support system of mothers who are also becoming my best friends.

In my heart of hearts, being in Seattle is starting to feel like home.

This time—because I've learned my lesson—I'll discuss it with my husband before making the final call.

Chapter Fourteen

A Few Weeks Later

JACE, ZANE, AND I stand on the stage at the new Mission as our roadies load in our gear. We've rehearsed some over the past couple weeks, and I'm so ready to play. It will be a welcome distraction from the storms blowing through my family.

Da's returning home after the long stint in the rehab facility. It's been months of recovery, but he's resilient. He uses a walker now. Talks up a storm. Gives my brothers and me hell. I'm glad that chapter is behind us.

Unfortunately, we have bigger issues in my household. Last week, despite Ronni's PR efforts, including a People magazine feature on me, her, and the kids, she's been asked to step down from the movie project. Even though they're giving her the opportunity to control the narrative, to say Ronni is devastated is an understatement. She's hurt. Betrayed. Kris flew up to tell her in person. She promised both of us that she's in Ronni's corner but explained that the legal situation had to play itself out.

Which is true.

I have a bit of perspective, and honestly, the situation is feckin' impossible. If Kris keeps Ronni on board, the financiers will back out. By allowing Ronni to withdraw from the film, the film can go forward. She wasn't "fired," so when we've got everything cleared up, she should be able to pick up the pieces. She retains her behind-the-scenes credit and profit participation for originating the project. If the film's successful, Ronni will make crazy money.

It's not any consolation to her, though. Not yet. The movie was her dream.

Hopefully tonight will be a fun distraction. Gus is opening. LTZ is playing. Our first show in well over a year. The entire inner circle will be together for a night of celebration. New babies. New businesses. New era for my band. Even if Ronni can't see the forest through the trees, she's excited for Fiona. And for me and the guys.

I gaze down into the smattering of folks wandering around. Bar staff. Ty's foundation artists. Roadies. This place is so much nicer than the original Mission but has managed to keep all of the charm. An entire wall adjacent to the bar features the show posters for the past thirty years. The LTZ show that changed everything for us is smack in the middle. Fiona and Zane have done her father proud.

Glancing around, my heart swells with another kind of pride. We were four lads with a pipe dream. Now our songs are embedded in music history. I can't wait to feckin' play tonight. It's been too long. "This is fantastic, Zane, so it is. But where the fuck is Ty?"

"He's still in the car talking to Zoey on the phone. She's not been feeling well. He'll be here soon." Zane caresses his Gibson, the pride and joy of his collection of guitars. Jace, Zane, and I sit on the edge of the stage chatting about gear when our elusive lead singer graces us with his presence.

"My brothers. I'm so fucking excited. I'm ready to go." Ty swaggers in with more spring in his step than I've seen the past couple of weeks.

Jace shoves his drumsticks in his back pocket. "While the gear's getting set up, let's have a quick meeting. It's time we finalize some stuff with the band."

I'm surprised that it's Jace who instigates the conversation we all want to have but have been putting off for various reasons. We pull some chairs into a circle in the green room to make the final decision on who's going to manage us.

"Isis Management. Discuss." Jace leans way back in his chair. His legs spread wide.

"I'm on board, they've been feckin' great for my wee brothers' band." I'm fidgeting for some reason. Essentially, I'm willing the guys to get on board with making some significant changes to how we do things. There's no way I can keep up the pace our current manager, Katherine, had us on for years. She's put so much pressure on all of us this entire year to record an album. Start touring. Get LTZ back up and running. It's been a lot when none of us have been ready.

Zane pulls no punches. He stares us down and states, rather than asks, "So, Katherine is out, correct?"

"She's pressuring us to do all the things that burned us out over the years. We're not kids starting out anymore. It feels like the time to make a change." Ty juts his chin out defiantly. "After all, we're all family men, or soon-to-be family men now."

Jace surprises me when he says, "Yeah, but I still want to play. And tour. Are we all up for that?"

I know this is my opportunity to take control of the situation. "Yes, I'm on board on one condition. We each need our own bus. If we can agree on that, I'm cool because I plan on having my family with me if we're gone for longer than a couple of days. That's my non-negotiable." I slump down in my seat and cross my arms across my chest. Decide I've come across too demanding, so I try to lighten the message. "You don't want to be woken up by my evil twins. Trust me."

The rest of the guys toss in their own non-negotiables. All in all, what we want is reasonable. With our future decided, we pick a date to fly down to LA to meet with Isis.

After the meeting and sound check, Ty summons Carter and Zane to the dressing room to chat about something. Jace and I are, once again, sitting on the stage talking shop with the musicians from the Rainier Foundation. Not ten minutes later, everyone's startled by a thunderous crash from the dressing room. Zane and Ty are screaming at the top of their lungs. Loud crashes. Angry yelling.

Jace and I jump off the stage and tear across the floor to the dressing room. Before we go inside, Jace threatens everyone with murder if they film or post anything. I throw the door open to find Ty categorically hammering the clean shite out of Carter, who appears to be unconscious. Zane, in turn, is trying to knock the bollocks out of Ty.

I run to pull Zane off Ty, but not before he smashes Ty's face in and breaks his nose with his knee. With the upper hand, Zane pins Ty to the ground. Jace and I manage to hold him back before he does any more damage. He's like a wildcat, it takes effort to avoid taking our own licks.

Until he spots his unconscious father. Every ounce of fight drains through the bottom of his soles. Zane drops to Carter's side and starts CPR. Kneeling next to him, I growl into his ear, "What the actual feck? What happened?"

Zane points at Ty. "He fucking killed Carter."

Ty moans and rolls over, attempts to get to his feet and crumples. Jace helps him up.

Zane snarls as he continues to work on Carter. "You're so fucked up, Ty. Seriously. Stay the fuck away from us."

EMTs burst through the door and stabilize Carter. As they load him onto the gurney, Zane bends down next to Ty and in a voice so evil I cannot believe it came from our guitarist, hisses, "Fuck you."

Ty's manages to sit up. His face might be a bloody disaster, but he bellows after Zane and Carter. "No, fuck you. And fuck Carter. You are both fucking dead to me."

Jace tries to calm him down, but Ty whirls around and cocks his fist. "Don't you fucking touch me, Jace. You have no idea how sick to death I am of you treating me like a fucking child. Leave me the fuck alone."

Jace shoots me an exasperated look, holds up his hands and joins me where I'm standing, transfixed at the absolute feckin' disaster the night's turned out to be.

It's clear to me, Ty's had some sort of mental break. My heart's beating a million miles an hour. The man's complicated, there's no denying it, but this has gone too far.

I'm debating silently in my head whether to go to him when he stumbles to his feet and roars the place down. "What? Do you want a piece of me too? Have I been a big joke to all of you? All these years? Wind Ty up. Put him on stage. Use his songs. Rip his soul out. Pat him on the head. Fucking repeat. We've made our money, right? It's all fine, right? You're all rich now, right? Well fuck this. I fucking quit."

Like zombies, Jace and I watch Ty as he rages and roars, bursting from the dressing room and tromping toward the loading dock. He screams at us over his shoulder, "There's no more LTZ. It's fucking over. If I never see any of you again it will be too fucking soon."

If that weren't bad enough, he points at his crying, horrified foundation artists, who have been looking forward to this show for months, and growls, "There won't be a show tonight, kids."

My mind can't catch up to the absolute shite show I've just been witness to. Jace and I push through the doors to the loading dock to see Ty slammed against the wall and cuffed. The face that's broken a million hearts looks bloodied and beaten. He crumples to the ground. The officers roughly yank him up and shove him into the back of the police car. Farther down, Zane's huddled next to Carter in the ambulance.

Jace grabs my elbow. He's as utterly freaked out as I am. "I need to get to Alex."

"Feck. Let's go." In all the chaos here at The Mission, Ronni's still next door at Gus. Holy feck. Fiona. She probably has no idea that her night's about to be ruined too. The devastation of our LTZ family is unbearable. I can hardly believe that a day that started out as a reboot for LTZ will now go down in history as the end of my band.

I can't lie, I feel hopeless. Ronni's career is in trouble. Mine is nonexistent, apparently.

I have no idea what to do. No idea what to think. I need my wife. I need my kids.

They're all that matter now.

Chapter Fifteen

The Same Day

SOMETIMES WHEN YOU'RE FEELING like absolute dogshit you still have to suck it up. Today is one of those days.

Rather than wallow in the misery this defamation lawsuit is bringing me, I'm taking the night off to celebrate Fiona's restaurant opening and my husband's return to the stage. Alex and I are utterly enthralled watching Fee command her kitchen staff with quiet confidence. She's in black chef gear with a tall, white chef hat. My badass friend's pink hair is plaited in a long braid. She's so ready. You can just feel her energy permeate this entire restaurant.

So yeah. Even though I'm having a severe career setback, I'm thrilled to see Fiona's dream come true.

It's fascinating how the chefs move at their individual stations. Together, it's like an intricate dance to plate the most beautiful food. It's almost eerily quiet, but everyone embodies their role. The front-of-the-house staff watches and waits. Their part is key. The food and the service together are how Gus will receive a Michelin star. Or maybe two.

The choreographed hustle and bustle continue even when Fiona disappears into the office for a bit. When she reappears, she approaches us with bottle of vintage Dom Perignon. "I thought we deserved to have a little toast with the expensive stuff. Zoey can't drink anyway, so we won't feel bad she's not here yet."

"Holy shit. I haven't tasted this stuff in years." I reach for my flute when she pours it to nearly full. The three of us clink glasses. Fee and I take a healthy gulp, savoring the bright, fruity flavor. It's such a treat. Tonight, I've decided to give myself a break and let loose. There's no way I'm going to miss anything she has in store for us. Not when she's worked so hard.

I can't help but notice Alex took barely a tiny sip. Discussion for later, perhaps.

Fiona hands Alex and I the menu for the evening. "Well, this is it. I can't believe tonight's the night. I've put my heart and soul into this opening. I hope everyone loves what we've prepared."

"OMG." I can't stop myself from licking my lips. "Crab with avocado, ginger lime, and cucumber? No, wait. Foie gras seared with sunchoke, dates, and water chestnut? I hope you know I'm going off my diet to eat this, Fee. It's going to be sooooo worth it!"

The three of us relax with our champagne and chitchat for a while. The atmosphere is super chill until we hear an incredibly loud crash next door at The Mission. It's so startling, Fiona jumps up and rushes through the kitchen into the dish pit. Alex and I follow close behind. She presses her ear to a strange-looking panel, which she explains is the hidden catering door to the green room at the club. She jiggles the tiny knob, but it's locked. Now we can hear screaming and yelling. It sounds like Ty and Zane.

All three of us pull out our phones to call our significant others, to no avail. We hear shouting. Well, that's an understatement. Ty's bellowing at the top of his lungs. We can't make out what he's saying, but he sounds out of control. More crashes, swearing, and thumps. Are they fighting? Did someone break in? Has there been a shooting?

None of the options are optimal. That much we know. But with so many horrific possibilities, the three of us are frozen in place. Staring at each other. Downright petrified and unsure of what's happening. Or, what the hell we're supposed to do.

Fee snaps out of it quickly. Takes a deep breath. Directs her staff. Keeps a cool head. I have every intention of following her lead when I hear Connor's deep, booming voice through the wall. Now that my man's involved, I can't help it. I take off running toward the front door. "What the fuck is happening?" I can't help but cry out.

Fee and Alex follow me outside and over to The Mission, where we pound on the main door, which is still locked. None of us can get ahold of our men, but Alex responds to some texts from Zoey, who's in a car on the way to meet us. Since we can't get in the front door, the three of us run to the loading dock behind the building without giving a second thought as to the potential consequences.

My heart sinks when I hear sirens approach. Seconds later, five police cars scream into the back parking lot, followed by two ambulances. They burst through the loading dock. Fee is sobbing now. Frantically calling both Zane and Carter with no answer. I'm feverish with worry. Just when my patience runs out, the EMTs wheel Carter out on a stretcher. Zane trails behind him, wailing. Clutching his dad's hand.

Fee stands there with the most broken expression I've ever seen. Her face is streaked with tears, but she's almost comatose. Like she's seen a ghost. She's clearly in shock. Rather than go to Zane, who's with Carter in the ambulance, she looks at the two of us and steels her expression. "I'm going back to the restaurant."

I'm about to follow her, because she's clearly not okay, except Ty's shoved out the door, shackled in handcuffs. He looks like hell. It's all too much. We're in a nightmare. Watching Fiona's dream explode. LTZ's reunion go up in flames. Needing comfort, Alex and I embrace.

There are no words.

"Fucking chaos. It's a fucking disaster," Jace roars as he bursts through the loading door followed close behind by Connor. It's clear they don't see us standing there.

Our men stand at the edge of the concrete platform. Surveying the aftermath. Ty crumpled in the back seat of the police car. Zane draped over Carter in the ambulance, wailing like a dying dog.

Alex and I peer inside the venue as the door snicks shut, hoping to get some clue as to what the hell's happening. All I can see is LTZ's crew and various kids from Ty's foundation milling around, tearful and slack-jawed. Our expressions mirror theirs. I'm unable to fully process what I've seen—what I'm seeing.

Strong arms suddenly wrap around my waist. Connor pulls me against him. "Come here, my love. I've got you."

"What in the world is going on?" I turn in his arms and clutch his t-shirt. In my peripheral vision, I see Jace and Alex wrapped up together.

He smooths my hair. Speaks to me in a calm voice that I know masks his true feelings. His eyes are wild. Scared. "I don't know, Mae. Ty went berserk. I had to pull him off Carter. He beat the absolute shite out of him until he was unconscious. Then, Zane beat the shite out of Ty. I truly couldn't tell you what the feck is happening now. Ty quit the band. He said some nasty, nasty words."

"Ohmygod." I bury my face into his chest.

He disengages from our embrace to look at me with sad eyes. "I'm gonna take charge and smooth things over. It's going to be up to me to talk to those poor kids. And our crew, of course. This is an absolute disgrace."

I nod to Jace, who's on the phone with someone, Alex firmly tucked into his side. "Is he handling press?"

"Aye." Connor glances down to a black car pulling to the edge of the lot. The police are waving it away. Out pops Zoey, clutching her protruding belly. When she spots Ty in the police car, she run-waddles toward her husband, wailing in grief. Alex breaks free from Jace and rushes past me, Connor, and Jace, down the loading dock stairs to intercept Zoey.

Zoey collapses to the ground in Alex's arms when the police door closes, and Ty is whisked off to the station. Jace runs down the stairs toward them, but the EMTs in the second ambulance already are loading her on a stretcher. Connor and I watch him have words with Alex before she climbs into the ambulance with Zoey.

Seconds later, both vehicles are headed to Harborview with their patients.

Jace paces like a panther. He's clearly pissed. It's unlike him to display any emotion in a public setting. I clasp his wrist. "We should go in. I'm sure we're being filmed. At the very least, we can try and do some damage control until we can figure all of this out."

"Aye. Let's go." Connor takes my hand. Jace follows.

Once inside Connor grabs a mike and jumps on stage. "Ladies and gents. None of us have words to describe what just happened. All of you are valued members of the LTZ and Mission community. We ask that you co-operate with the police and remember you're all under NDA. No one may talk to the press or post on social media without running it past our management. For those who are here with the Rainier Foundation, the same thing applies."

The police aren't there for long. Once they're finished, Jace and Connor manage to get everyone to depart. I can't help but shudder. What occurred tonight changed LTZ's history. My husband's identity is tied up intrinsically with his band, which means his life has just been forever altered.

We're quite the pair.

The three of us go back to the dressing room. I'm flabbergasted. It's utterly trashed. The walls have jagged holes in various places. The furniture has been turned over. Paper is strewn everywhere. The catering table has collapsed, squished fruit, meat, and cheese splays across the floor. Connor and Jace start cleaning up when I realize no one's checked on Fiona for at least forty-five minutes.

Kneeling next to him, I hook my arm through Connor's. "I think it's best if I go to Fee. After all her hard work, her night is ruined too. Everything she planned for so many months is destroyed. Zane's with Carter. Someone needs to be there for her."

"Mae, my love. Go to her. That's very kind of you." Connor kisses me sweetly. "Jace and I will clean up as best we can."

Once outside, I'm grateful to be back in the fresh air. I can't help but lean against the back wall and take cleansing breaths. My stress level is through the roof. I'm trying so hard not to make assumptions about what happened. It's a well-known fact that Carter was the one who broke Ty and Zoey up all those years ago. He's since redeemed himself, but who's to say what happened? I can't help but wonder what Carter did to cause Ty's visceral reaction.

I make my way back to Gus. Inside, Fee is curled up on an ornate couch in the waiting area by reception. I sit next to her. Gently take off her chef hat and brush a hair out of her face. "I know you're not okay."

"I'm trying not to make this whole thing about me, but fuck, Ronni. Every time I think everything's on track, the rug's pulled out from under me. It's hard to keep fighting." She sluggishly sits up and slumps back against the cushion. "I'm trying not to feel sorry for myself, but there's a nugget of rage bubbling inside me. It started when I had to call the food critics and tell them we weren't opening. Based on the reaction I got, it's unlikely they'll give me another chance."

I move so I'm sitting sideways, cross-legged. My back's against the armrest. "This is just as much your loss as Zane's, babe."

"I know, it's not that. It's everything. Zane texted me. Carter had a heart attack." Her shoulders slump forward. She buries her face in her hands and cries. I scoot over and pull her into me. Hold her as she lets out her grief.

"Carter will be fine. You'll reopen. The band will work it out," I say decisively.

She shakes her head sadly. "Zane needs me, but they won't let anyone else in Carter's room. He's just wrecked. It's like déjà vu."

Fiona tells me a story I'd not heard before about when she and Zane were six and they found Carter OD'd in the park. "I just don't know if I have the stamina to start from scratch. My menu is seasonal. God."

"Just take some time. You might want a project to distract you from the LTZ stuff." I can't help but think the idea sounds kind of nice. I'd give anything to get out from under the shitstorm of my own life.

Like a bolt, she reaches over and grips my hand. "Shit. Ronni. I'm the bad friend. I haven't even asked you about all of what you're going through."

"Oh, it's all legal bullshit." I wave my hand across my face like it's nothing.

Her eyes narrow. "Uh. No. Try again."

"I've been asked to step down from the movie I was producing for Finnegan O'Rourke." I try to keep my voice from quivering, but it's hard. The news is raw. "I'm beginning to wonder if all the work I did to bring these bastards down was worth it."

"I never thought about how the allegations would affect your work." Fee rests her head on her hand. "Are people truly believing it?"

I can't help but laugh. "You have been in the dark. Yeah. The tide of public opinion is most definitely moving against me currently. Kircher has social media bots trolling me. Spewing out trending hashtags. It's a lot."

"You seem so poised. How are you getting through this?" She looks at me with awe. Not pity. I love her for it.

"Connor."

It's a simple, but true statement. There's no way I'd be able to handle the wave of negative press that's crashed me to the beach without my husband. He's the stability in life.

"Zane's always been my person, you know?" Fee nods. "Do you mind if I go call him? I should check how Carter's doing."

"Don't ask a second time. Go." I point toward the kitchen.

When she leaves, I lie down on the couch like it's a bed. Stare at the ornate gold carvings on the ceiling. My God. We're all going through it. Every single one of us. It's hard not to be scared. Hard not to be pessimistic. Or negative. Or downtrodden.

The people that preach positivity and manifestation? I call bullshit. If you never have any expectations in life—or, no. If you always believe the worst will happen but hope for the best—or, no. If you just keep to yourself and never take any stupid risks...

No.

No. No. No.

I hold up my arm. Read my tattoo.

Be fearless in the pursuit of what sets your soul on fire.

I'm not going to let anything bring me down. Or Fee. Or the band. Or anyone I love. We're a family. Family sticks together, and family helps each other through hard times.

I'm under no illusion. Hard times are ahead.

Connor and I will stay strong to overcome our own obstacles.

So will the rest of LTZ.

I'll do anything to make it happen.

Chapter Sixteen

The Same Day

LEAVE IT TO MY wife to prioritize Fiona. I watch her fine ass walk out the door and feel proud. My woman's going through a crisis much bigger than this one could ever be, yet she's thinking about everyone but herself.

Jace mumbles something about how mad he is about Alex chasing after Zoey, which strikes a chord. I can't help but admonish him. "Ack. No, Jace. Alex and Zoey have been friends since they were wee lasses. She should be by her side. Don't make this situation worse by taking out your frustrations on your missus."

"Aren't you furious?" He paces back and forth. Throws his hands up in exasperation.

"Aye, I'm furious at what happened to the band and the night in general. But we don't have any further insight, do we? There's no way for me to know what set Ty off tonight. But I know the man. I've traveled with him. Spent time in the studio with him. I've had my own issues with him, but never, in the history of our friendship, have I ever seen him react this way. And neither have you."

Jace is completely fed up. "I have an idea," he says in a high-pitched mocking tone. "More of the same." He plops down on a chair. "Maybe this is all for the best. I don't want to do this anymore."

I pick up another chair and place it across from his. "Jace, my brother. You've lived a privileged life. As have I. There's a lot about Tyson's past that I relate to, though. We both had to grow up too soon and support our families because of addiction. It fucks with you. I'm not excusing him, but Ty's a gentle soul. Let's at least try to remain neutral until we know what's what. All of us need to stick together."

"With all due respect, you heard him. LTZ is through. He killed our band, Connor." Jace punches his fist into his hand repeatedly. He's so incredibly agitated, it's a bit disconcerting.

"Aye. So it seems. But before all of this happened, he looked happy. Genuinely happy. So, I'm going to reserve judgement." I stand and go to the door. "I'll get the crew to start loading up the gear. Let's ask Ty's foundation kids to clean up a bit. I just want to take some of the burden off Zane and Fiona. They're going to have a lot to deal with."

Jace follows me. "You're a stand-up man, Connor. A caring man. I'll do my part too, I'll call Katherine. She's still officially our manager. I'll sort out social media. Draft a press statement. All the usual damage control."

"Right. Let's reconvene in a bit." I salute him with two fingers and go out into the main room.

Under my direction, the remaining crew and foundation kids straighten up the main room. Mop. Put things back in order. It looks satisfactory. I'm chatting with our crew when Ronni's text comes in.

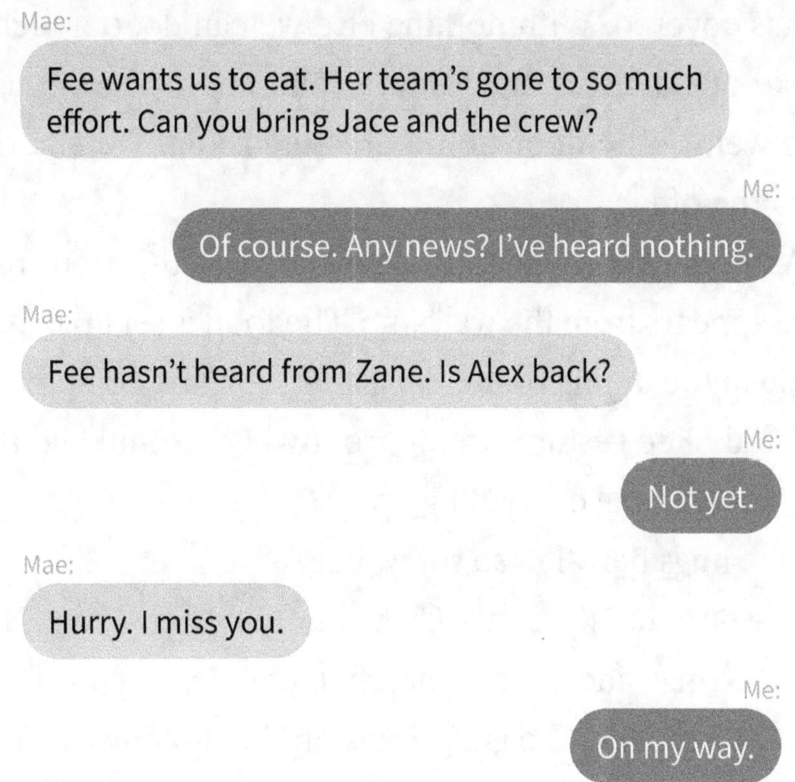

Jace emerges from the dressing room. "Shit's still scattered all over the floor, can I get the broom?"

"Leave it for now. Fee wants to feed us. There's a ton of food that's going to spoil if it's not eaten." I gesture toward the crew. "I say, let's bring them over to salvage their evening at the very least. When will they get a meal like this otherwise?"

He agrees. We lock up the loading dock and other doors too. Security is in the parking lot redirecting the fans that were supposed to see us perform tonight, so that's covered. With nothing else we can do, our techs, Pokey, Rex, Angus, and Kimora, follow us to Gus through the weird little door in the dressing room. We emerge into the office.

As we walk through the dish pit and into the prep area, Fee appears from the walk-in. "The food is set up family style in the dining room. I'm glad it won't be completely wasted." Fee gestures to the front where Ronni and the staff are setting everything up.

Jace hugs her. "I'm so sorry, Fee."

She bites her lip. Nods. Clearly holding back tears. Her phone rings and buzzes, nearly launching itself off the nearby counter. She grabs it just in time. "Zaney, talk to me." She moves briskly to the office for privacy.

Ronni hands both me and Jace a fully loaded plate and takes one for herself. "We need to eat this food. She worked her ass off for this and now it's ruined."

"I love it when you eat." I kiss her temple. She blushes. Her constant dieting is not a fun topic for us.

The three of us sit at a table still set for tonight's opening. The food is exquisite. I can't even imagine what this night could have—and should have—been had Fee been able to present it in the manner she intended.

Halfway through the meal, Alex returns from the hospital. The four of us move to a table away from the crew.

"Zoey's fine, they're releasing her after she has some tests done. Zoey's dad is handling Ty's situation, but I don't have any updates there. Carter's in ICU. He's beaten up badly. He had a heart attack but seems to be okay. Zane wouldn't tell me anything else until he talked to Fiona," Alex word vomits all she knows.

"She's a mess, understandably." Ronni hands Alex a plate of food. "We're eating what she made for us in solidarity."

"Should we check on her?" Alex gestures to the office.

"Aye. In a while. She was on the phone with Zane. How about we sort out what's left to do for tonight to ease her burden." I call over the crew and the kitchen staff to organize cleaning up the restaurant and transporting the gear home.

Ronni glances over at Alex. "Jace didn't have time to finish before dinner was served, so I think we should go straighten up the dressing room. You boys take a rest; it's been a long day. Get a drink, there's some phenomenal shit in the bar."

Our girls leave us. I move behind the bar and peruse the selection of fine spirits. I'm thrilled to see Midleton, my favorite Irish Whiskey. I don't indulge that often, given my family history, but when I do...

"Are you calmer?" I pour two fingers for both of us and hand Jace a glass.

Jace literally falls back into the sofa. He looks exhausted both mentally and physically. "Yeah. I texted Mike Pearson, he's working on getting Ty out of jail. Apparently, Carter and Zane aren't pressing charges."

"Good. Good." I hold my glass up to the light, swirl the amber liquid, and have a taste.

Jace downs the entire glass in one gulp and squeezes his eyes shut. "Alex is pregnant."

I'm surprised, but just nod.

"She's been having serious health issues." He shakes his head. Clearly broken up.

I savor another sip of my whiskey. "We all have things we're dealing with outside the band, my man. That's life, isn't it?"

"I was looking forward to playing tonight." His voice breaks a bit.

As sad as I am, I didn't realize Jace would be this emotional. He rarely lets on that he has problems. I'm likely the only one of us he'd ever confess to. Doesn't mean he wants me to solve things for him. I'm like a big brother. A sounding board. He's capable of figuring out his own shite. "We all were."

"Don't move back to LA." Jace opens his eyes. His gaze is pleading.

I'm about to fill him in on my own news when Alex and Ronni fly through the restaurant toward us. Alex thrusts a piece of paper at Jace. "Holy hell, you guys, we're not supposed to know this, but Carter is Ty's father. We found this DNA test in the dressing room rubble."

None of us can speak for a minute. This news is feckin' mental. I manage to find my voice. "We've got to assume this is going to get leaked. Jace, you should call Katherine."

"No, we aren't supposed to know about this." Jace shakes his head definitively. "It's their private business. In fact, none of us should say anything. We can't embarrass Carter, Zane, Ty, and Zoey like that."

Silence.

Jace kicks the ground. "With all of that said, what the actual fuck?"

Alex takes the paper from him. Folds it up and puts it back into the envelope. "Ronni and Jace, I know you're better at this celebrity damage control stuff than I am. What I do know is I should be the one to bring this to Zoey. She deserves to know before anything else happens. I'll head back to the hospital before she's released. It's what any best friend would do."

"Okay, Poppy." Jace lovingly strokes her hair. "I'll drive you. We've done all we can do for now. At some point, the chips are going to fall where they fall."

I grab our empty glasses. "Aye. Agreed. As for us... Mae, we should get the kids."

Ronni wraps her arms through mine and clasps my hand. "Actually, no we shouldn't, Connor. I talked to your mom. She's keeping the twins tonight. We need to stay here with Fee until she's ready for whatever the next step is."

Alex and Jace leave. Not long after, we let the restaurant staff out. I hand each of them a hundred-dollar bill on the way out. It's not going to make up for the tips they would have received tonight, but it's all the cash I have on hand.

The place is eerily quiet. "Should I go check on her?" Ronni sits on my lap and strokes my beard.

"Aye." I thread my fingers through her hair and pull her toward me. Our foreheads touch. "How are you, my love?"

"It's hard to tell. I thought I had problems." She shudders in my arms.

I squeeze her tightly. Her arms loop around my neck. "I feel like I've been run over by a semitruck."

"I'm worried about Ty." She pulls back to look at me. "Really worried."

"Me too. I've never seen anything like it, Mae. He was like a rabid, caged tiger. He could have killed Carter." I stroke Ronni's back, taking comfort in her mere presence.

"Ty is Carter's son." Fiona's voice startles us. We didn't tell her earlier. Now, she looks as defeated as I've ever seen a person look. "Which means, Ty is Zane's actual brother."

Ronni scoots off my lap and throws her arms around Fee, who's like a limp rag doll. She collapses in a booth seat, aided by Ronni, who sits next to her. I move over to where they're sitting. "Can I get you guys anything? A shot? A glass of water?"

"Can you rewind the clock so we can have a do-over?" Fee peers up at me.

I sit next to her opposite Ronni. She leans on my shoulder, and I wrap my arm around her shoulder. "You'll have a do-over, love. I promise."

"You're the strongest person I know, Fee." Ronni sandwiches her in. "This is just a little setback."

"Zane's incredibly upset, you guys." Fiona sits upright. Drums her fingers on the table. "I'm working up the energy to push down my feelings to meet him at the hospital and give him the support he needs."

"You should go." Ronni places her hand over Fee's. "We can all go. You need to be with your husband."

"I know, but he's all over the map. Talking about suing Ty. Scared about Carter. Furious at Carter. I love him. God, he's my life. He's put everything on hold for me to focus on the restaurant. You have no idea how much he needed LTZ to reunite. Now? I'm fucking scared for our families." Fiona gives in to her emotions and collapses on the table. Her entire body is wracked with the kind of grief that only happens when everything you held dear in your life is ripped away.

We should know.

Ronni and I glance at each other and, almost in tandem, sandwich her from both sides. Fee is not a cuddly, needy woman. She's always quick-witted, a bit abrasive, and wickedly funny. In the years I've known her, I've never seen this broken side of her. Even when she was going through Mia's custody bullshit, Fiona always exuded confidence. Something tells me, she needs us.

So my wife and I continue to sit with her.

For hours. She cries a bathtub full of tears until, exhausted, she falls asleep in my arms. I cradle her like a child. Ronni strokes her hand. We give each other a little smile. We're not going anywhere anytime soon.

And that's okay.

I can't help but stare at my beautiful wife. She leans against Fee's shoulder, keeping hold of her hand.

Despite her own crisis, which is monumental and has the potential to ruin her professional life forever, Ronni's here. Supporting me. Supporting my bandmates and their families.

Unconditionally.

In this moment, despite the fact two of my bandmates found out they're related and LTZ is very likely done, nothing is clearer.

As long as Ronni and I are together.

Nothing else matters.

Chapter Seventeen

The Next Morning

HOLY MOTHER OF GOD, my neck is killing me.

My eyes blink awake. It takes me a minute to figure out where the heck I am until I realize I'm staring at the polished concrete floor of Gus. Stretched out across a booth, my head is resting on my arm like it's a pillow. It's numb. Using my abs, I hoist myself to a sitting position and shake my wrist vigorously when the pins and needles start. I'm still fully dressed in my black satin jumpsuit. My six-inch platforms are strapped to my feet.

Yawning, I glance around the room. No sign of Connor or Fiona. I turn my head from side to side. Up and down. Reach around to massage my nape. I've never slept in anything but a bed. I never had any of the normal high school and college experiences high school and college kids had.

"Ah, Mae. You're awake. I had to take a piss." Connor emerges from the back, stretching his long arms behind his back.

I can't help but yawn again. I'm exhausted. "Where's Fee?"

"With Zane. They're in the office." He sits next to me. "Ty was released early this morning. Zane is...well, he's not good."

That wakes me up. "Of course he's not. How's Carter?"

Connor peers past me toward the kitchen and his gaze flicks back to me. He keeps his voice quiet. "Two stents. He'll be in the hospital for a few more days. Apparently, the injuries from the fight were bad. His nose was smashed to bits."

"God." I continue to rub the back of my neck to try to work out the kinks. Connor notices and takes over. I moan when he hits the exact spot that needs attention. Whine a bit when he withdraws his hand.

"I think we should get our boys. We can check in with everyone later. I talked to Jace, he and Alex spent the night at her mom's. They're on the ferry heading home with Mia." Connor stands and holds his hand up to me.

"Yeah, this wasn't the best place to sleep." I tilt my head left and right to try to release some tension. "My purse is back in the office, though."

"I've got it." Fiona holds my Valentino clutch out to me. Zane follows her, his designer jeans and black sweater rumpled. Connor's right. Zane, who's normally lit up from within like a firefly, looks like his switch was turned off.

Ignoring my purse for the moment, I gather Fiona to me and hug her hard. "Babe, are you okay?"

"Honestly? No." She crosses her arms around her middle when I let her go. "We were just talking. I think we're going to close the venue and postpone opening the restaurant until later this year. It's not definite, but when Carter gets home from the hospital we may go to Hawaii. Mia has a couple months before school starts. I think the three of us need to get away and do nothing. Recalibrate."

Zane doesn't say anything. He's eerily devoid of emotion. Like the events of the past day have sapped all his energy. And his personality.

Connor flexes his hand against my neck and squeezes gently. Uses his thumb to knead at the knot. "We're off to retrieve our wee boys. My ma wanted me to invite yous over for some Irish stew tonight. Just us, my folks. I think Cillian and Seamus might join. Might be an opportunity for us to have a peaceful night."

"Can I call you later? We need to go back to the hospital for a while." Zane's voice is flat. He sighs. "My mom won't leave Carter's side. I don't get it. She just found out he fucked an underage homeless girl and fathered a child a couple of months before she was pregnant with me. Why she didn't fly back to Denver, I don't know."

Fee tenderly strokes Zane's face. "She loves him, Zaney. He's her person. It's not all that different than our story."

"It's not the same." He shakes his head. "It's not the same."

"It's going to take a bit for this to all sink in." Fee cradles Zane's head when he crumples against her. "Our family has so much healing to do. It's hard to fathom that Ty…"

"Fucking Carter." Zane bolts up and smashes his fist against a table to stop her from saying the thing that has ruined LTZ. We all jump at the loud sound. Repercussions from the night before, no doubt.

Realizing that he's startled us all, Zane's chin hits his chest, wild, dark curls hide his eyes. Connor takes a step toward his bandmate. Slides his hand up Zane's back. "Aye. Feckin' Carter."

Zane peers up from under the curtain of his hair. Shakes his shoulders out as he straightens back up. He loops an elbow around Connor's neck and raises his other hand in a fist. "Fucking Carter," he yells at the top of his lungs.

Just like that, I know he's going to be okay. It might take a while, but he'll get through it.

As for Fee? The sadness behind her eyes is just a little deeper. She says tiredly, "We should let them get their kids, Zane. I'd like to pick Mia up from my mom."

"Yeah. I'm ready." Zane holds his hand out to her. She takes it. We follow them out. Luckily, the news cameras left hours ago when all activity ceased. I don't even want to know what was reported. Or how far this story has spread. I have enough bad publicity as it is, this is simply going to fuel the fire.

Fee and Zane get into Carter's fancy Audi and speed off. We both wave. When the car disappears, I look up at Connor. His expression is unreadable.

"Well, in the light of day, what do you think about all of this?" I slip my hand under his arm.

Worry creases his brow as he examines me. His eyes flick around my face before he shakes his head. "It's hard to believe that both of our professional lives have blown up in the span of a couple months."

"I guess we're in the same boat now." I squeeze his bicep, disengage myself and move toward the passenger side of the car.

"Maybe we should take a page out of Fee and Zane's book and hide out in Belfast for a while." He toes the asphalt with his black boot. "At least we can lick our wounds in a place without paparazzi."

"I have a better idea," I say as he buckles himself into the driver's seat.

"Aye?"

"Let's buy a house here." I turn in my seat to face him. "Somewhere gated. With security. We can't keep staying at the town house. I'd be surprised if we don't pull up to news vans out front."

Connor glances over at me, his brow knits together. "Bollocks. You're right."

I turn toward the window. We don't say much on the way to Connor's folks' house as the reality of the latest setback permeates the air.

The quaint little storefronts in Columbia City whoosh by, replaced by industrial buildings leading to the back roads to Capitol Hill. I'm beginning to know my way around Seattle now. At least to and from Connor's most-visited locations. When the scenery changes and we're in the middle of what looks to be an old-growth forest of evergreens, I whirl around.

"Where are we going?" I grab Connor's wrist.

He flashes me a toothy grin. "Thought I'd show you a house that has some significance to me."

I cock my head, puzzled as he parks on the street across from a beautiful old craftsman. Connor taps into his phone and stares, seemingly waiting for a response.

When his phone pings he nods and gets out. Trots to my side of the door and opens it for me. "Where are we?"

"This is Carter's house. The neighborhood is called Madrona. All of us have keys and codes to the alarm, Zane just confirmed Carter's never changed them." Connor leads me down a walkway to a carved wood door. He pulls out his key ring. Jiggles them until he finds what he's looking for.

I'm not certain why I'm here, but I figure Connor has a reason. The house is beautiful in a traditional way. Beige walls. Thick crown molding. Custom hardwood floors. Impeccable decorating, even if it's a bit dated. I can't help but gape at the rock memorabilia lining Carter's walls. I've seen Limelight play and liked them, but they were never on my radar until I met the LTZ guys. Well, until Carter allowed Kris and I to hitch a ride with LTZ on his private jet to Australia.

Connor stands beside me. "I can't tell you how many hours we all spent here when we were starting out. I was so starstruck. Can you imagine? One minute I was running the family construction company and hating my life. The next, I'm in a band with Carter Pope's son." He sighs and touches a picture of Zane and Ty when they were teenagers. "Two of Carter Pope's sons."

"Why did you want to show me Carter's house?" I smile at a picture of Limelight posing in front of the old Mission. The toddler in a stroller must be Zane.

Connor spreads his arms wide. Turns leisurely in a circle, taking it all in. "This is what I always dreamed of, Mae. A house on the lake. A place to raise a family."

"It's a beautiful house." I look around with a fresh perspective.

He grabs my hand and I barely keep up with him as he crosses the living room to the floor-to-ceiling windows. "Look." He points to the view of the lake, which is accessible across a vast lawn.

"Do you want to buy a place in this neighborhood?" I clasp his big hand with both of mine.

"I don't know. We're both essentially unemployed. Maybe we should wait." He looks down at me and cocks a brow. "Although, if we combine our resources..."

"I think we should do it." I nod. "Let's get a realtor."

Connor steps forward, eliminating the minuscule space between us. My palms splay across his chest and roam to the broad planes of his back. He rests his cheek on top of my head and moans when I skim down his spine and dip my fingers just below the waistband of his jeans. His hips jerk against me, his rigid cock nestles against my stomach.

Hooking my thumbs in his belt loops, I grab his muscular butt and squeeze. Yank him in toward me. He returns the favor by banding his arm under my ass and lifting me. I lock my legs around his waist as he turns and hustles across the living room and down the hallway lined with pictures. He stops at the last door. Manages to haul me inside without dropping me.

We burst into a room full of amps and instruments. "Is this Carter's practice space?"

"Aye," he growls. "It was LTZ's original practice space too. You have no idea how long I've fantasized about fucking you here, Mae."

Tenderly, he sets me down on an amp. I waste no time unbuckling his belt and opening his jeans. He rips off his Henley. I look up into his feral, amber eyes. "Let me."

He nods, grinding his teeth in anticipation. I pull out his cock and wrap my hand around him. Using the beads of precum from his crown, I pump my fist up and down his hard length before guiding it inside my mouth. Connor leans into me, bracing himself on either side of the amp with flattened palms. He cants his hips as I suck. Lick. Lave. Swirl. Hollowing out my cheeks, I suction the tip of his shaft down my throat.

"Christ, Mae." He cups my head and pumps, nearly choking me. Saliva spills out of my mouth, but I don't stop until he pulls out abruptly. "I'm too close." He steps away, his wet cock bobbing against his flat stomach.

I lean back on the amp, though there's not much room. Connor kneels in between my legs and unzips my jump-suit. He looks down at my midsection and then up at me, perplexed. I shrug. I'm wearing constricting Spanx that stretch up to my bra line. "I didn't expect to get fucked in the practice room, babe." I unclasp my front-loader black bra and give him an assist in rolling down the tight undergarment. The process is not sexy by any stretch of the imagination, but then again, we're an old married couple now. I guess it's time he discovered my secret to looking tight and toned in my clothes.

"You're not making this easy." Connor grins when he flings my undergarment to the floor. Returning to the matter at hand, he grips my jaw with gentle pressure. Drags his fingers through my soaking folds. Every nerve ending in my body ignites when he lines himself up with my opening and guides himself inside. I grip his forearms and lock my feet around his waist. Watching him disappear to the root. Slide out and push back in.

Each time his cock drags along my channel, sparks shoot up my spine. "God, Connor. Faster."

Reacting to my frenzied need, Connor lowers his chest to mine and brackets my head on the stack of amps behind us. He dips his chin down to capture one of my nipples with his teeth. Sucks it in time to his thrusts. I can't help but murmur words of encouragement. What we're doing here seems so forbidden. So hot. It reminds me of the years when we were separated for long stretches of time and his dressing room became our den of debauchery.

Connor drives into me, hitting my clit at the exact precise angle, sending me spiraling into release. He doesn't stop, merely buries his face into my hair. Bucking into me. Hot. Frantic. His hips slap against mine. Our fingers are tangled in each other's hair. We're kissing, sucking, biting any bit of skin we encounter. His fingertips dig into my ass. He slams me against him, swiveling his hips, sending me over the edge again.

As I'm seizing around him, Connor bucks into me with abandon before stilling and spilling into me, prolonging my orgasm. Our chests rise and fall together. Our breath mingles. I can't help but sigh with contentment. "I needed that."

"Aye. Me too." He watches himself ease out of me, leaving behind a pool of our combined pleasure on the top of the amp. I lean back while he searches for something to clean me up. "Christ, let me grab a towel from the bathroom across the hall."

I can't help but giggle when he shoves himself into his pants and scoots out the door to return thirty seconds later with a wet washcloth. He wipes me up and cleans off the amp. I shimmy my jumpsuit back on—without the Spanx this time. "We're taking that washcloth with us." I wag my finger at him. "Carter won't miss it."

"We're so bold." Connor can't help but laugh as we walk to the front door.

We're about to leave when the front door opens. Lianne stares at us, shocked. "Well, I didn't expect to find you two here."

Our faces are definitely the shade of a tomato. Connor stutters, "Uh, Zane said I could show Ronni the, uh... view. We're..."

"Looking for a permanent house in Seattle. Connor thought I'd like the neighborhood," I smoothly take over. "How's Carter doing?"

She glances at both of us. "His vitals are better. They will likely release him in a couple days."

"If you need anything..." Connor tilts his head.

She sighs. "About twenty-four hours of solid rest."

"I'm sorry for the intrusion, we were on our way out. We'll check in on you in a couple of days." I grip her elbow and we scoot past her out the door.

On the way to Connor's parents' house, we can't help but sneak knowing side looks. Chuckle every now and then. It's going to be a good memory.

I can't help but think that even if our lives are entirely up in the air, there's no one I'd rather be on this adventure with than my husband. Getting up to some mischief. Loving our kids. Meshing our lives into one functioning unit.

Both of us were fully capable on our own.

Sometimes we revert into old patterns.

Together is better, though. Even when it's hard.

Together is how we'll get through all of this.

Chapter Eighteen

A Couple Weeks Later

I'M TRYING TO GAIN some perspective about what happened at The Mission a couple weeks ago.

Jace has done his best, but as far as the press is concerned, LTZ is done. We've flamed out. Exploded. Broken up. Never to be heard from again. Most of the negative stories might focus on Ty and his meltdown, but the rest of us haven't fared very well either.

It's funny how fast people want to take you down. I've been riding on the success of my band for a decade. Ty's taken the brunt of any negative publicity we've ever had, but it's all added to his mystery. His allure.

Not so much now.

It's not like any of us are speaking yet. Ty and Zoey are at some clinic in Arizona, he's in an intensive rehab program. Zane and Fiona are at their house in Maui for the rest of the summer. Alex is dealing with some significant health issues. We've offered to take Lena , but they've gone radio silent. I get it. They keep to themselves. Seamus told me what he can, but he's Alex's surgeon. He won't divulge much. It was touch and go, that much I know.

Which leaves Ronni and me in Seattle. We're thinking about house hunting. Halfheartedly. The reason we planned on moving here was to be with my family and the band. My family's still a draw, don't get me wrong, but our little family is a bit unanchored at the minute.

Tonight, we're having dinner at my folks' place. Everyone's in town. Ma's making a feast.

"Rory, let me set these guys on your lap so I can get a picture." Ronni's positioning Torin and Tristan on my da's lap. His movement is mostly back, so he clutches the boys around their middles. Miraculously, they settle instead of squirm and Ronni's able to get a shot.

He's surprisingly adept at handling them. Liam and Padraig prepared him years ago. "What nice wee lads." He boops them on the nose.

"Okay, now all of you brothers gather by the fireplace." Ronni attempts to herd us and is met with various intonations of grumbling. I clasp Brennan and Cillian by the neck and guide them to where I want them. The twins follow. Seamus trudges over, looking exhausted as usual. Surgical residency is grueling.

The six of us plaster big smiles for my wife. "Perfect!" She claps gleefully and shows all of us the snaps. "I'll get these pics blown up and framed for your mom, Connor."

"She'd like that, my love." I lean down and place a kiss on her sweet lips. She's been handling the stress of everything like a champ. I know she's disappointed—no, devastated at the state of her own career, but she's helped me navigate some extremely bleak days.

Ma calls us to dinner. We get the twins situated in their highchairs and take in the tremendous spread. Roast ham. Roast beef. Dressing. Roasties, of course. Mashed potatoes. Parsnips and carrots. Fresh soda bread. I can't help but pile my plate high. It's been a long time since my entire family's been together for such a feast.

"How's the Amazon project, Cillian?" Ronni asks my brother. He took over McGloughlin Construction and has grown the business to, quite possibly, the biggest game in town.

He chews thoughtfully. "It's insane. I've hired three project managers just to keep up with the expectations."

Padraig and Liam are quiet. Liam hasn't come out with his relationship to the family yet. Padraig's still uneasy about the entire situation. I steer clear of their own band drama. "Is your tour set for this album, guys?"

"Yep." Padraig glances at Liam, who nods but doesn't say anything. "We're getting slotted into some of the LTZ shows on the festival circuit."

"Oh, aye?" I'm surprised, mostly at how much the news sends pangs to my heart. We were supposed to take our families on the road for some shows this fall. It was one of the scheduling situations Ronni and I were dreading, considering she was supposed to be in Ireland filming the movie.

Liam shrugs. "Paddy didn't want to do it, but he was outvoted. You understand, brother? Right?"

"Of course." I swallow a bit of a lump. "You should take the opportunity. As of now, LTZ is through." The words burn my throat when I say it out loud.

Ronni grips my knee under the table and squeezes. I don't look over at her, though.

"You lads will find yer way back, so you will." Da's raspy voice surprises the feck out of me.

"Da?" I steeple my fingers under my chin.

He looks over at my ma, then flicks his eyes to me. "It seems like the lot of you have dealt with yer share of personal shite. Taking time off can give yous all perspective. Yer talented. They're like yer family. Give it a bit of time, lad."

In all honestly, it could be the nicest thing my da has ever said to me. It means a lot, considering what a shit show the past couple of weeks have been. It helps me out of my funk, truth be told.

On our way home, Ronni takes my hand across the console of the Range Rover. "Let's take the house hunting seriously. Regardless of what's going on with LTZ, I feel like I can breathe here. Your family is here. We should be here, don't you think?"

"Aye. If that's what you want, it's what I want." I glance over at her. "The money from your house burning a hole in your pocket?"

"Ha. Ha. A twenty-million-dollar profit is nothing to sneeze at. Can you imagine the house we can get here for half that much?" She leans back against the seat rest. Turns her head to check on the boys, who are sound asleep in their car seats. "In all seriousness, your mom's still young, Connor. I know your dad's health issues have taken up much of her time, but she's not even sixty years old yet. We were talking, and she'd love to be there for her grandkids. She's so sweet with them. We'd never have to worry about a skanky nanny again."

"You've got a point there, love." I smile at her. My breath seizes for a moment at the mention of Yolanda. Nothing's happened since the day she showed up on our front door in Malibu. We haven't heard a peep. Still, something niggles at me. It may be trite, but it feels like the calm before a storm.

We arrive home and go through our nightly bedtime routine with the boys. I brush my teeth and dive into bed, where I watch her go through her own nightly rituals.. All she wears is a tank top and a tiny pair of panties.

For all her grousing of losing the baby weight, I swear she's more beautiful now than before she was pregnant. I can't help but grow hard when she approaches our bed. Her nipples poke through her top. A little slice of her flat belly peeks above her panties.

I fling back the covers to let her into bed. She slides against me, her back to my front. Wrapping my arms around her middle, I drag her against me. My bare cock rests in the middle of her ass cheeks. She wiggles her butt against me and cranes her neck to look back at me. I skim my hands down her sides and hook my thumbs into the waistband of her panties and drag them down. She kicks them to the floor and turns in my arms.

"Ride me," I command.

As instructed, Ronni straddles my thighs, fists my shaft and hovers her pussy over my shaft. Inches down so I feel her slickness. As she undulates her hips, getting my cock slick and wet, I pull her tank top above her perfect, round tits so I can watch them bounce to her rhythm. Then, I reach above my head and grab the iron slats of the headboard.

Tonight is the Veronica Mae Miller show, and I'm going to enjoy every single god damn minute of it.

"You're letting me do the work?" She yanks the tank all the way off and throws it on the floor.

I waggle my brows. "Aye."

She cups her breasts and pinches her nipples. Wee Connor literally jumps at the sight of her. Laughing, Ronni lifts her ass from my thighs, grips my shaft and drags it through her pussy lips to her clit and rubs it with my crown. Her mouth parts and her eyes close. She rotates her hips from side to side so the tip of my cock hits her little nub from all angles.

Mesmerized, I watch her sway above me. Taking her pleasure. Listening to her little moans and breathless pants. My cock pulses and weeps in her grip, it wants inside her so badly.

"Ride me, Mae. Now." My knuckles are white from how hard my grip is on the headboard.

She splays her hand on my chest and guides me inside her until I'm stretching her opening wide. I get lost in the sensations of being inside my exquisite wife and grit my jaw when she comes with a keening moan.

Releasing my grip on the slats, I wrap my arms around Ronni's ass to keep her still when I roll us over. Now it's her turn to reach up and grip the headboard when

I drape her leg over my elbow and spread her legs wide. Pressing my knee to the mattress in between her thighs, I cup and squeeze her breast, rolling her nipple with my thumb and forefinger.

She arches her back, allowing me to go deeper. I lean down and catch her earlobe with my teeth. Grind my pelvis against her clit, knowing I'm hitting that spot deep inside her when her eyes begin to blink rapidly. "Again, Mae. Come."

"Connor, I don't think I..."

"Aye, You can." I swivel my hips as I pound into her faster. Harder.

Her pussy clamps down around me. Hot. Slick. Holy feck, I'm not going to be able to hold on. I band my arm around her to keep her fastened to me. Pump. In. Out. Hard. Rough. Her walls flutter. "Connor, Ah—" Breaking off, she moans, deep and guttural.

Jerking her tightly to me, white heat explodes along my spine and I spill inside her, buried as deep as I can possibly get. "Aye. Mae. Holy Jaysus."

Coming down from such an epic orgasm, I feel Ronni digging her fingers into my scalp. My face is buried in her neck. Our mouths meet. Our kisses slow and sweet.

Making love to my wife is my favorite thing in the entire world. Even after all these years.

Especially after all these years.

It's feckin' everything.

Chapter Nineteen

Two Weeks Later

WHO KNEW THE PACIFIC Northwest could rival Los Angeles when it comes to wealth and opulence?

We're driving through a tiny municipality across the lake from Carter's house called Hunts Point. Connor and I are riding in a sleek, black Bentley Bentayga EWB SUV driven by Astrid Gustafsson, a stunning woman with silvery-blonde hair. She's about my age and, apparently, is the most coveted luxury real estate agent in the area.

At least that's what Jace's dad told us when he introduced her. She works on referral from high-net-worth individuals. After an extensive financial review.

Our house-hunting journey started in earnest a couple weeks ago. Jace called Connor after seeing an IG post I made with Clover at the Polo Lounge in LA. Thinking we'd moved back to LA, Jace called Connor to ask if we'd changed our plans to stay in the Seattle area. Connor alleviated his concern, explaining I'd flown down to meet with my lawyers.

I returned a couple days later, feeling more positive than I have in a while. That night, me, Connor, and the boys were invited to Jace's parents' house for a family dinner. Imagine my utter shock when Jason Deveraux, Seattle's most famous tech executive next to Jeff Bezos and Bill Gates, opened the door. Connor's still mocking my slack-jawed reaction.

To say I fell in love with the Medina neighborhood is an understatement. Jason made the introduction to Astrid. Now, we're touring five off-market houses that meet our simple criteria: Security. Seclusion. Serenity.

With so much chaos, it's the simple things that matter now.

"Hunts Point is a tiny municipality, and extraordinarily private. It's like living in an urban forest, yet every house has waterfront access to Lake Washington," Astrid coos in her smooth, whisky-tinged voice. "It's arguably the most exclusive neighborhood in the Pacific Northwest. I'll drive you through the commercial area. Lots of cafes and little shops. You're also near a beautiful nature preserve. Many local celebrities call it home."

We turn down a winding road and pass mansion after mansion. Some look old and iconic. Some are new and modern. It reminds me of Malibu, substituting lakefront for oceanfront, of course.

"What are the schools here like?" I grip Connor's hand tightly and squeeze, still watching the houses whiz by as we approach our destination.

Astrid turns into a long, paved driveway. "The best in the state. Whether you want your kids to go to public or private, one of my services is to help jump you to the top of the waiting list. I'll send some materials for the two of you to look over later tonight."

"This neighborhood is class." Connor looks around the thirty-foot-high trees surrounding us.

We emerge from what, essentially, is a forest into a clearing where a sprawling, modern prairie-style home takes center stage. Located on the point, the property sits on two acres. The juxtaposition is incredible. While the drive in feels like the wilderness, once we get to the clearing everything opens up. An acre of full waterfront access lined with manicured lawns and sleek stone walkways.

I step out of the Bentley onto the intricate chevron-patterned driveway and instantly feel at home. It's the first place we've looked at and I already know it's the house I never knew I needed. Without even seeing the inside, somehow I know—this is the perfect home for Connor and me to raise our family.

"Jaysus, this is something else." Connor runs his hands along the heavy steel panels embedded into an old-growth wood front door. It's twice as tall as he is. "I've never seen workmanship so beautiful."

"Everything you'll see is custom. From the finishes to the paint. There is nothing in this house you could buy off the shelf in any store." Astrid, wearing a vintage ivory wool tweed Chanel suit paired with nude Louboutin's, is every inch the image of every high-end realtor I've met in LA. Minus the entitled attitude. She's stylish, down to earth and friendly.

We enter a foyer into a seating area filled with oversized plush cream couches and gray-and-cream-striped chairs in the middle of two floor-to-ceiling steel fireplaces. The entire back of the house is glass. Lake Washington seems like it's in the room. I notice a covered dock, with a huge boat moored at the end of it.

"Wow, this is something else." I can't help but look out the windows and gawk.

Connor joins me at the window. Wraps his arm around my shoulder. We both gaze out at the calm lake lapping at the shore. "Growing up, there's no way I'd have even dreamed of visiting a house like this, let alone owning it."

He takes my hand and squeezes, letting me know he's as much in love with this place as I am.

Astrid takes us on the rest of the tour. When I see the kitchen, I silently celebrate. It's the closest thing to Fee's kitchen I've seen. It's smaller, and the design is sleeker and modern, but I'm not the professional chef in the group. It's astounding. Fiona will be proud.

It takes about an hour to tour the entire place. We learn about every custom feature of the house, and they are endless. The bedrooms are perfect. The bathrooms are perfect. There isn't one thing I'd change.

"Will the owners sell the furniture and art with the property?" The three of us are sitting in what Astrid calls a "whiskey" room, which is more like an old-time gentleman's lounge with a fully stocked bar with half-a-dozen oversized chairs set up in a semicircle facing the lake.

She taps her phone. "I just asked. Are you ready to head to the next location, or do you have any other questions about this property?"

Connor and I catch each other's eye. He nods then takes my hand. "Astrid, love. I think this might be the place for us."

"I thought it might." She smiles as she finishes her text but doesn't look up.

"As we mentioned, we're all-cash buyers," I remind her, suddenly nervous that maybe we're not the only ones interested in this house. It's a steep price tag, I can't imagine there will be a bidding war.

"There's one thing to discuss. As you may have heard from Jason, I pride myself on my ability to be discreet."

Astrid leans forward on her elbows, flicking her gaze to both of us.

Rather than answer, I lean back in my chair and hold eye contact. It's a power move I learned from Kris. Men never lean forward; the body language is too urgent. Desperate. Leaning back gives you control over every situation. You're in a receptive position—people are likely to be drawn in.

Connor mirrors me. "Go on."

"Do you covet press and paparazzi?" She looks directly at me when she asks the question.

I brush a lock of hair out of my eyes. "Why do you ask?"

Another negotiating tactic. Never answer a question from a relative stranger unless you have some idea what their end-game is.

"Privacy. The residents in Hunts Point pride themselves on discretion." Astrid does her best to speak to both of us, but she clearly is addressing me. I get it. "Despite the, uh, situations you find yourself in currently, you're both well-known in your own professions. Most of the residents here set up shell companies to hold the real estate in to avoid detection. If you're of the mindset to cultivate press and publicity—say, social media or otherwise, we may need to look at less-exclusive neighborhoods."

Relief washes over me. She's alleviated one of my biggest fears without even realizing it. "No. We want to raise our kids in a quiet, secure location where we're safe. I loved my house in Malibu, but everyone knew where to find me. It's currently impossible to leave the house without being photographed. It's one of many reasons we're relocating to Seattle."

"Aye. This place is perfect. We love the water view. It's relaxing. Helps us escape from the madness of our lives." Connor nods.

Astrid smiles like we've answered her questions perfectly. "Well, should we write up an offer?"

With our fate decided, Astrid drives us around what we hope will be our new neighborhood. Shows us the harbor at Carillon Point. Her favorite bistros and restaurants. Grocery stores. We get a great feel for the location, including where the schools are. We stop in nearby Bellevue at John Howie Steak for lunch.

Over the most delicious Cobb salad I've ever tasted, we hammer out the details of the offer. It's hard to believe that we'll be able to buy the house outright and still bank several million dollars from the sale of the Malibu house.

Just before we finish, Astrid looks at my husband. "Would you mind if I asked you a question, Connor?"

His eyebrows raise. "Uh, I'm not making any statements about the band. Or Ty." His voice is gruff, annoyed.

"No, I'm sorry." She waves her hand in the air as if to erase what she just said. "I'd never ask about that. I was wondering if your brother Brennan is back in town."

Connor squints at her. "May I ask why?"

I give her a curious look as well.

"I went to high school with him. I have something of his I'd like to return, but I've got to be the one to give it to him. I know that sounds...uh, sketchy. How about this. If I give you my card will you pass it on to him?" Astrid's cheeks redden a little when she asks.

Connor leans back and crosses his arms. "Surely you have alternative ways of getting ahold of him?"

She shakes her head, now clearly embarrassed. "Forget I said anything. It's stupid. I didn't mean to offend..."

"You didn't." I encircle her wrist with my hand. "Give me the card, we'll get it to Brennan. Then he can decide."

I look over at Connor. "It's not like she couldn't have asked Jason."

Connor allows a smile to creep over his face. "Ah, you've piqued my interest, Miss Astrid. We'll at least text him your number."

An hour later, we're back at the town house with the twins. After touring the Hunts Point property, to say it feels cramped is an understatement. There's no backyard. We're in a busy neighborhood with lots of noise. Assuming the owners accept our offer, if all goes well, we'll be moving in three weeks.

We're changing the boys' diapers and getting them in their pajamas when Connor's phone pings. "You can take that, I've got this covered."

"It's Brennan, I sent him Miss Astrid's number." He waggles his eyebrows, flashes me a cheesy grin and heads out to the living room.

I take my time with the twins. Read them stories in their big-boy beds. We gave up trying to keep them in their cribs. Now, everything in the room is kid-safe, nothing to hurt them. They can roam around to their hearts content without us worrying. They conk out thirty minutes later. I change into yoga pants and a sweat-shirt and collapse on the sofa in the living room.

"Hey, big guy. You hungry?" I direct my comment to Connor, who's standing at the window. He glances over at me; his expression is strange. "Should we order in?"

"Aye. You pick." He looks back out the window.

Ever since Fiona's thwarted restaurant opening and I lost my production projects, I've loosened up on my dietary restrictions. Shockingly, I've dropped a pound, not gained twenty. "Pizza?"

"Fine. No olives." He sinks into the couch next to me. Clicks the TV on.

I can't help enjoying the splendid mundaneness of our evening. Binge-watching shows that I've never had time to watch. Ordering delicious carby pizza. I'm not going crazy, but it feels great to eat like a normal person. No, it feels great to live like a normal person.

I'm giddy with excitement when I snuggle up next to my husband. He puts his arm around me. Kisses my head and pulls me close. I poke his rock-hard abs. "Is Brennan going to call Astrid?"

"Huh?" He looks at me, puzzled. Then he nods. "Oh, aye. He remembered her."

"Is everything okay, my honey? Are you having second thoughts about the house?" I thread my fingers through his. Rest my cheek on his shoulder so I can look up at him.

He smiles, but it doesn't reach his eyes. "I'm grand, my love. Perfect for us."

I'm not sure why he's acting weird, but I decide to let it go. Pointedly ignoring the prickles down my spine, which have started their macabre dance of doom.

The prickles make me mad.

Today is such a happy day. A day of hope and new beginnings.

What else can be taken away from us?

Chapter Twenty

Later That Night

SEATTLE ISN'T A TOWN filled with people who give many shites about celebrity.

Oh, I get stopped. So does Ronni. Sometimes when we're at the grocery store. Or at the park with the boys. We always agree to selfies if we're asked. It's not that often, surprisingly. Generally, everyone in the Seattle area is chill. No one bothers us. Or harasses. Despite the bad LTZ publicity and Ronni's ongoing back-and-forth war with the media over her lawsuits.

I'm not stupid, though. We're exposed. Barry's based in LA, so he didn't make the trip to Seattle with us. Without security, my family isn't fully safe, and that's a problem. One the house in Hunts Point would solve.

Too feckin' bad we can't move in tonight.

It's three in the morning. I'm up pacing the living room. Sometime during the night, I received a creepy text from an anonymous number.

Ha ha. Your life's about to be ruined.

I don't take kindly to receiving a threat from some anonymous gobshite. Ordinarily, I wouldn't worry too much about it. Everyone in my band's attracted negative attention from all sorts of people. Stalkers. Obsessed fans. Trolls. Rejected groupies. All in all, I've suffered the least. Makes sense. I've been in a committed relationship for most of my adult years. With Jen Deveraux. Then Ronni. The two years in between? Aye. I indulged in a bit of sexual debauchery. Even then, my behavior was tame in comparison to that of my bandmates.

My dick hasn't been hard for anyone but Ronni from the day and hour I comforted her on the private jet ride to Australia all those years ago.

Even when we split up, I didn't fuck anyone else. How could I? She's always been it for me.

Something about this text raises my hackles. A lot. I sent a screenshot to Barry hours ago. Standard protocol. His security company logged into my phone. They're analyzing where it originated from. I won't keep it from her forever, but I haven't mentioned it to Ronni yet. Not until we learned something concrete.

My mind keeps flashing to the day in Malibu when Yolanda showed up on our doorstep.

Somehow, I know it's from her. Before the day Tristan hit his head, I never got vibes that she was into me. I was blindsided by Ronni's so-called intuition. Which was justified, obviously. Yet, everything about that encounter in Malibu felt staged. Why? I don't know what she wants. I don't know where she is. I don't know what to do.

This entire situation makes me want to rage and punch walls. No one is going to fuck with my family. I'd die before anyone hurt Ronni. Or my kids. I feckin' mean it. My family is everything to me.

Jaysus.

I've seriously lost the plot.

"Connor?" Ronni sleepily pads out to the living room. She walks straight into my arms, which I wrap around her shoulders.

Shite.

"Go back to sleep, my love." I kiss her temple. Thumb her cheeks. "I got a creepy text from a fan. I'm just waiting for Barry to clear it."

Ronni's been through this before with me. "I wonder if it has something to do with the news about my lawsuit."

"Why would you think that?" I keep hold of her shoulders, but look into her green eyes. The court dealt Kircher a major blow a couple weeks ago when the raw film of Ronni's interviews was allowed as evidence to prove the truth of her statements. A major part of his case hinges on Ronni's editorial choices in editing her "documentary" about his victims and her First Amendment right to do so.

She yawns. "Well, I wouldn't put it past Kircher to try to fuck with us now that he lost the motion today. He has your number from the poker games."

"Ah. Excellent sleuthing. I forgot about that. The old 'if you can't bring Veronica Mae Miller down, go for the tall Irish guy' strategy?" I can't help but grin.

"Something like that." Ronni strokes my beard. "Come to bed, I hate waking up with you not there."

Obediently, I follow her back to the bedroom. Cuddled up under the covers, it takes Ronni mere minutes before she dozes back off. With the dozens of gerbils running races in my mind, I don't fare quite so well. No matter what I do, I just can't fall back asleep. Eventually, I turn away from her and face the window to gaze into the night through the slats in the blinds.

Silvery-blue skies filter through around five. It's a warm morning, and like many Seattle houses, ours doesn't have air-conditioning. We kicked the sheets off long ago. When I turn back over, Ronni's still sleeping. She's so exquisite. On her back, her hair fans out over the pillow. Plum lips puff out silent breaths of air. One arm is flung above her head, the other rests on her flat stomach. Her dusky-pink nipples are puckered tightly and are too tempting for me to resist.

Leaning over, I suckle one taut nub . Lick and kiss it. Ronni shifts a little but keeps her eyes shut tight. I give her other nipple similar attention. Feasting on my wife's breasts is a great distraction, so I continue when Ronni's little mewls egg me on.

"God, Connor. You're making me so wet." I look up to find her watching me through hooded eyes.

I gently roll her so her back is against my front. My stiff cock nestles in the crease of her ass. "Let me feel." I skim my hand down to her pussy, to her wet heat. Gradually insert two fingers inside her and stroke. Her hips move in time with each plunge.

My arm bands around her stomach when I enter her from behind. She twists so she's on her back, resting her thigh over my waist. I fold my long body around hers, caging her head with my arm. My other hand cups her breast and thumbs her nipple as I roll my hips in lazy waves, building us to a languid but powerful release.

"Mmm," Ronni purrs. "This is my favorite way to wake up."

Tangled together with me still buried inside her, our bodies have a light sheen of sweat in the warm glow of dawn. I sneak my hand down to her clit and rub her gently. "Keep going, Mae."

She's still coming down from her previous orgasm. Her groany little breaths reinvigorate my cock. "I'll never get enough of you, my love." I fasten my lips to her neck and continue pumping into her while circling her swollen nub gently but vigorously.

She digs her heels into the bed and grinds her pussy against my hand. "Ahhh, Connor." She bites her lip and squeezes her eyes shut when she comes. I'm about to flip her on her stomach and fuck her doggie-style when Ronni's phone pings. She ignores it, but then it pings again. And again. And again.

My phone starts buzzing too.

"Leave it." I order, my thrusts are faster and harder.

Buzz. Ping. Buzz. Ping.

Thrust. Thrust. Thrust.

Buzz. Ping. Buzz. Ping.

Feckin' cock-blocking phones.

"Goddamit." I pull out and rise to my knees. My dick, wet with Ronni's juices deflates to half-mast. "Who's trying so hard to get ahold of us?"

Ronni sits up, pulling the sheet around her naked body. "I don't know, but it must be important."

A feeling of doom washes over me. Ronni's expression doesn't help. Nothing beneficial comes from texts this early in the morning. It's a toss-up between LTZ bull-shite or Kircher bullshite, neither one pleasant.

She twists, grabs her phone from the nightstand and swipes it on. Presses the screen. Her face blanches. My stomach lurches, instinctively I want to protect my wife in that moment of suspension where I know it's bad but not how bad it is. Ronni taps her phone furiously. Watches the screen.

"Mae?" My voice is dry.

She ignores me. Her brow furrows and her mouth forms a little "o" but she doesn't look away from whatever it is she's watching.

When my phone buzzes again, I'm on autopilot. Still watching Ronni from the corner of my eye. Another buzz prompts me to glance down where I see a flurry of texts incoming from the same anonymous number.

I can't wait to see her bitch face when she sees us fucking.

She'll cry for days when she sees your cock in my mouth.

How will you explain your lips on my pussy?

Your wife is the biggest cunt on the planet.

She deserves everything she's getting.

What the actual fuck?

My entire body goes rigid with horror. My eyes dart to Ronni, who's still staring at her phone, her expression one of devastation and disgust. Tears stream down her face in rivulets. She taps her phone vigorously. Stares at the screen. Taps. Watches. Wipes the wetness from her eyes furiously with her wrist.

Yet I'm paralyzed. I have no idea what to do. What to say. Ice runs through my veins until I'm able to croak, "Mae what's going on? I just got another batch of fucked-up texts."

She still doesn't answer me. I reach for her, but she holds up a palm. Intently stares at her phone. I'm going feckin' mad. "Ronni. Talk to me."

"All that time you were fucking Yolanda. I'm such a complete idiot." Ronni throws her phone at my chest.

My mind goes totally blank. I'm certain I'm staring at her with a big, dumb look on my face because, what the ever-loving fuck? How could she know about the texts on my phone before I showed them to her?

Ronni tears out of bed and sprints toward the bathroom. Slams the door behind her. Locks it. I'm behind her in a flash. Thundering my fist on the door. "Mae?

Mae? What do you mean? I never fucked Yolanda. Never. I'd never."

Through the door I hear wracking sobs. Horrible, choking, life-ending sobs. Like her entire world has fallen apart.

But it hasn't. Has it?

What was she looking at?

I'm a crazed bull. I tear back to the bed and grab her phone. Enter the password and scroll to her texts, which are merely a series of links. I click on one.

It's a grainy video, as if it's been taken from a nanny cam. It's not very well-lit. There appears to be some sort of light source in the background. Although the picture is in black and white, Yolanda, clear as day, comes into view on what looks like the front porch in Malibu. Her entire face takes up the screen as she adjusts the angle of the camera. She moves away when a man opens the door and comes into view. Tall. Wearing jeans. Baseball cap. Dark t-shirt. They talk for a while. He backs away, but she kneels to unbuckle his pants. Pulls out the guy's cock and starts blowing him. Halfway through, he pulls off his cap. Shakes out his long, curly hair. Looks into the camera and smiles.

Every single part of my body seizes. It's me. It's fucking me.

My breath comes in short bursts. I feel like I'm about to have a heart attack. I never fucked Yolanda. Never had a blowjob from her. How does this video exist? Where was it filmed?

Am I losing my mind?

I click on the next one. Looks like the master bedroom in Vancouver. This time the camera zooms in on Yolanda's bare pussy. Clone me is licking her. Suckling her. Spreading her pussy lips with his fingers. Eating her out like she's dessert. Clone me speaks. "I feckin' love going down on you, Yolanda. Your pussy is the sweetest I've ever tasted."

Every hair on my body stands on end. It's my voice. It sounds a little strange but it's my fucking voice.

Anguished beyond belief, I cry out, "No, this isn't happening. That isn't me."

Because it isn't. But it is. Isn't it?

My mind's a sickening, brain-twisting whirl. I can't stop. I watch the third video. Clone me is fucking Yolanda against a nondescript wall I don't recognize. He turns to the camera, bouncing her on his cock. "Fuck me, Yolanda. Give me that sweet pussy."

This guy looks like me. Sounds like me. Has my same tattoos in the exact same locations. Same nose. Same hair. Same hands. Same fingernails.

But it's not me. None of this ever happened.

Somewhere in the chaos of my mind, I hear her emerge from the bathroom. Ronni storms over to me and snatches the phone out of my hand. "You need to get out of this house. I can't be around you. What you've done is...beyond words. I mean, fucking the nanny. I don't even know who you are right now."

"That wasn't me," I say, weakly. Because, well. I don't know. I have no idea what is going on. I just know that I feel like my body is being pulled apart by ten thousand red ants. White-hot pokers puncturing my flesh.

Ronni points at our closet. "Pack your things and get the fuck out."

I wonder how my morning went from making love to the woman I love more than life itself to being cast out of my own house. But, here we are.

"It's not me," I whisper, but I'm defeated. My mind's spinning into a vortex.

Who knows what I throw into my duffle bag. I don't care a whit. If these videos are real, I have no memory of it happening. I guess it's possible. Jace was roofied years ago and he was tricked into thinking he fathered Helena. Ty fucked a thousand girls over the years and often didn't remember anything the next day. Hell, our publicist filmed herself giving him a blowjob and he had no recollection. It happened when they were broken up, but Zoey was so distraught when she found out she ran into traffic and was nearly run over by a taxi. Ty nearly lost her.

That's when it hits me. Ronni is never going forgive me for this. If I thought my life was up in the air before, now I know the truth. It's blown to smithereens. I've lost everything. The most important thing.

My family.

Hell, if I fucked Yolanda all those times, I wouldn't forgive myself for this. I'd expect Ronni's reaction.

If I did it.

Except, I didn't do it. I didn't feckin' do it. I wasn't drugged. I wasn't drunk. I can recall every single encounter with Yolanda. Except for that scene in Malibu, I'd never even come close to touching that woman.

So, no. The guy fucking our former nanny wasn't me.

It. Wasn't. Feckin'. Me.

Except?

That guy in the video was me.

What the feck is happening?

Chapter Twenty-One

The Same Morning

IN MY PERIPHERAL VISION, I see Connor standing in the closet doorway with his duffle bag slung over his shoulder. He's openly weeping, swiping his eyes, not bothering to hide his tears. The part of me who's loved this man with my entire heart and soul wants to comfort this man who so rarely cries.

The part of me who's been betrayed by the bastard who was fucking our nanny wants to stab him between the eyes. No, in his balls.

I can't look at him directly because I will very likely burst into a ball of flames if I do.

"That isn't me." His low, mournful voice catches. "It isn't me. It isn't me. It isn't me," he chant-whispers, each time punctuated with a wracking sob.

Something makes me glance down at my tattoo.

Be fearless in the pursuit of what sets your soul on fire.

What a fucking joke. My life is a fucking joke. Everything I've done? For what? For this? To be cheated on by my husband? Humiliated?

Yolanda already sold her stories. Connor's indiscretion is plastered on every major entertainment site. The videos are posted everywhere. I had to uninstall my social accounts. Too unbearable to read the comments about my cheating husband's cock.

I'll never, ever be able to show my face again. Neither will Connor. If he thinks Ty's meltdown killed LTZ, well, he's in for a rude awakening. Cheating on America's sweetheart won't win you any fans, that much I know.

"Can you please just leave, Connor?" My voice is stone cold. Definitive.

He moves toward me, I feel him though I refuse to look at him. Keeping my head down and eyes averted, I hold my hand up. "Don't come any closer, I mean it."

"What about the boys, Mae?" he pleads. "Don't take them away from me."

I whirl around and charge him. He stands there like a marble statue while I pound on his chest. "Why would you do this? Why? How could you hurt me like this?" I know I'm out of control. I can't stop myself, which makes me furious. Decisively, I scream at the top of my lungs, "Get the fuck out of this house."

Connor's wracking sobs fill the room, but he doesn't say another word. He just...leaves. Thunders down the stairs. The front door opens. Slams shut. Moments later, I hear the Range Rover peel out of the driveway.

That's when I start to panic.

I'm alone here in Seattle. I have no infrastructure. No support. Connor's family isn't an option, obviously. I've got to get out of here. It's nearly seven in the morning. If they aren't there already, there will be news vans lining the street in moments.

I've got to pull my shit together and get out of here safely. The boys aren't awake yet, so I hurriedly pack a couple of suitcases. Next, I tiptoe into the nursery and throw some of the boys' things in a duffle bag. Torin wakes up, I pluck him and bring him into the living room where I call Kris.

"Did you see the headlines?" Torin sits in my lap when Kris answers.

I've clearly woken her up. She sounds exhausted. "No, what's going on?"

"Connor fucked Yolanda. Multiple times. Videos are posted everywhere. I kicked him out." I cannot believe the words are leaving my lips. They feel false. This entire situation is amiss. Except, I saw what I saw. The man in the videos is my husband. The woman is Yolanda. I watched his cock disappear into her mouth. I watched his mouth on her pussy.

My stomach lurches. My heart seizes. It's too much for any wife to see.

I'm going to be sick.

Kris is awake now. "What the fuck are you talking about? I don't believe that for a second."

"Just go to any gossip site. Any news site. It's all there for anyone to see." I dig the heel of my hand into my forehead. Willing the images to magically erase themselves from my mind.

The phone goes silent except for the sound of Kris tapping on her phone. I hear her audible gasps. "What are these videos?"

"Sex tapes. I'm chartering a plane. Me and the boys are moving back to LA. Can we stay with you until I figure out where to live?"

"Of course." Kris moves into fix-it mode. "Give me a couple hours and I'll call you back. I'll get Allison on it immediately."

Torin is quiet in my arms. He looks up at me and giggles, oblivious his family has been torn apart. My God, he and Tristan are so handsome. They look exactly like their father. I set him down and he toddles behind me as I return to the nursery to get Tristan up. Methodically, I go about the morning tasks, which take twice as long without Connor. By some miracle, the boys are subdued this morning. Unquestionably, the vibes in the house are affecting them.

At least mothering allows me to forget what I saw for an hour or two. My phone pings. The sound gives me a visceral reaction. I'm scared shitless to see who it's from.

I can't bear to see another video of Connor with that cunt. It will slice me in two. Well, four. Or six. I'm already in tatters.

Connor:

> Barry's sending three security detail for you and the boys. They'll be there at ten.

Me:

> Thank you.

Connor:

> I love you, Mae. Please, let's talk. I don't know what's happening.

Me:

> You gave up that right when you put your dick in her.

I shut off my phone. I'm not about to get in a text war with Connor about something I could clearly see plain as day. He made a choice. I won't be with a man who cheats. Period. End of story. Even if my heart never recovers, it's a hard no for me.

I give the boys baths and dress them. Put them in the playpen with their blocks while I speedily wash up and get dressed in yoga pants and a sweatshirt. I grab a baseball cap and tuck my hair under it, ready to leave at a moment's notice. I don't want to be recognized until I can get somewhere safe.

I'm so adrift. Connor has been my anchor for so many years. To have it yanked away without warning is jarring. Devastating. My mind is in so many places. I zone out for a while. I have no idea how long.

The stillness is what snaps me out of my trance. Realizing that Kris might be trying to reach me, I turn the phone back on.

Fatal mistake. The news alerts pop up one by one before I can adjust my Settings to shut them off.

> Nanny Yolanda Gomez Claims Affair with LTZ Bassist Connor McGloughlin

> Who Is Yolanda Gomez? 5 Things to Know About the Nanny Who Claimed She Had an Affair With LTZ Bassist, Connor McGloughlin

> Nanny Yolanda Gomez Releases Viral TikTok Video Claiming She Had a Months-Long Affair with Ronni Miller's Husband

Hot Nanny Shares Cryptic Message after Revealing Affair with Ronni Miller's Husband.

Hot Nanny Apologizes to Ronni Miller about Affair with Connor McGloughlin.

Kris will have to wait. I can't bear this shit.

I click the phone back off.

I'm in the middle of a nightmare. An absolute nightmare. I've never felt so alone in all my life. Connor's honor is so important to him. Never, in a zillion years, would I dream he'd cheat on me. Hell, I'd peg Ty, Jace, and Zane as cheaters before I'd have believed it of my husband. None of those guys would ever step out on their women.

Not in a million years.

As I obsess over the entire situation, one thing is for certain. Something about all of this is off. Yet, I can't deny what I saw with my own eyes. While I can't bear to ever watch one of those videos again, it was Connor. No question. It's just...it didn't seem like Connor.

How could that be?

With a sigh, I turn the phone on again to call Kris, who answers on the first ring. "Charter set for two thirty. Car will pick you all up and bring you to my house. Do you need beds for the boys? What else?"

"God dammit." I want to crawl out of my skin. "I need everything. Highchairs. Beds. Toys. It's too much to ask, Kris. I'm stuck here. For now."

"Ronni, you need to take a minute and think about things. Don't throw away your marriage—"

I can't help but interrupt, "What part of 'he cheated on me repeatedly' do you not understand?"

Kris sighs heavily. "I'm just saying, take a breath. You don't always have to be on the run. I can have whatever you need delivered, babe. Come. Don't come. It's up to you."

I'm quiet for a minute. Hearing myself talk makes me take a pause. "Kris, I owe you an apology."

"For what, babe?"

"My heart is broken, there's no doubt about it. Before I make any life-changing decisions, I should take a minute. I've crashed your morning, you've rearranged whatever it is you're doing to accommodate me and the kids. No questions asked. You always do that for me and you never ask for anything in return." My entire body aches with grief. Not just for what's happening with me and Connor, but for how I've failed my mentor. Over and over. "I can't think of one time you've needed me to do something for you. All you've wanted is for me to try and be your partner. Which I've sucked at. For years. So, yes. That's my long-winded way of saying I'm taking some time to figure things out. Get my head on straight."

Kris sniffles. This is a woman I've rarely seen cry in nearly two decades. "I just want what's best for you. Ever since your mom died, I feel like you're mine to protect."

"I appreciate that. I love you. You're family. I've got to figure out what I want to do with my life, Kris." Tears stream down my face. What's happening is so horrible. I never imagined I'd be in this position.

We end the call with a promise that I'll check in later.

The boys are crashed out in the playpen, cuddled together. I sit cross-legged on the floor, leaning on the side of the apparatus watching them sleep. Clutching my phone tightly. Hoping Connor will text. Hoping he won't.

Mostly wishing all of this were a dream I could wake up from.

Losing my family. My career. My dignity? My deep soul-crushing sadness is suddenly replaced with a jolt. Almost like I've been hit by lightning. I bolt upright.

Because-- holy fucking shit.

I've been so blind. So naïve.

Enough's enough.

It's time for me to truly be fearless.

Chapter Twenty-Two

Present Day - Belfast, Ireland

WHAT CAN A MAN do when he's lost everything and has no idea how it happened so fast? Last month feels like a distant dream. My band was reuniting. My family was moving to Seattle. Ronni had decent news about the lawsuit. Things were great, so they were.

I could feel it.

Our lives were about to become settled. Under control.

I really thought Ronni and I could have it all.

It's all over now. Bloody hell, I'm beginning to understand why my da started drinking after his accident. If he felt even an iota as helpless as I feel now? Drinking yourself into oblivion doesn't seem like such a bad idea.

As for me, it's not how I'll handle things. I'd never do that to Tristan or Torin. Never. Not after what I went through. The best I can do is set their mother free, so she can distance herself from me. I still have no idea how it's me in those videos, but I'm also not stupid enough to try to deny it.

I've seen the headlines. There's no way to get away from the news coverage of this debacle. Whining about how clone me isn't me will make me look even more like an eejit.

And no one will believe you anyway.

I know with certainty I never fucked that woman. I never let her suck my cock. I do not cheat. I never have. Never will. I physically get ill thinking of being with anyone but Mae.

I. Am. Not. A. Cheater.

Doesn't feckin' matter. Everyone in the whole world believes it's who I am now. I'm just another bollocks in a long line of bollockses who broke Ronni Miller's heart.

I'm forever a cheater. Ronni believes it. She never even gave me a chance to talk it through. Sure, she's here now—to what end, though? How she spoke to me was cold. Unfeeling. I could tell how much she hated me.

It's devastating. My sons will grow up hating me. Not knowing who I am and what I stand for. They'll believe I wronged their mother somehow.

I. Am. Not. A. Cheater.

I. Am. Not. A. Cheater.

I. AM. NOT. A. FECKIN' CHEATER!

With nowhere to go, I chartered a jet to Belfast. I've ignored every attempt by my family and band members to get a hold of me. I cannot face them. Maybe never again. I might just stay here forever.

Truth be told, I'm angry. Really feckin' angry. The irony of this situation is not lost on me. I loved and supported Ronni for years even when she was still manipulating the media to convince the world she was in love with men who weren't me—including Ty. Her entire public persona was based upon carefully cultivated lies. And I'm the bollocks who put up with it.

I was complicit. For feck's sake, if I had brains I'd be dangerous.

So, here we are.

I finish putting together the furniture in the playroom. Tromp downstairs and across the yard back to the main house. It's dark, just the way I left it. Hopefully, Ronni went back home to the boys. Saoirse is away in Cork for a wedding, so my plan is to try to relax. Watch mindless television.

I'm just putting the kettle on for tea when her voice startles me. "Connor."

I still for a minute to calm myself, then resume making my tea. "I thought you'd left."

"Can we talk?" Ronni walks up behind me, places her hand at the small of my back. She peers up at me. "I came at you all wrong up in the playroom."

I sigh. Shake my head. "Haven't we said all that needs saying? You kicked me out. I left. We can't come back from this."

"You weren't with Yolanda." She says this as though it's the truth. Definitively.

I look her dead in the eye. "No. Of course I wasn't."

Her body crumples with relief. She folds her arms around her middle. "I'm so sorry I reacted the way I did. Can you ever forgive me?"

I'm so shocked, all I can do is stare at her, dumb-founded.

"They were deepfakes." She grips my forearm.

I have no idea what she's talking about. My face must say as much.

"Deepfakes are created by using artificial intelligence technology. I realized what was going on after I took the time to calm down and think about it. Kris and I were planning on using similar technology to create realistic crowd scenes without paying for hundreds of extras. The software is so phenomenal nowadays, an entire movie can be created with one or two images." She looks exhausted. Defeated.

I have to brace myself on the counter for balance, this is shocking. "What the actual feck, Mae?"

"It's a thing, Connor. A real thing. You can download free apps. There are websites dedicated to morphing celebrities' faces onto the faces of porn artists. They're so convincing, it's hard to distinguish real from fake." Ronni grabs her phone and taps into it. Turns the screen to me. It's a website with hundreds of graphic videos of celebrities having sex.

"Jaysus feckin' Christ." I can't breathe. My heart races. My arse thunks down on a chair at the kitchen table. I bury my face in my hands. I'm not sure what to think. Or do.

Ronni sits next to me. "I'd should have believed you, my honey. Can you forgive me for overreacting? You had the jet, Zane let me use Carter's. I got here as soon as I could."

"After seeing those videos, I didn't know what to do. I was distraught. I didn't understand. I've never felt lower than I did in that moment. You didn't believe me. You truly thought I could do that to you. You thought I could stomach being inside another woman who wasn't you." I let out a giant puff of air. Ronni's heart might be broken, but mine is too. I pound the table with my fist.

Ronni's hand covers mine. "I was wrong. I was in shock. I'd have never believed it if I hadn't seen it with my own eyes. After you left, my mind was whirling. I made plans to move back to LA. Then I realized I wasn't right in the head. So, I took a moment, sat with the boys. Gave myself a little space to think. It was so obvious. So stupidly obvious."

"Who would do this to us?" I feel like I'm mortally wounded.

She cocks an eyebrow. "Do you need me to say his name?"

"Ach. Kircher? He took it this far?" I scrub my beard with my fingers. "Obviously. Was Yolanda involved too?"

Ronni barely contains a snarl. "I don't know. I'd guess yes considering she showed up at the house. Sent you texts. She could have been working with him."

"I'm so upset, Mae. I truly don't know if we come back from this." I pull my hand away. Squeeze my eyes shut. "Those videos..."

We sit in silence for what seems like hours. Eventually, Ronni speaks. Tentatively. "Your mom told me where you went, so I came here to bring you home."

"Is she watching the boys?" My hands are shaking from stress.

She nods.

"Mae, I'm not going to sweep what happened under the rug. I can't." I bury my face in my hands. Shake my head.

I hear her get up and cross the room. Some rustling. She returns and sits next to me. Grabs my wrist and pulls it down. I look sideways to see her holding her iPad.

"What's that?" I flick my eyes up to hers.

She pulls up her Instagram page. The latest post is recent. It's our family portrait. Me, Ronni, and the boys in the living room at the town house.

Don't believe everything you see. Come for me, I can take it. Come for my family, I won't stand for it.

"So?" I look at it and glance at her hopeful expression.

Her face crumples. "We'll get to the bottom of it. To-gether."

"Together?" I stand abruptly, knocking the chair over. "I can't take it, Mae. You did it again. Don't you understand? You kicked me out on a gut reaction. I understand the videos were horrifying. Jesus Christ. This Kircher thing is the gift that keeps on giving. Fuck all of it."

"Connor..." she calls as I storm out.

I make it to the living room.

Staring out at Belfast Lough, the deep hurt washes over me. This evil man has permeated our lives for years. His abuse damaged my wife so deeply she can't fully trust me. She's spent thousands of hours seeking revenge.

Sacrificed her reputation to bring justice to his victims. I was a fool to think this was behind us.

It will never be behind us.

Not when he still manages to find ways to try to destroy her from behind bars.

This time through me.

Will our sons be next?

How can I protect her?

How do I protect them?

Fear permeates every molecule in my body.

"Connor," she whispers against my back. Her arms wrap around my waist.

I turn and fold her against my chest. Rest my cheek on the top of her head. Inhale her lemony scent. "This has to end."

"I know," she says so softly I can hardly hear her.

We stay that way for a long while. Holding on for dear life. Absorbing each other's energy. Not knowing what the future holds.

Not knowing up from down.

Knowing that life apart will be unbearable. Unfathomable.

And perhaps, unavoidable.

For now, I reach down and grip Ronni's heart-shaped ass. Hoist her up. She hooks her legs around my hips. Wraps her arms around my neck. I carry her to the bedroom. Set her on the bed. Crouch to unzip her boots and toss them on the ground.

I stand and rip off my t-shirt. She unbuckles my jeans. I kick off my shoes and peel them off while she sheds her jeans and top. Her green eyes blink up at me, uncertain.

"Lie back," I command.

Ronni scurries up the bed and relaxes back against the headboard. Her taut nipples poke through the sheer fabric of her black bra. Her knees splay apart, revealing her pink, glistening pussy.

I stroke my cock, though I don't need to. I'm harder than a steel pole. Ronni licks her lips but says nothing. Tears stream down her face as she watches me kneel before her.

Tears stream down mine too.

I plunge inside her. Holding her knees apart so I can watch myself disappear in my wife's body. Her cunt sucks me in and holds me there when she squeezes around me like she never wants me to leave.

I skim my hands down to grip her ass. Pull her up so she's pressed against my chest. Sitting on my cock as I fuck up into her. Every part of our bodies is touching.

Controlling her movement, I hold her in place. I'm so deep inside her. We're one grinding, writhing being. Then all bets are off.

Our mouths smash together. Teeth gnash. Hair is pulled. She scratches my back. I spank her ass. I slam into her. She grinds her pussy furiously. We're anger fucking. Hurt fucking.

Catharsis fucking.

We detonate like a nuclear bomb at the exact same time. She screams like a banshee. I roar like a caged lion.

Then I flip her over and we do it all again.

Hours later, we both look like we've been through a tornado.

The sheets are sweaty and full of our combined releases.

Somehow, it feels like the storm has passed.

The question remains... Will we make it to shore?

Chapter Twenty-Three

Three Weeks Later

MY ENTIRE BODY FEELS relaxed. Loose. Free.

I find it nearly impossible to wake up, I'm so incredibly comfortable. This new bed is seriously like a drug. I never want to leave it. The mattress envelops me in a warm embrace. I want to melt into it.

Except for one thing. The hot, wet fire intensifying in my pussy. Connor's beard drags across my inner thighs, where he's kissing me. Blowing hot hair against my folds.

Dipping his tongue into me so softly, I can scarcely feel it.

My fingers thread through his curls. My eyes flutter open to find him grinning up at me. "Good?"

"Ah-may-zing." I rake my nails along his scalp and push him back down. Obediently, he grips my hips with his big hands and holds me against his mouth, keeping me still so his tongue can caress me every-where. Along my seam. At the crease of my thighs. Along my outer lips. Lapping at my sensitive nub. Delving inside, swirling around my opening.

Out of nowhere, he kisses then suckles my clit. Unable to help it, my back arches off the bed. His fingers grip me tightly so there's no escape from the incredible sensation. Not that I want to escape. "God, keep doing that. Don't stop."

"That's just to take the edge off." He uses the flat of his tongue to lick up my juices. "Now we're going to get serious, my love."

Connor wastes no time burying his face in my pussy. Eating me like he can't get enough. He moans and utters words like "delicious" and "so sweet" against my clit. His worship makes me feel like he'd gladly wake me up this way every day for the rest of my life.

"It's so, so, soooo good." I'm mewling. Rolling my hips to meet him.

My orgasm washes over me like a tidal wave, building. Rolling. Crashing. He laves me and coaxes a second, then third more languid, rolling release. I'm overheated. Overstimulated.

I never want him to stop. Never.

"I need you, Connor," I cry out. His hands sneak under my ass, where he cups me and pulls me even tighter against his lips. He's moaning and grunting against my pussy. Devouring me like I'm the most delicious meal he'll ever have. I tug his hair because it's too much, but he's relentless. He inserts two fingers inside me and strokes my G-spot. Sucks my clit hard with his lips. Grazes it with his teeth. Swirls his tongue in tight circles on my nub. Repeats the cycle until I'm shaking from head to toe, ready to detonate.

"Please. Fuck me, Connor. I need your cock inside me." I shriek when I do, in fact, go over. Gushing my release all over his face.

He looks up at me from between my thighs. My heart melts. After what happened, I never thought I'd see the love and adoration in his eyes again. But there it is. Utter devotion. Pure love. All communicated in one look.

Which changes to fiery desire as he rises to his knees. "I'm going to fuck you hard, Mae. Are you ready?"

"Yes. Yes." I attempt to pull him toward me, but his plans are already in motion.

He takes his time, kissing my everywhere, leaving trails of heat as he works his way up. To my breasts. He bites my nipple, then licks. It puckers into a tight nub. Smiling up at me, he repeats with my other nipple. Caging my head with his arms, Connor sinks into me. He's in no hurry. His hips rock into me as he kisses his way up my neck until he reaches my lips.

Our mouths mash together. Tongues war, then dance. My arms wrap around his back and trail down his ass. I grip him and pull him into me, holding him still as we kiss. Feeling him buried inside me. Like we are one. Knowing our connection is unbreakable.

It's everything.

"Ride me, Mae." His thumbs caress my cheeks. His beard is coated with my juices. His amber eyes bore into my soul.

I nod.

Connor deftly rolls us over, never allowing us to lose our connection. I squeeze my knees against his thighs and undulate my hips to find my rhythm. His thick cock is so deep inside me, where it belongs. I'm so tender and wet, even the slightest movement causes little fires to ignite. I move faster, with more intention. Slamming myself on his cock. Furiously grinding.

He watches me so intently, I shut my eyes because it's so much. "No, Mae. Look at me when I'm inside you."

I do as he asks, and his intense look is replaced with utter adoration. Like I am perfect. His goddess. I slide my hands up his chest and he takes over the pace. Gripping my hips and rocking me against him. Thrusting up to meet me. Hitting my inner walls at just the angle that makes me lose my mind.

"Grind yourself on me. Take what you need, my love." He presses against my lower back, giving me an assist to get the exact level of friction against my clit I need to get off.

I moan, "Connor. Oh God."

"That's it, Mae. That's my sweet girl." He fucks up into me harder, faster, and I go over the edge, nearly sucking his cock into my body when I come.

Connor rolls us to our sides. "Jaysus, Mae. You're killing me." He pulls my leg up over his arm and jackhammers into me so deep it feels like he's hitting my stomach. He groans and grunts, his face contorted into an expression of pure agony mixed with pleasure. My hands grip his jaw. "Fill me, babe. Let it go."

With a loud lion's roar, Connor floods me and collapses, but holds my leg in place so he can stay buried inside me. "You're incredible. That was incredible."

We wind our arms around each other until he eventually softens and slips out. Our kisses are gentle. Passionate. Sweet.

"This is the best bed ever," he mumbles against my neck.

I giggle into his damp hair. "Magic sex bed."

I turn in his arms so I'm the little spoon. Gaze out the floor-to-ceiling windows in our bedroom. Lake Washington is calm. The morning sun is beginning to permeate the sky, leaving little pink streaks.

Morning sex in our dream house is my favorite pastime.

We moved in a week after returning from Ireland. Bought all the furniture except for the bedrooms. Our adjustable king-size cooling Tempur-Pedic bed is, quite literally, the most amazing piece of furniture I've ever owned. It was delivered five days ago. We've spent a fair amount of time christening it.

The unusual angles it allows...well, if our sex was incredible before...

"What time is our appointment?" Connor's voice is sleepy.

Considering all we've been dealing with, Connor and I decided to dedicate ourselves to a more intensive couple's counseling program with Lisa Kinkaid. He and I both see her separately as well. "Not until later this morning. Our flight's tonight at five."

"Okay. I'll catch a wee nap," he mumbles before emitting a slight snort. Soon, he's sound asleep.

When his hold on me slackens, I slip out of bed. Put on a robe. Linger in the doorway to enjoy the view of Connor's naked body at rest. My gentle yet fierce giant.

The man who'd never hurt a hair on my body. My man who protects his family with everything he has.

I try not to think about how I almost lost him. It's too painful.

The past three weeks have been an absolute whirlwind. If all goes to plan tomorrow, I'll put an end to the madness. Once and for all.

I'm willing to sacrifice myself this time. For the greater good. To stop hiding and pretending I came out of Hawaiian High unscathed.

I've been living with trauma. Reacting accordingly. My survival instinct has been on high alert for too long, even if I wasn't conscious of it. I've hurt Connor. Hurt Kris. Hurt myself. It's time for a change.

Through hours of therapy, Connor and I came up with a plan.

Together.

I'm taking my shot.

This time, I'm not going to miss.

Chapter Twenty-Four

The Next Day

RONNI CAN'T SIT STILL. Her knee is bouncing. She fidgets with her water glass. Clasping it. Letting it go. Tracing little patterns in the condensation. I know she's nervous. Today's a big day.

If all goes well, it will be the official start of our new life. Well, a reimagining of our old life is a better description. I slide my hand across the table and encircle her wrist. Work my fingers up to clasp her hand. I bring it to my mouth for a kiss, then keep our clasped hands safe against my thigh.

"I'm a bit tense." She squeezes my leg.

I chuckle. "Aye, you could say that."

"I felt bold and empowered yesterday, why does it feel like ants are crawling all over my body now?" She shivers a bit.

"Well, love. That's quite a visual." I lean over and touch my forehead to hers. "There are no ants, my love. You've got this."

The door opens to the glass-enclosed conference room we're sitting in. Five attorneys of various ages, sexes, sizes, and shapes, all in either blue or gray suits, settle in across the table. They introduce themselves to me. A couple even look a bit starstruck.

To me, they're essentially insignificant. If they do their jobs correctly, my wife should have this Kircher mess behind her. Hopefully with a fat deposit into her bank account to boot.

Once the lawyers are settled, the eldest of the blue-gray suit crew addresses Ronni. "As I mentioned on the phone, Ms. Miller—"

"It's Mrs. McGloughlin," Ronni interrupts to correct him.

The suits exchange glances. The guy coughs. "My mistake. Mrs. McGloughlin, as I mentioned on the phone, we're nearly at the discovery phase. We believe if we can get Kircher to sit for two or three days during his deposition, we'll be able to crack him."

"I'm not interested in proceeding to that phase. As you are fully aware, we have proof the sex videos of Connor with our former nanny are deepfakes. You have a forensic report showing the software program and precisely how and when the videos were made. We've traced the account's origin to Caspar Kircher, Don's son." Ronni's voice is forceful. Authoritative. My chest swells with pride.

"That's not going to be sufficient to shut this down." He looks exasperated. Like Ronni's annoying him to no end.

"Well, I have something else. I'm going to show you an authenticated video. Kircher has no idea I have it." Ronni looks over at me, takes a deep breath and looks each of the suits in the eye. One by one. "What you're about to see is something I've worked hard to keep secret. I was ashamed for so many years. I've come to realize my story is important. I'm ready to share it. Especially if it will help prevent this stuff from happening again."

The suits mumble amongst themselves. I stand and lower the shades on the glass conference-room windows facing the office. I'm here to give Ronni moral support and back up her decision. Doesn't mean the entire floor needs to see what she's going to show them.

Ronni connects her phone to the big screen at the end of the conference table and presses play.

I can't help but tense up. I know what I'm about to see. I also know I'm going to have a horrific time watching it.

The video starts. It's a bit grainy, but clear enough to see Kircher and his three schlubby counterparts sitting in what looks to be a barren room with auditorium-style seating.

I can't help but ball my free hand into a fist. I clench and unclench it. My throat constricts painfully when fifteen-year-old Ronni follows Hannah, her longtime stylist into the room. The two women look like absolute babies. Ronni with a backpack slung over her shoulder. Hannah with bright-orange hair wearing purple Chucks.

"Good afternoon, I'm Veronica Mae Miller." Ronni's voice is the identical lyrical, sweet tone. A little less refined. More sassy, perhaps. She has a strange, fake smile on her face as she looks over at Kircher, who wears a tailored blue suit and two older out-of-shape guys are in dad attire.

One of the older guys licks his lips. His beady eyes travel up and down Ronni's body. "Are you wearing the required attire?"

Ronni looks like she's about to vomit. Tentatively, she holds up a polka-dotted bikini, but says nothing.

"You can change there." Hannah apologizes to Ronni with her eyes, but gestures to a short, blue curtain hanging from the ceiling, which is virtually see through and stops short of the floor by at least four feet.

The low growl emanates from me and Ronni snaps her eyes to mine. I shake my head in apology. I press my lips together and puff out a short breath. Give her a smile. Squeeze her hand. I pray for some self-control over my reaction to seeing her this way, or Ronni may not get through the meeting.

I want to dive through the screen and slit every one of the bastard's throats.

"Um… Sure, sounds good…" Ronni sticks out her chest, gives the men a smile that looks more like a wince. Her eyes flick over to the curtain. A wave of fear washes over her. She bites her lip, uncertain as she stands and stares.

The men glance amongst themselves. Chuckle and leer at Ronni. "In this lifetime, please," Kircher snarks. He rubs his hands together menacingly.

My heart breaks for the younger version of my wife. I can tell she's on the verge of bolting. Her thoughts are at war. You can essentially watch each emotion pass across her face as she wrestles with a decision. To stay? Or go?

Terror. Determination. Uncertainty. Resignation. Calmness.

Ronni marches into the changing area. Turns her back to the men. Pulls down her pants and underwear in one motion. Steps into her bikini bottoms. Clearly unaware that when she bends, the men get a flash of her pussy. One has the audacity to grab his cock and squeeze.

Beside me, Ronni gasps. Tenses. She's determined, though, and doesn't take her eyes off the screen.

Kircher looks at her like she's his prey.

Next, Ronni strips off her top and ties on her bikini. Even though she's not facing these assholes, they get a flash of her fifteen-year-old nipples. I find myself shifting uncomfortably in my seat. She's my feckin' wife, and even I feel like a creep watching her this way.

These guys? You can just see on their faces that this is a normal day at the office for them.

Disgusting. Utterly disgusting.

On screen, Ronni sucks in a breath as she adjusts her bikini top. Her lips move, though she's silent. Resigned. Then she blows out a long gust of air. Turns and strides out to address the men. She catches each of their eyes. Smiles at them. Thrusts out her breasts. Bends her knee and juts her hip to the side. Two of the guys lick their lips, not bothering to hide their leers, as she recites her lines.

When she's done, they stare at her. Eyes roaming up and down her body. She stands, frozen in her pose, while grown men openly comment on how hot she is. How fuckable. How they can't wait to write in a "losing her virginity" scene. Ronni doesn't move. It's hard to tell if she just doesn't hear what they are saying or is so traumatized she's just tuned out.

After five or six uncomfortable minutes, Kircher sucks in a breath and nods to the door. Coldly dismisses her. "We'll be in touch."

"Thank you all, very much. I truly appreciate the opportunity." Ronni walks backward, smiling that weird smile. She tentatively dips down to pick up her backpack, turns and hurries out the door.

When she's gone, the three men laugh heartily. Kircher grabs his dick. "She's definitely the lead. Hot damn, I'm going to make it my personal mission for that little honey to suck my fat cock as often as possible so I can come all over those tits."

The video fades to black.

Ronni's shaking. I put my arm around her in comfort. We look over at her legal team, all of whom are staring, slack-jawed, at the screen.

"Is it enough?" She glances around the room. "If so, you may release this to Kircher's lawyers so long as it's under an iron-clad protective order."

"Um...Uh..." Blue-gray lawyer dude squirms in his seat. "How do we prove the origin of this video?"

Ronni pulls out a folder, hands it to him. "It circulated around the inner circle of predators that I've been speaking out against and goes even further. There's a sworn statement in the folder you should read. I can get more. At least five people promised me they are willing to testify should it come down to that. Including my stylist, Hannah. She was there. She saw it with her own eyes."

The women on the legal team are beside themselves. One is openly crying. Another gazes at Ronni empathetically. "Are you okay?"

"I will be. Tell him my price is ten million dollars. Not a penny less. It will be donated in equal parts to each of these charities." Ronni slides a printout of five assorted nonprofit victim's groups. "I want a permanent contractual restraining order with a hundred-million-dollar penalty if he harasses me in any way again—either on his own or using anyone else to do it on his behalf. It's time for this man to leave me the fuck alone." She levels her gaze on the older guy. "Both components must be agreed to, or I will go on a media tour. I'm more than willing to share this video with anyone who will watch it. Tell the world exactly what I lived through. Because if it will help innocent young women and men avoid what I endured, it will be worth it."

The older man coughs. "He won't believe you'd take this public. Frankly, I don't either, Mrs. McGloughlin."

The tall woman snaps, "Shut up, Howard. Do you know how many women put up with this type of shit every day? It doesn't matter what our profession is. Men like those assholes lurk everywhere. Did you see the look of terror on her face? If you won't honor Ms. Miller's wishes on this, I will."

"For the record, Howard." Ronni stands and leans over the conference table. Glares directly into his eyes. "I have no problem at all releasing this. Part of me wants to do it. I have been terrified of this video surfacing for years. My business partner took great pains to obtain each and every copy of this before I started filming She's All That. Just to protect me. But, make no mistake, everyone in the industry knows about it. If it helps me wash my hands of this asshole forever and take my life back, it's worth it. I'm not ashamed. I was exploited."

"Are you certain, my love?" I grip her hand. Checking in. Making sure she's truly okay.

She nods definitively. "Yes. I'm through letting Don-fucking-Kircher think he can control me. If what he did to me as a teenager wasn't enough, my private investigators have evidence that he planted Yolanda in my home. I let that woman care for my children. When I fired her, he struck back and created deep-fake videos to hurt my husband. It all's traced back to him."

The lawyers shuffle through the folder and the paperwork. Consult wordlessly. Scribble notes.

"You have the evidence on all the rest, this should be the nail in the coffin. Here are my terms: he drops this suit within forty-eight hours, deposits the funds into my designated charities and I keep the video from being released. If he won't agree—and I'm not negotiating this--I'm sending the video and all the evidence to every major news outlet."

Howard shuffles some papers. The lawyers talk amongst themselves before he grumbles, "Yes. Okay. We understand perfectly. We'll be in touch once we speak to his legal team."

"You forgot this." Ronni slides a flash drive to him.

His eyes dart around to his colleagues. "Uh. Right." He snatches the device form the table. Gathers his things. Departs in a hurry. The others follow.

"We're in town for three more days," Ronni calls after them.

When they leave, I pull her into my lap. Cradle the love of my feckin' life. "You are one brave woman, Veronica Mae Miller."

"Not that brave. A big part of me wants him to take the deal so we can move on with our lives. The thing is? I've agonized over that video for nearly twenty years. From the second I realized they were filming me. Do you know how humiliating it's been to know men have been beating off to my teenage naked body for years?" Ronni nestles into me. I clutch her tightly. "After Kircher fired me, I was positive he'd let it leak publicly. Try to convince my fans what a slut I was. How I deserved to be ostracized. Banned from Hollywood. Now that I've seen it, I realize that's not what it shows at all."

"No. You were a wee baby, my love. You were terrified. It makes me crazy to know that happened to you. I want to kill that bollocks." I stroke her hair. Rub her back.

"I'd built it up into something it wasn't. I remember seeing the flashing red light. Feeling like I was going to throw up. Knowing it was a setup for their dirty, perverted minds." She cries softly.

"Mae, you didn't know any better. How could you?"

"I realize that now. At the time, my mom was working three jobs. I figured if I could do what it took to get hired, we would solve our money problems. When I did get the job, we moved to Hawaii and our standard of living improved dramatically." She looks up at me with a tear-streaked face. "Until I was fired after his failed attempt to rape me on my eighteenth birthday. It took me a year to recover. Acting lost its sheen, but I didn't know what else I was qualified to do. Then I met Kris. Got lost being a sit-com star. America's sweetheart. The celebrity life pulled me in. I bought into it. I'm not saying I didn't—don't—enjoy it. It's just time for me to take my own break and decide how and if it's what I want to do going forward. No matter what, I want to be with my kids when they're young. I'm not going to miss their milestones for a career I don't even know if I want anymore."

We sit locked together for a long while. Ronni's shared her thoughts in our counseling sessions. I'm learning a lot about the long-term effects of sexual trauma. Of my own trauma. Day by day we're healing. Together.

Ronni pulls away. "My God, I looked terrified. Like a lamb being led to slaughter. In my mind, I exuded confidence. I remember repeating my mantra. Sticking my chest out. Cocking my hips so they'd think I could handle the part. I didn't realize that they wanted me to be scared. It's part of what they got off on. The power. the control."

"They were counting on it. He's used the video to keep you in line." I gaze up at her. "No wonder you've developed such a survival instinct. As Lisa explained, when you get backed into a corner, you react to save yourself."

Ronni surprises me by laughing. "It's true. I'm ready to put it behind me, though. Let's get out of here. Your mom's at the hotel with the kids, and I want to spend the evening with them. Maybe even take them into the pool."

"Sounds like the perfect evening, so it does." I let her pull me out of my chair and we depart the law offices hand in hand.

Barry greets us at the car with a crooked grin. "Everything okay?"

"Better than okay." Ronni scoots close to me. "No matter what comes next, today I'm a free woman."

In this moment, I realize without any shadow of a doubt. My love for Ronni is deeper than any pond, lake, sea, or ocean.

No storm will ever topple us again.

I wind my arm around her. She looks up at me with her sparkly green eyes and I melt. There's something about getting through a crisis together. It brings you closer. Makes you more resilient.

It deepens your love.

Makes you fearless.

Chapter Twenty-Five

A Month Later

TODAY IS MY INAUGURATION into the concept of a play date. Connor helped me get the boys into the Range Rover. It's up to me to get them out and safely into the house.

My days of panic and woe at being a bad mom are long behind me. Every day I get to spend with my sons is magical. They change so much. Whether it's a gesture. Or a sound. Even how they interact.

I've turned into one of those moms who says things like, "You just don't know until you have kids."

Oh, I'm fine with it. It's who I am. Veronica Mae Miller, wife of Connor, mother of twins.

My favorite role I've ever had.

I manage to hoist Torin into my arms and take Tristan's tiny hand and ring the doorbell. Fiona answers within minutes, Mia peers around her leg.

"Get your ass in here." She motions me in, snatching Tristan up. "Aren't you two the most handsome boys?"

"Can the twins play in my room?" Mia is adorable in black leggings and a skull hoodie.

I'm about to protest—now that they're walking, the boys get into all sorts of mischief—but Fiona takes charge. "Meems, how about we put up the baby gate in the kitchen? The three of you can hang out in the sitting room where we set up the Play-Doh and racetrack. You can put on a movie too if you want. Then Aunt Ronni and I can be in the kitchen in case you need us."

"Okay." She smiles, dimples drilling holes in her cheeks. Mia is a truly stunning child. Huge blue eyes. Dark lashes. Long, black hair. She's the double of Fiona.

We get the kids settled and sit in Fee's impressive kitchen. She's added to it. Personal touches like family photos. It's starting to look lived in. "I can't get over this kitchen. I never will."

"Zane texted me a pic of the house. Seems like you're doing okay." Fee pours us each a healthy glass of Pinot Grigio.

"Yeah." I can't help but smile to myself thinking of Connor reuniting with Zane and Jace at our new home. "Things have settled down. We definitely had a rough patch."

Fiona wrinkles her nose. "For the record, no one believed Connor fucked that woman. Not for a second. I'm glad that shit's behind you. Still. How are you holding up?"

"Oh, I'm okay. When those videos were released, I jumped to conclusions. It made me physically ill to see Connor boning our former nanny. I'm embarrassed to say, it devastated him that I believed it even for a second. I didn't handle it well." I twirl the stem of the wine glass between my fingers.

"Sure, but your reaction was understandable." Fee purses her lips. "I know firsthand. It was rough on me when Zane and I were broken up all those years ago. Seeing him in public with the beautiful, perfect models and actresses. I was so jealous. Insecure. I've always had meat on my bones, so…"

I scoff good-naturedly. "You're one of the most beautiful women I've ever seen in real life. I'd kill for your curves. Restricting myself to a certain weight is something that was drilled into my head by that bastard, Kircher. He kept a red laser on set. Would point out any areas on my body that he thought were 'chubby.' Always when cast and crew were present." I stare at the plate of cheese and crackers Fee's set out. Another beautiful charcuterie spread. I make myself a little sandwich. Take a bite. Savor.

Yet one more phase of my life—I can enjoy food again.

"I saw the lawsuit was dismissed. I'm so sorry you had to go through so much, Ronni. You essentially survived a predator." She stares at me intently, then looks down. Like she's dying to know more but doesn't want me to be uncomfortable.

Unfortunately, I can't say too much because of the settlement agreement. Despite my theatrics at the firm, the lawyers negotiated what I can and cannot say. Everything I'm allowed to reveal about my time on Hawaiian

High is already out there. One interview. Vetted by both sides.

I could have fought it harder, but having the suit dismissed was enough. Well, the payments to the charities, of course. That was non-negotiable. Helping victims is why I got into this mess. Hopefully, the money will help some deserving people.

Of course Yolanda's testimony against Kircher--complete with a public statement and apology to me and Connor about the fake "sex" videos--didn't hurt. Some of our fans will always believe the worst, but at least they've all been taken down.

What's most important is Connor and I know the truth.

"Yeah. It's true. I'm forever free of Kircher." Saying these words never gets old. "I'd love to give you details, but the dozens of women who are sharing their hellish encounters will give you some idea of what happened to me."

Fiona glances down at the kids, who are playing happily. She lowers her voice. "Do you know how Mia was conceived?"

"Uh, not really. Just that she's not Zane's biological daughter." I hold her gaze. It's the truth, Connor would never share one of his bandmates' secrets, even with me. He also would never pry into Zane and Fiona's private business, so it's possible he doesn't know the story behind Mia's paternity.

Fiona leans in closer. My guess is to be positive Mia can't hear her. "Zane and I had an arrangement that I never took advantage of. He did. We even had rules... um, we thought we came up with a perfect plan." She gives me a pointed look.

I put my hand over my mouth to cover my surprise. "Wow. That's, uh..."

"Yeah. Well. When he got home, he let it slip that he'd slept with hundreds of women. I was devastated. He was devastated. Anyway, we broke up." Fee seems almost transported back in time, that's how wistful her expression is. She catches me watching her and shakes it off. "One night a handsome guy came into The Mission. We started talking. Flirting. Kissing. Once we were, uh...well, it just turned. The condom broke. Mia was born. He nearly bankrupted me with the legal shit around her custody.

"Holy shit, Fee." I grasp her forearm. Squeeze. I remember Connor saying something about the custody battle, but wow.

She raises her wine glass and I mirror her gesture. We clink. "To surviving."

"To overcoming misogyny." I smile.

"Fuck the patriarchy." She grins back. "You did good taking that asshole down. And that nanny too."

I nod. "Thank you. I nearly lost Connor. So many times."

"He was never going anywhere. You're Ronni fucking Miller. He loves the fuck out of you." She raises her glass again.

"He does, and I love the fuck out of him." I laugh. We clink again.

"Mommy juice is the best." Fee moves to pour a bit more into both of our glasses.

I hold up my hand. "I've had enough. I've got to drive us home. No need for any drunk-driving scandals. There's been enough press about me and Connor to last a lifetime."

Olga, Zane and Fiona's nanny, has the night off. We both stand to check on the kids, who are now playing dress up. Well, Mia is dressing the boys in her clothes. I'm confident they'd let her do anything, that's how much she has them in the palm of her hand. "She's an absolute natural." I point to them with my nearly empty wine glass.

"She'll be a great babysitter when we're all on the road." Fee gazes lovingly at her little girl. "If the boys can get their shit together, that is."

"Hopefully the three of them will get their game plan together. Tomorrow's a big day. Connor's convinced Ty's going to quit." I broach the subject tentatively. Fiona's been furious at both Ty and Zoey for not reaching out after his meltdown.

Fee visibly shakes it off. "God, I'm trying not to be a bitch. It's just that Zane has suffered so much. I know Carter's bullshit is not Ty's fault. I'm disappointed in Zoey. I thought we'd become close when they got back from their trip. Considering what happened, it hurts she hasn't reached out."

"She's not been in touch with me either. Or Alex. I'm keeping an open mind. I understand needing a break. Connor mentioned Zane saw Ty—oh, God. tell me if I'm prying." I finish my wine and set it down.

Fiona bites her lip. Squints at me. "No, it's fine. Yeah, Zane's been in a couple sessions with Ty and Carter. They're trying to work things out. Zane's in a bit of a regression when it comes to Carter. He's trying desperately not to be resentful, but their history is very—um—challenged."

"Because of Carter's addiction issues?"

"Sure, that comes into play. It's more about abandonment. I mean, he and I were six—Mia's age--when we saw Carter OD in the park. That night at The Mission? Serious flashbacks for me when I saw Carter unconscious in the ambulance. I shut down."

Holy shit.

Fee doesn't notice my astoundment. "Anyway, when Lianne and Zane moved to Denver, I saw more of Carter than Zane did for years. He's working through it. Well, we all are." Fee stares off into space. "At least, I hope we are."

I decide it's time to switch subjects. "Will you reopen Gus soon?"

"Oh. Yeah..." Fee's face lights up then dims. "Maybe. I'm not going to count my chickens. Let's get through tomorrow and see if we're going to be band widows."

"Did you get a bus customized?" I grab my phone and scroll through my pictures to find the renderings for ours. "Ours will be ready by March. We're psyched to tour as a family."

Fee uses her fingers to expand and contract each image. "I haven't had time. Wow. This is super fancy, Ronni. Well done. Are you on board with going on the road with the band though? I mean, don't you have a ton of projects in the works?"

"Not right now. You knew the studio took me off the movie when I was sued?"

She nods. "Uh-huh. You mentioned it."

"Well, surprise, surprise. With the Kircher situation resolved, they asked me to come back. I declined. To make a point. In Hollywood, men are rarely pushed into the background if they are part of a scandal until there's some hard evidence. It's a double standard for women. I'm not allowing my integrity to be questioned by anyone. They should have stood by me. It's risky, but I have two boys I need to set an example for."

"So bold. I love it." Fee's eyes shine with admiration. "I need to bottle up a little of that confidence and spray it on myself."

"The thing is, the people at Netflix were concerned, but they stood by me. Before I settled with Kircher, they'd already re-upped our series. Kris and I will be back in Vancouver to film Season 2 but not until next spring. Their support gives me the confidence to be more choosy about where I spend my time and energy." I take my phone back and set it face down on the counter. "Truthfully? A lot of decent offers have been rolling in."

Fee looks wistful. "I don't know if I want to take Mia out on the road. She loves her school. Her friends. Plus, I've not had my chance yet. All of you ladies have amazing careers. I want to live my own dream."

"It's funny." I take a swig of wine. "When we were filming the show in Vancouver before all of the lawsuit madness, I was miserable knowing that Connor got to spend all day with our sons while I worked. After everything we've been through this year, I realized I needed a break. A huge, huge, break. This Kircher bullshit has taken its toll. The videos put me over the edge. The band stuff hasn't helped. On the glass is half full side, it's also forced me to take stock of my life. It's funny. I'm seriously questioning whether this industry fulfills me."

Fee nods, her eyes wide at my confession. "Yeah. Wow. I totally get it. It equally kicks ass and sucks being a grownup. It's like we must pretend to know all the things when we know nothing at all."

"So profound." I burst into laughter. "And so true."

"God, look at them." Fee rests her chin on her hand. Her legs swing from where she sits on the stool.

I glance toward the seating area where Mia now has the boys draped on her sides. She has both arms wrapped around them. Adorable. I nod to where they're cuddled together. "That's what I want my boys to have. Family. We're all family."

"Yeah." Her face softens. "We are."

"Speaking of which, have you talked to Alex? She never answers any of my texts." I'm worried about my friend, who has withdrawn from all contact. It's understandable. I hope she knows we're all here for her.

"I haven't." Fee grimaces. Pinches her nose with her fingers.

I grip her shoulder. "Fee, are you okay? Tell me the truth."

We sit in silence for a bit. "I don't...know." She looks at the ceiling then back at me. "Ronni, I'm going to confide in you. I've been wallowing. I'm still angry. I'm trying to be rainbows and puppies, but I worked so hard on Gus. I'm bitter. It's hard not to be resentful. I want to follow my dreams but I truthfully don't know if I have the energy to do it all again. Or if it's worth the investment of time. Money. Zane spent a small fortune on the renovations for the club. My restaurant..."

It's too much. Tears stream down Fee's face. I slide off my bar stool and embrace her. Her pink hair is a curtain on my shoulder as she sobs. Moments later, she pulls away. Uses her thumbs to wipe under her eyes. Sucks in a deep breath.

"I'm sorry." She breathes out. "I think I just needed to vent."

I pat her knee. "Don't apologize for having feelings. Better out than in."

"I can't seem to stop crying. Or eating. I hate myself for it. I hide. Zane's the one whose band imploded. He's the one who has the family drama. He's the one who's wife won't give him a baby because, well.... My Zaney is the one who should be sobbing and he's spending all his time comforting me." Fee shakes her head sadly, then reaches for her wine glass.

I sit back down across from her. "Why do women always take on so much?"

"Says the woman who brought down the slimiest men in Hollywood. Not once, but twice." Fee drums her fingers on the table and studies me.

"Ah, well. Maybe so, but I'd argue all of us LTZ women are overachievers. We're badasses." I cock an eyebrow. "If you want my advice, maybe don't put too much pressure on yourself. We're all behind you so try to enjoy your downtime. Gus will reopen when you're ready. I'll go back to work when I'm ready. So will Alex. And Zoey. I do hope the guys can get their own shit together, though."

"What do you think they're talking about?" Fee eases off the barstool.

I shrug. "I'm just glad they're talking. Their future essentially hinges on seeing Ty tomorrow."

The next room is quiet except for whatever Disney+ show is on in the background. I crane my neck to check on them. All three are asleep. Mia's wrapped around Tristan. Torin's head rests on her hip.

I check my phone. I missed a text from Connor. "Zane's going to be home soon, they left an hour ago. I should get going."

"You guys should get here a little earlier than Jace and Alex. If you can, that is." She leans in the doorway holding Tristan while I load Torin in the car seat.

I come back for Tristan. "Sure. We'll leave early." I finish buckling Tristan in his car seat. "By the way, thank you for tonight."

Fee shoots me a halfhearted, mischievous smile. "I'm glad you guys moved to the area."

"Me too." I wave from the driver's seat. "I love having a BFF."

Fee's shocked expression delights me. I meant what I said. Fiona Rocks is fast becoming my bestie.

On the drive home, I turn on the radio.

Of course, it's Rise by LTZ.

I mouth the words rather than sing them, no need to wake up my kids.

No matter what happens with the band tomorrow, there's a path ahead.

I, for one, can't wait to see where it leads all of us.

Chapter Twenty-Six

The Next Day

TODAY IS GOING TO be interesting. I don't quite know what to expect. None of us, including Zane, have much information about Ty's rehab program. We know our singer is troubled. I've been confused because when I've been around him, he's never seemed drunk or high.

To say I'm nervous is an understatement.

At least Ronni and I are on solid ground again. She's finishing her morning routine. I turn my attention to the latest article about Kircher. It seems the nails are firmly driven into his coffin.

"Don Kircher, disgraced producer and director pled guilty to fifteen criminal counts related to his abuse of eleven prominent actresses on Friday afternoon. Actress Ronni Miller, whose relentless behind-the-scenes work exposing Merv Sofer and Kircher released a statement via her publicist.

"This man started grooming me when I was a teenager and horrifically abused so many of my colleagues on Hawaiian High for years. I've come to learn through extensive therapy that I was brainwashed and manipulated into submission and silence. My husband and I are finally free of living in fear of retaliation, slander, and blackmail. I applaud all who have come forward to expose this dangerous man, including the people and industry which enabled him. I'm excited to get back to work, but for now I'll be concentrating on spending time with my extended family."

"Kircher faces sentencing later this year. Experts predict he'll spend the rest of his life behind bars thanks to the dozens of victims who've come forward. Miller faced an additional scandal this summer when explicit sexual videos of her husband, LTZ bass player Connor McGloughlin and the nanny to their twin sons were plastered online.

The nanny, Yolanda Gomez, subsequently confirmed Miller's assertion the videos were deepfakes made at the direction of Kircher. In a coalition led by Miller and other celebrities, California is currently finalizing an anti-impersonation statute which will impose criminal penalties on those who misappropriate images to create fake sexually explicit media."

God, my wife. She's the most amazing, stunning, brave woman in the world. As horrific as some of the shite we've been through this year has been, we've survived. I'm more in love with her now than ever before.

"Connor. I'm ready. Is your mom here yet?" Ronni calls from the boys' bedroom.

I hear the keycode beep. "Aye, love. She's just arrived."

I greet my ma, who adores helping us with the twins, thank God. She's the perfect nana. It doesn't hurt that Tristan and Torin are her first grandkids. Ronni and I are grateful to have her help. She shoos us away. The boys don't give us a second glance when we leave the nursery.

Half hour later, we're at Zane's house. I stare out the window at downtown Seattle. Waiting for Ty. A bit on edge. The meeting at our house last night didn't solve anything. Zane and I want the band to continue, even though Fee plans on opening Gus again at some point which would make it hard for her to be on the road with him. Jace is on the fence because of Alex's health issues. We have no idea where Ty's head is at. Yet.

All things considered, LTZ is still in limbo.

I'm half-listening to Ronni and Fee's conversation with Alex about her recent health scare. Half-zoning out because, well, I feel a bit creepy for eavesdropping. I watch a huge cruise ship head out to sea and find it fascinating. The boat's filled with families on their way to Alaska. An adventure of a lifetime planned for months, if not years. Who knows, maybe an LTZ song is blaring over the sound system as they leave.

Conversely, I'm looking out over Puget Sound, watching them depart. Knowing the future of the band will likely be decided today. If the band breaks up, will Ronni and I be on that cruise ship with the boys in a year's time?

Life is strange.

My mind snaps back to the present when I notice Jace is close by. His arm is wrapped around Alex. We've not spent a ton of time with the two of them as a couple, but the way he looks at her reminds me of how I look at Ronni. I'm happy he's found his person.

Fiona fans herself. "You two are so freakin' adorable."

"Are you nervous seeing Zoey? She's due any day now," Ronni leans in and whispers to Alex.

She opens her mouth to answer when the doorbell rings. We all go silent. I stride toward Ronni and sit next to her. Everyone else settles around the living room as Ty, Zoey, and Carter walk into the room.

Carter stands behind Ty, who looks clear-eyed and confident, and grips his shoulders. "Guys, I appreciate you all coming here today. Ty and I have a few things to say. I sincerely hope that it will be our first step to healing."

Ty explains his diagnosis of CPTSD and why he was in treatment. We learn that his addiction was a symptom of coping rather than the problem itself. Zoey stands proudly next to him, looking like she could give birth at any moment. The two have never looked so united. Strong. They've been through the ringer. We all have, in our own way.

"What does CPTSD mean?" Ronni directs her question to Ty.

"It's a trauma and stress-related disorder, which is similar to PTSD that developed because I was exposed to repeated trauma throughout my childhood. I'll be honest, Ronni. I was ashamed when I received my diagnosis. That's why I kept it from all of you and why I'm here to ask for forgiveness. Regardless of what you might think, I love each and every one of you in this room. I haven't done well in expressing it. I hope that's behind me. I don't want to hide anymore."

I catch Jace's eye. Ronni and I exchange glances. She leans into me. Grips my thigh with her hand. I keep my arm around her shoulder. I didn't expect this from Ty. I'm hopeful. Optimistic.

"I know all of you have some idea of how I grew up. My mom was an addict. But, there was a lot more that I never told anyone," Ty continues. His story is captivating and devastating. No one suspected the level of abuse he endured. The secrets he carried. How the experiences have so permanently affected his psyche.

Now? He seems peaceful. Humble. Authentic.

I've never been prouder to know a man. Doesn't mean it's easy to hear, I have a huge lump in my throat. I'm afraid to speak for the fear of bawling my eyes out.

I'm not alone. Ronni bursts into tears, I tighten my arm around her. Tears roll down Fiona's face. Alex sobs next to Jace. None of us, except maybe Zane, had a clue. Even if Zane knew part of it, from his expression, he wasn't privy to the entire story.

Ty takes a deep breath and very deliberately looks at Jace, Zane, and then me. "I'll shut up now, but before I do. I'm sorry. I said horrible things to all of you. Things I truly didn't mean. I can't expect any of you to understand. This information is, well… It's a lot. I just need you all to know while I'm never going to be cured, I've done everything in my power to learn how to manage my CPTSD. I understand if you don't want anything to do with me. If the band is truly broken up. I hope that isn't the case, because I was so fucking excited to start things up again. No matter what happens, all of you are my family. I hope you'll find it in your hearts to forgive me. To learn more. To talk to me. I'm an open book. I'm not hiding anymore. And I'm not going to let what happened fucking define me anymore."

My wife jumps up, still sobbing, and crouches next to Ty. She takes his hands in hers. "I understand, Ty. I'm sorry you felt so alone for so long. You're a good man, sweetheart. You deserve happiness. I'm here for you. Connor too."

I nod. Touched at Ronni's big heart. Even better, I realize I don't have an ounce of animosity left at the fauxmance situation that plagued my mind for so long. I glance up at Zoey who smiles at me. Grips Ty's shoulder and squeezes.

Everyone begins murmuring and whispering. As we process what Ty's just told us, I know with certainty we're going to be okay. There's no question.

We're family.

Zoey jumps in to quiet the room. Ty finishes his tale, confirming that Carter is his biological father and he's grateful for it. We also learn he's inherited a shite-ton of money from his mother's side of the family, who are icons in the community. Talk about a life-changing experience all the way around.

Carter chimes in because, well, Carter. My eyes flick to Zane, who's hard to read. He's gained a brother. Then again, from the moment they met, Ty has always been his brother. What a strange turn of events.

Rather abruptly, Jace and Alex say their goodbyes. Ty hands them some sort of flyer and they're gone. Some of my anxiety returns. I thought Jace was on board with reuniting. Hopefully he hasn't changed his mind.

Their abrupt departure has us all talking softly amongst ourselves. Zoey claps her hands sharply. "You guys, if we could just say one thing I'd appreciate it."

We all snap to attention.

"If any of you are like me, you're probably feeling a lot of different things. I handed Alex and Jace something we put together that will give you the basics." Ty picks up the conversation. "Rather than leave here today and let you speculate, I think it will explain a lot."

They hand out the flyers. The room buzzes again with various groups of us chatting softly about what just happened. Fiona speaks inaudibly to Zoey, I can't hear what they're saying. Before I can speak with Ty or Zoey, they say goodbye and leave. My optimism begins to turn. It's not a great sign when fifty percent of LTZ isn't even in the room.

Maybe this didn't go as well as I thought it did.

Moments after Ty and Zoey leave, Ronni jumps up and pulls Fee in a huge bear hug. She pulls away and looks her square in the eye. "Are you okay? That was a lot."

"I'm fine." Fiona's jaw is set.

Zane pulls her down into his lap. Cradles her head. Whispers into her ear. She presses her temple against his. They sit that way with their eyes closed for five minutes or so. Comforting and calming each other too, so it appears.

I stand and place my hand on Ronni's shoulder. Bend to speak calmly in her ear, "Should we go?"

Lianne, who's said nothing during this entire time, is adamant. "No, Connor. Ronni. Please stay. Let's talk this out for a bit."

"Yes, I'd like that." Ronni cranes her neck up at me.

I kiss her lips. "Aye. We'll stay."

Zane gestures to the kitchen. "Fee always has delicious stuff in the fridge. Let's go eat."

"I have some soup I can heat up. Artisan bread." Fee wipes an errant tear from the corner of her eye. "I'd like us to have some time to decompress after all of that."

The six of us follow them into the kitchen. We sit around a huge marble-covered island while Fee and Zane bustle about, pulling a feast together, in addition to the soup.

"I heard you visited the house." Carter sits next to me and waggles his brows.

Lianne smacks his arm. "I told you not to say anything."

"Ohmygod." Ronni folds her arms on the table and buries her face on top of them.

Carter nudges me. "She just gave herself away, eh?"

"I plead the fifth." I make a zipping motion in front of my lips. "Don't remember a thing."

Ronni looks up. "He was showing me the view…" Her face reddens when she realizes she just dug herself in deeper.

Lianne, Carter, and I burst into laughter. Zane and Fee set a load of food down. When we recount the tale, they join in the hilarity.

God, it feels terrific to laugh with my bandmates again. I've missed it, so I have.

"So are we back together or what?" Zane says before dunking a chunk of bread into his soup and stuffing it in his mouth.

I nearly choke on a piece of chicken in my soup. Ronni thunks me on the back a couple of times. "Were you in the same room as me?"

"Uh, yeah. Ty's back in. Jace is in too. Alex wasn't feeling well, that was obvious." He shrugs.

Fee glares at him. "Don't be ignorant, babe. It's unbecoming. Alex was struggling because Zoey's about ready to pop. She's suffered an enormous loss. Jace isn't going to be touring anytime soon."

"Maybe we should just ask." He ignores Fiona's comment.

Carter is watching Zane thoughtfully throughout the exchange. "Do you need some time, Zane?"

"No." He keeps his eyes on his soup as he spoons it into his mouth.

Lianne and Carter exchange glances. Ronni and I do too. It's apparent that we need to leave soon to let the family dynamics play out.

"Do you all mind if I go pick up Mia?" Fee spins keys around her finger. "She's at my mom's. I didn't want her to hear any of this. We haven't told her about Ty yet."

Zane glances at her. "Can we please have a conversation about this, Fee? I'm trying to wrap my head around everything. We need to talk it out..."

"Fee, you know I'm mortified. I'm so sorry..." Carter stands and attempts to hug her.

She ducks out of his embrace. "You should be. I can't help but have sympathy for Ty. The way he grew up. You're equally as responsible, Carter for what he endured. You know that, right?"

"Now, Fee..." Lianne attempts to interject.

Fiona whirls around. "No. Don't make excuses for him, Lianne. You're so confusing. You push Carter away. You…"

"Wait." I hold my hand up. "Ronni and I are going to leave. This is family business."

Ronni stands. We say quick goodbyes and depart.

On the way home, Ronni reaches over and places her hand on my thigh. Squeezes. I cover her hand with mine. Glance over. Her smile is radiant, which surprises me.

"Why are you smiling, Mae?"

She shrugs. "I love you. I'm proud to be your wife."

"Why's that?" I fish a little.

"You're a stand-up guy, Connor. For the record, I think they'll all be okay back there. I'm glad we left, though. It's important for the four of them to have some conversations that are probably a long time coming."

I flick my eyes to hers. "Aye?"

"Aye," she lovingly mimics. "Talking with Fee gave me great perspective. It will all work out. I'm certain of it."

"I hope you're right." I glance over at her. She's perfection. Utter and total perfection.

Regardless of whether my band and I can pull ourselves back together, life is always uncertain. No matter how much control you think you have.

What is certain?

You can survive whatever life throws at you if the person you love is also the person you trust.

She and I have been through it all. The good: love, marriage, babies, fame, fortune, hot sex, family, and so much laughter and fun. Also, the bad: separation, lies, scandals, lawsuits, public scrutiny and fear.

We've made mistakes. But, we've put in the work.

I'll spend the rest of my life with this woman, of that I have no doubt.

I can't help but believe everything's been worth it.

Chapter Twenty-Seven

A Few Weeks Later

I'M IN THE MIDDLE of packing up the load of crap Connor and I drag with us whenever we take the boys to his parents' house. Which isn't quite as often these days, considering Maureen spends so much time at our house. We're due at Ty and Zoey's shortly.

"Can I help you, love?" Rory hovers next to me, resting on his cane.

I glancc up. "No, I'm nearly done. I swear, the stuff we tow around multiplies."

"Oh, aye. The joys of twins. Double the fun, so they are. Padraig and Liam were born ten months after Connor. We called them our wee Irish triplets."

"I'm not sure how you did it." I stuff some toys into my giant tote bag. "I'm not looking forward to the terrible twos. They seem to already have their own language that Connor and I don't have translations for."

Rory throws his head back and laughs. "Yer alright, so you are."

"Let me help." Maureen hurries toward me.

Connor emerges from the bedroom with Tristan and Torin under each arm, both boys squealing with laughter. He whirls around, eliciting shrieks and giggles. "Pa Pa Mow. Pa Pa Mow."

"You want more, wee lads?" Connor's smile lights up the room. He grips their little bellies with his big palm and flies them around the room.

My heart melts.

"Don't wind them up after a nap, you eejit," Maureen scolds her oldest son. She intercepts him and plucks Torin and hands him to me.

"Thank you for dinner, Maureen. Rory." I give her a side hug. "See you later guys."

Padraig, Liam and Cillian turn from their seats on the sofa where they're watching the Seahawks play Kansas City.

Connor leans down and hugs his brothers. "Give Seamus and Brennan my best, I'm sorry to miss them."

We finish our goodbyes and load the boys into their car seats. I relax back against the leather seat when Connor drives away. "Christmas Eve at Ty and Zoey's is going to be a thing now?"

"Aye. I'd say so." Connor turns onto Alaskan Way so we can take the faster route to West Seattle. "Or maybe we rotate homes. Who knows."

"Tonight should be rather epic," I say when we pull into Ty and Zoey's driveway. "It's hard to believe it's been two years since their engagement."

"Can you believe it's been a whole year since we were in Los Angeles with Zoey's family? This year, you and I have a lot less pressure, thank Christ." He hands Tristan to me while he gets to work on Torin's seat belt.

Ten minutes later we've hauled in our stuff with the boys in tow. We follow Ty and Zoey into the living room. I take Torin. Connor lifts Tristan and hands him to Ty, who's now very comfortable with kids. He's a dad now, getting plenty of practice with his infant son Oliver.

Connor gets to work on unfurling the playpen. "You'll thank me later, so you will."

I side hug Ty, who is radiant. "You look great, Ty. I'm so excited to help out with the foundation."

Ty squeezes me back. "We really appreciate your support."

"Thank you, Ronni." Zoey embraces me from behind. "We can't wait to include mental health awareness and implement technology education. Your donation will help make it possible."

Given my traumatic background, I decided to team up with the Rainier Foundation to help them provide more than just arts education. With his contribution and my endowment, hopefully we can help underserved community kids gain access to mental health resources.

Connor helps me settle the twins in their playpen with a multitude of toys. Lianne and Carter hover and I realize they haven't seen the boys in months. Zoey brings her and Ty's newborn son, Oliver, out to say hello.

The door opens. "We're here, motherfuckers." Zane bops in. Fiona and Mia follow. Mia ignores the twins and runs to Carter, who's holding Ollie. Ty and Zane hug. It seems a bit awkward, but things are a million times better than a couple months ago when Ty got home from intensive therapy.

"How are you?" I embrace Fee. She looks a bit weary.

She cocks an eyebrow and plucks some sort of hors d'oeuvre that a caterer is passing around. "Oh, I'm fine. You know."

We haven't had the chance to spend much time together over the past couple months. I've been getting the house put together. She's been gearing up for the new restaurant opening. The guys have spent a fair bit of time together, all four are doing group therapy with Lisa Kinkaid before they embark upon the next chapter.

The wives have agreed to lay low so our men can work out their own dynamic for the time being.

Zoey disappears to her bedroom to feed Oliver. Alex and Jace arrive minutes later. We manage to say a brief hello before Alex joins Zoey to put Lena down for a bit. They've traveled twenty-four hours to be here, all of them look utterly exhausted.

While we wait for dinner to be served, Ty, Zane, Fee, Jace, Connor, and I make small talk for a while. It's light.

Fun. Chatting about Jace and Alex's latest adventures. Fee's new menu. Stories of our kids' shenanigans. Ty fills us in on a couple of the foundation artists he's producing.

We all turn around when Carter clinks a spoon on his glass. "Before we sit down to dinner, I just have something I want to say—"

"Wait, Carter." Ty jumps up. "Zoey and Alex are in the back with the kids."

Zoey appears holding Alex's hand, they look like they've been crying. "No, we're here. Go ahead."

Carter gazes adoringly at Lianne. "Exactly two years ago, Ty stood here and proposed to Zoey in front of all of us but you, my love."

"Best decision ever." Ty embraces Zoey. "I can't tell you how much it means to me that you're all here with us this Christmas Eve. You're all my family, and I love you."

Carter bores a good-natured hole in Ty's head. "Well don't steal my thunder, son. I've got a little proposal to get through."

I can't help but squeal. I reach for Connor's hand. How utterly delightful. It appears to be a surprise, Lianne's face says it all.

"Lianne, you are the only woman I have ever loved. The only woman for me. You've been there for me throughout all of the hell I put you and Zane through. You've been my best friend and only lover for many years now. Life is short, babe. I've lived too long without you being officially my girl; will you marry me? Finally?" Carter dramatically sinks to one knee and thrusts a little black box toward her. Opens it to reveal a stunning diamond ring.

My gaze wanders to Zane and Fiona, who look as stunned as Lianne does. Clearly, they weren't in on the proposal. Ty and Zoey, who obviously were in the "know," gaze lovingly at the couple. It doesn't take a rocket scientist to figure out which of Carter's sons was given the heads-up.

Lianne accepts. of course. Everyone, except Fee and Zane, swarm around the happy couple. My phone buzzes. I've stopped feeling dread, but still. It's Christmas Eve. Who would need to get a hold of me tonight?

Kris. That's who.

We text back and forth. I hear Connor say my name, I hold a finger up to stall him, knowing he hates it when I don't answer with words. I can feel his gruff gaze upon me, so I look up from my phone and wink.

This elicits the smile I love so much. I mouth, "I love you."

"Aye," he mouths back. Points between us, then goes to the playpen to check on the boys, who are fighting over some toy. Mia and Lena follow him. Connor is so amazing with children, I'm beginning to reconsider whether we should stop at two. For now, I feed the boys and put them down in Zoey's bedroom so we can all eat dinner. Lucky for us, Tristan and Torin are great sleepers.

When I return, I sit next to Connor at the dinner table. "Who was on the phone?" Connor keeps his voice low and quiet.

"Kris." I grip his wrist. "They changed the working title of the series to the official title, it's called Why Choose."

Connor raises an eyebrow. "Oh, aye?"

"Yep. Produced by Kris Blakely and Veronica Miller." I grin.

He hugs me tightly. "Congratulations, my love. When does it air?"

"Drops on Valentine's Day."

Mia startles us by yelling, "Uncle Connor. Aunt Ronni. It's not polite to whisper."

"Aye, wee Mia." Connor turns to her. "You're undeniably dead-on. Should I share Aunt Ronni's news with the group?"

"Yes." She crinkles her nose just like her mom. Fee rolls her eyes and tucks her daughter's hair behind her ear.

Zane laughs. Slings an arm around Ty. "Do share, miss television star."

"Okay." I stand and address the table. "If you all want to see my husband, your esteemed bass player, make his television debut as a shirtless hunk, we all have a date on Valentine's Day. That's when the series I produced drops. It's getting such a great buzz, Netflix ordered seasons two and three."

"I want to be a shirtless hunk," Zane cries out. "Ty too. Jace, are you in? You have the best abs out of all of us out-of-shape blobs."

Ty pats his abs. "Speak for yourself."

Jace just grins.

"Don't be trying to steal my thunder, now." Connor snakes his arm around me.

The rest of the night is a flurry of tasty food. Friendly conversation. Mostly, an overall feeling of rightness. I'm so incredibly grateful be part of the LTZ family,

Knowing that Connor and I made it to shore after such a stormy year, I'm excited for what next year brings.

For all of us.

Epilogue - Valentine's Day

ANOTHER DAY. ANOTHER WEDDING.

Alex and Jace got married earlier this evening. Me, Ty, and Zane stood up for him, along with his college friends. I was touched when he asked me to be his best man. Zoey was Alex's maid of honor. Ronni, Fiona, my ex, Jen, and Jace's two sisters were Alex's bridesmaids.

It's the biggest LTZ wedding yet, which makes sense considering Jace's dad, Jason invited some of the who's who of the tech community to witness his only son get married. Over a hundred people have filled the Deveraux family home on Lake Washington, in the Medina neighborhood just down the road from our house.

The dances are complete. People are filtering out. The kids are all asleep. The night should be wrapping up, but we still have one final part of the evening to get through.

I'm so feckin' nervous, I swear I can hear my knees knocking.

"You look like you just sucked on a pickle. Did old Connor return to the building?" Jennifer Deveraux hip checks me. Her wife, Becca smirks.

I can't help but laugh. Jen likes to tease me about how gruff and serious I used to be. Before Ronni, that is. "Aye, maybe just for a second. I'm beginning to think this was a terrible idea."

Jace and Alex return to the ballroom—yes this house has a feckin' ballroom. "Pops says everything is set up. It's just the inner circle left. Let's go, I want the honeymoon to start uh, yesterday. No offense."

"We don't have to do this tonight—"

Fiona interrupts me, "Oh, yes we do. You're not getting out of it."

"Fine. Fine." I lift my hands in surrender. "Where's Ronni?"

Alex points to the staircase leading down to the theater room. "We're set up down there. She's waiting for us."

I trot down the steps to my impending doom. Ronni greets me at the door. "You'll be fine."

"You owe me at least an hour of sexual favors," I growl, baring my teeth. "I can't believe you wouldn't let me see it before everyone else. I'll never live this down."

Zane slaps me on the back as he passes with Fee close behind him. "Oh, I can promise you won't."

The eight of us plus Jen and Becca settle into the theater seats. Ronni presses play. Everyone cheers when the title of the show appears on the screen and whoops and hollers when Ronni's name shows up as producer.

"Yay, Ronni," Zoey and Alex squeal.

I cannot believe how witty and fast-paced the show is. Everyone's engrossed in it. They laugh at the appropriate spots. Ronni, however, is in her own world. Immersed for special reasons. Likely cataloging things she likes and dislikes in her mind for future reference. I'm surprised at how fast time passes until suddenly, without warning.

There. I. Am.

A slow-mo close-up of my abs. The camera pans up at a sickeningly snail-like pace. My entire band snickers. The girls ooh and ahh. Make kissy faces. I try to bury my face in my hand, but Ronni turns and pulls my arm down. "Watch yourself, you gorgeous hunk of a man."

Thankfully, this isn't an episode where I have any lines. It's one gratuitous study of my naked abs and chest. The show ends with Clover waggling her brows at the camera.

The room explodes with applause.

"Way to go, Connor." Ty smiles at me. "We have another actor in the LTZ family now."

I scrub my beard. "I didn't even have a line."

"Oh, he has lines. Wait for the next couple episodes. He ad-libbed. Charmed all the ladies on the set." Ronni clasps my hand. "When you get back from your honeymoon, we'll have a binge night of Connor at our place."

Jen jokes, "Ronni, had I known he had the charisma he has on screen, I may have never ditched his ass."

"Hey!" Becca puts her hands on her hips.

Jen smooches her wife. "Just kidding, babe. Connor's abs and big dick are Ronni's property now."

"Okay, if the night is devolving into dick references, we're outta here. I'm going for the real thing." Alex grabs Jace's hand. "It's honeymoon time. Time to go."

Everyone shuffles out, including Ronni and me. After the wedding, my mom and dad took the twins to their house for the night, so we have a rare night alone. Fifteen minutes later and we're pulling into our driveway.

I'm in the bathroom brushing my teeth when I notice Ronni slip out the sliding glass door to our private patio overlooking the lake. She has an armful of blankets. I follow her outside to find her lighting the firepit and several heaters arranged around our custom pod. It's an upgraded replica of the ones we used to nestle in at the Malibu house. Made with material that's resilient to the weather in the Pacific Northwest.

"Whatcha doin, Mae?" I shiver. I'm shirtless, wearing just boxer briefs. My nipples are tight from the cold.

She looks up from where she's tossing the blankets. "Get over here. Don't stand out here in the cold without any clothes on. At least not yet."

"What are you up to?" I stalk her.

She backs up and scurries deep into the pod and pulls up the blankets. Pats the spot next to her. Looks down at the prominent bulge in my boxers and licks her lips. "I could ask you the same thing."

"You ready for a shagging to end all shagging?" I strip off my boxers and crawl next to her, forgetting the cold. With the heat of the fire and the thick, plush blankets, we'll be warm enough on this crisp, clear night.

"You didn't think I'd let all those people ogle you without a reminder of who actually owns all this." She gestures to my body. Winks. Pulls back the covers to reveal she's wearing the sheerest of sheer nighties. Her ripe, pink nipples jut out. No underwear.

I take her in my arms and kiss the bejeezus out of her. "You own me, there's no question, Mae."

Ronni takes me in her hand and pumps. Rubs her thumb over my crown as our tongues dance and swirl. I grip the back of her head to hold her in position. Her hand works me faster and harder until I nearly lose my shite. I grip her wrist. Shake my head. Lay her back against the cushions.

She lets go and stretches her arms above her head so I can pull off her lingerie. I feast on her perfect breasts and stroke her clit so lightly, she squirms to make contact.

Her little huffs of frustration are so cute. "Lie still, my love. Let me make you come."

Her fingers thread through my curls as I sip and nibble on her nipples. Swirl my finger in tight circles around her perky nub. Slide it through her slickness to her opening. I work my way down her body and bury my face in her sweet cunt. Drag my beard along her inner thighs while my tongue traces every millimeter of her pussy.

"You're driving me insane." Ronni bucks against me. "I'm so close. So far. Please."

I suck her clit between my lips. Gently, at first. Then, hard. Her body seizes.

"Ohhhhmyyyygodddd." Ronni's shriek echos across the lake. I don't stop, though. Who the feck cares if someone hears me pleasuring my woman? It's not like they'll know it's us.

Her stomach is still contracting from the epic orgasm when I kneel, press her thighs apart so I can cup her ass and drag her body up until her overstimulated pussy rests against the base of my cock, which twitches against my belly. Anxious to plunge inside its home. I want to draw it out a bit for us both, though. Using my thumbs,

I spread her lips apart. Cant my hips slightly so the backside of my cock gets good and wet.

"Jaysus." My eyes roll back in my head.

I slide my hands back down to Ronni's hips and yank her closer. "Ohhh." Ronni's head thrashes from side to side. She clasps my wrists in her hands to keep the contact steady. We're not moving, but tingles rush down my spine. My dick head slides against her sweet cunt. I thrust and the energy between our most private of parts sparks.

I can wait no longer.

I guide my cock inside of Ronni. She moans. I lean forward and cage her head with my arms. My hips roll in a wavelike motion. "My God, Mae. My God. I could fuck you like this forever."

She wraps her arms around me. Our lovemaking is not urgent. It's reverential. My hands roam over her body. I kiss and suckle her lemony essence wherever my lips can reach.

We roll and switch positions effortlessly. She rides me for a while, matching our earlier pace. Her fingers spread across my chest when she leans forward and undulates in circles. I reach down to flick her clit, which is swollen and pulsing.

"Ahhhhhhh." Ronni clenches around me. My cock is squeezed tightly in her inner walls and I couldn't stop my impending eruption if I tried.

We lay wrapped together under the blankets for a long while. I stroke her back. She circles my nipple with her finger. Staring at the dark, starry night. Listening to the lake lapping at the dock below us.

"I wouldn't trade anything that happened, you know." Ronni's voice is so sleepy it sounds like she's slurring her words.

I kiss her temple. "Except the video shite. That wasn't my favorite thing, truth be told."

She leans up on an elbow and blinks her green eyes. "Yeah, it wasn't mine either, for obvious reasons. I'm feeling a little introspective though. Maybe it's the story-teller in me. Maybe I'm just happier than I've ever been, but I truly think that everything you and I have been through has brought us to this point."

"Aye." I give her a wee smile. "Surely that's true."

"We're stronger now, right?" She boops my nose.

I can't help but laugh. "Undoubtedly."

"We can get through anything, right?" She slides her leg over my thigh and straddles me, keeping her breasts pressed against my chest.

My cock springs to life again against all odds, considering how hard I came not an hour ago. "Uh…"

"Say it."

"We can get through anything." I grit my teeth and breath out a sigh of pleasure when I slip inside her again.

"Even another baby?" She wiggles her hips to allow me to go deeper.

I press her up by her upper arms so she's looking down at me. "You just had the IUD taken out a month ago."

"And yet, this is where we find ourselves." She smiles.

I sit up, careful to keep her impaled on my cock. "You're filming the new season. We're interviewing new management. Everything's settling down after the Ty situation, are you…"

"Shhh…" She presses her finger to my lips. "Look at me."

I gaze into her eyes.

"Say it, my love." She presses her lips to my forehead before looking at me expectantly.

My eyes explore hers. Searching for what she wants. And then it hits me.

She rolls her hips, taking me as deep as I can get. She mouths, "Say it."

I cup her face in my hands. Understanding. There's nothing we can't do so long as we're together. And we are. For now. And for always.

"Say it, Connor. I want to hear you say it."

"Aye." I breath in deeply as I thrust up into her. "Deep breath."

She moans, "Yessss."

"Suck it up." I fasten my lips to the space below her ear and suck.

"Oh, yesss," she sighs and squeezes around me.

I press my forehead to hers. We stare deeply into each other's souls.

"Be fearless," we say in unison.

On the night of LTZ's failed reunion, Fiona's dream of opening her Michclin star restaurant was destroyed. Meanwhile, Zane patiently waited for his band to reunite only to have his own family drama explode - taking LTZ down with it.

As Fiona descends into self-doubt and despair, Zane's trying to come to terms with his new normal.

Don't miss the continuation of Zane and Fiona's love story in TIMELESS Encore, Book 8 in the Less Than Zero Rockstar Romance Series.

For special offers, promotions, news about LTZ and all of my upcoming releases and all sorts of behind the scenes stuff, please sign up for my newsletter.

Behind the Scenes

Fearless Encore Edition

THANK YOU FOR READING Connor & Ronni's Encore. It means the world to me that you're immersed in my LTZ corner of the world.

At the end of each book, I like to take you behind the scenes and share a few ramblings from my journey to publish.

Nothing in this section is edited or proofread, there will probably be typos (especially if I don't have my reading glasses on – don't judge, I just am in denial that I need them).

Ah, Connor and Ronni.

There is so much to unpack, I think I'll just tackle it by topic.

In some ways, I relate to Ronni the most out of all of my LTZ heroines – mainly because I have a tendency to take on too much. This year is a perfect example. I released three full-length books, four audiobooks, re-formatted all of the books and also attended three book signings and two writing conferences. I create all my own graphics, post TikTok videos and manage my social media accounts.

Not to mention, I still run full-time business, I chaired a fundraising gala for an arts organization, I've travelled to Ireland to visit my in-laws. Not to mention a couple of work trips.

WHEW!

So, yeah. Maybe I was channeling myself a bit when I gave Ronni not one, but two producing projects, twins, a move and a defamation lawsuit to boot.

My friends often ask me, how do you manage every-thing? The answer is... I LOVE EVERYTHING I DO! Nothing feels like work or a chore. Especially not writing all of the LTZ books.

I've said it many times – writing is the GREAT JOY of my life. It is so fun to create stories and characters that readers fall in love with.

But... there are days when it's literally impossible to keep up. Even as I write this, it's nearly midnight on the day I'm supposed to submit this to my formatter.

Thank God for my very own "Connor" – my husband. He is a rock, holds down the fort. Fixes things .Makes dinner. Takes care of our pup when I'm doing 13 hour days. And always supports me. Encourages me.

He's also been known to dole out a dose of tough love when I make big decisions on things that I should ask him about so we can discuss together. Just so I can check something off the list. Nothing like not telling him about birth control, but stuff like "oh, by the way...I switched car insurance companies." Or "by the way, I invited house guests the week of..."

You get my drift.

Marriage is a constant dance of communication – and when communication fails, its up to both people to work on it. To NOT slip into comfortable – but bad patterns.

Ronni is so used to doing things on her own – even as a happily married woman and mother, sometimes it's easy to revert into behavior that isn't always cool. It's called survival mode. And for all you women out there who are balancing all the things? Maybe you can relate.

Doesn't make it right...it's called SURVIVAL! LOL.

DEFAMATION

I was RIVETED to the Johnny Depp/Amber Heard trial – not because I feel any particular way about either of them, but the law geek in me was fascinated by the legal process.

Note: Defamation is REALLY hard to win when the parties in the lawsuit are "public figures" – there is a heightened standard of proof. And, the absolute defense to defamation is the TRUTH. If you tell the truth and can prove that it was the truth, you cannot lose a defamation lawsuit.

Except... if you're sued – rightfully or wrongfully- defamation lawsuits are still super EXPENSIVE. The sheer amount of legal work needed to go to trial makes litigation expensive. Even to get to the point of having a case dismissed. And with defamation, you can't exactly take the stand and expect the jury to just believe your testimony – you need expert witnesses and even cor- roborating witnesses to back up your case.

This is why many lawsuits like this settle. And how much they settle for is largely dependent on a whole lot of legal posturing and the specific facts of the case. But, there's a level of uncertainty that makes it risky to go to trial.

Sometimes certainty is better than proving you're right. Especially in Ronni's case – she has other priorities now. Why spend the next two years mired in litigation and distractions, when her adorable boys are growing up. She's already missed important milestones by working too hard. At some point, staying fixated on a toxic person in your life—even if you are in the right – is detrimental to your own well-being.

It was time for Ronni to let Kircher go. Once and for all. And, get a big settlement check out of it.

By the way, I mentioned this in FEARLESS, but Kircher and the rest of the "schlumpies" are based on REAL LIFE headlines that I've followed for years.

DEEP FAKES

Did I scare you when the videos surfaced? Did you have a moment thinking that Connor wasn't the man you know him to be?

The reality is technology is BATSHIT. It stands to reason that a showrunner-turned-powerful director would have access to state-of-the art programs to really mess with Ronni and Connor. His own form of revenge, you might say.

How would you handle it if your own spouse confronted you with multiple sex tapes you never starred in?

Well, that's it for now. Please keep in touch! You can write me at kaylene@kaylenewinter.com

On a final note, I'd greatly appreciate it if you would leave a review of this book. Reviews help readers like you discover books they love, which is why it means the world to me when you take a second to tell me what you think."

Kaylene

Dedication

To G, MY OWN Irish honey, you have provided love and support unlike anything I'd ever dreamed of. Each one of my heros has a little bit of you embedded in him.

Acknowledgments

This book was an absolute labor of love, and I couldn't have done it without the help and support of the following awesome rock stars:

Cover/Graphic Designer/Finder of Hotties: Regina Wamba

Editor: Grace Bradley

Formatting: Willow Yanarella

PR: Dain Sanchez, Wildfire Marketing

Agent: Stephanie Phillips, SBR Media

Website Maven: Sherri Kiarsis, Sublime Creations

My Right Hand: Willow Yanarella

Models: Shorty Vest & Christine Klein

The character Brody Mason is from and appears courtesy of Jaine Diamond

YAY to **Kaylene's Krew!!!**

Beta Readers: Anna Theurer & Beth Carbutt

My Inspirations: Gareth, Sheila, Kris

Special shout out to all of my ARC readers, bloggers, Bookstagrammers, TikTokers & anyone who is new to the LTZ World. I hope to always make you proud and look forward to expanding into all sorts of new territory when this series is finished.

So, thank you thank you thank you to everyone—I'm overwhelmed by your love, support, kindness, etc. Thank you for making my dream come true!

About the Author

KAYLENE WINTER IS AN best-selling author of steamy, contemporary romance.

Each character-driven novel is filled with snappy dialogue, pop-culture references and enough steam to make you fan yourself. Kaylene weaves authenticity, emotion and angst into a turbulent rollercoaster ride of love, passion and soul-searing romance always ending with a delicious HEA.

Kaylene lives in Seattle with her amazing Irish husband and her Pomsky, Phalen. She loves creating art of all kinds.

Other Titles